GODLESS

Feathers and Fire Book 7

SHAYNE SILVERS

ARGENTO PUBLISHING

CONTENTS

CONTENTS

Shayne Silvers

Godless

Feathers and Fire Book 7

A TempleVerse Series

ISBN 13: **978-1-947709-27-0**

© 2019, Shayne Silvers / Argento Publishing, LLC

info@shaynesilvers.com

SLAUGHTER IS THE BEST MEDICINE...

Callie Penrose is back to murder vampires and chew bubblegum. And she's all out of bubblegum.

Callie has had a rough few days. Five minutes after discovering she had a Godfather, she learned that the future of the world depended on the two of them taking an immediate road trip.

To Castle Dracula—a place even the supernatural community believed to be an urban myth, dead and abandoned long ago when Dracula had perished at the hands of Van Helsing, Mina and Jonathan Harker.

Except...Dracula and his castle were alive and well. Worse, he had been secretly running the Sanguine Council—the governmental body of every vampire in the world—ever since his alleged death, with none the wiser. Not even the vampires.

And Callie's first Godfather-daughter dance was to go assassinate the Sultan of Suck once and for all.

But she soon learns that Dracula is the absolute *least* of her concerns. And that some bonds should never be forged. Because once made, they can never be broken...

Callie Penrose is about to show the world fear in a palmful of blood. Get your ponchos on...

DON'T FORGET!

VIP's get early access to all sorts of book goodies, including signed copies, private giveaways, and advance notice of future projects. AND A FREE NOVELLA! Click the image or join here:
www.shaynesilvers.com/l/219800

FOLLOW AND LIKE:

Shayne's FACEBOOK PAGE:

www.shaynesilvers.com/l/38602

I try my best to respond to all messages, so don't hesitate to drop me a line. Not interacting with readers is the biggest travesty that most authors can make. Let me fix that.

The Biblical passage from Ecclesiastes softly played in the back of my mind as I stared at the entrance to Hell on Earth.

To every thing there is a season, and a time to every purpose under the heaven: a time to be born, a time to die; a time to plant, and a time to pluck up that which is planted; A time to kill, and a time to heal; a time to break down, and a time to build up; a time to weep, and a time to laugh; a time to mourn, and a time to dance; a time to cast away stones, and a time to gather stones together; a time to embrace, and a time to refrain from embracing; a time to get, and a time to lose; a time to keep, and a time to cast away; a time to rend, and a time to sew; a time to keep silence, and a time to speak; a time to love, and a time to hate; a time of war, and a time of peace.

Or, in my words—a time for laughter, and a time for slaughter.

Dracula's season had come to an end.

It was time for a little K.C. Slaughter

I took a deep breath, forcing my pulse to slow. We stood only paces away from an open pair of thirty-foot-tall wooden doors that led into a castle unlike any I had ever seen—even in movies. Although I saw no monsters waiting inside to bestow upon us welcoming hugs and kisses—with their bloodstained fangs and razor-sharp claws—a formless, malevolent presence beckoned us to enter with a deceiving purr.

'Will you walk into my parlour?' said the spider to the fly...

The massive wooden doors were decorated with dozens of scratches, gouges and indentations from blades, axes, and all manner of tool. I even saw what appeared to be broken off claws, teeth, and fingernails firmly embedded into the wood.

All on the *inside* of the wooden doors—from people trying to escape.

Castle Dracula.

I shivered before I could stop myself. I concealed the movement by glancing back at the courtyard and the massive castle gates trapping us inside. I turned back to look up at least a hundred feet to the peak of the castle entrance above the doors. Gargoyles lined the roof every few paces and, rather than looking outward like good stone sentries, they were looking straight down.

At me.

Their eyes flickered with literal crimson flame, emitting occasional sparks and embers that lazily drifted down, extinguishing as they burned out. The stone gargoyles were each unique in design—sporting heads of eagles, lions, crocodiles, devils, and even pudgy babies—but all were grotesque, imagined hybrids birthed only in the darkest of nightmares. Some were tall, short, spindly, fat, or muscular, but they all had wings—just as varied as every other part of their body. A few clutched weapons, but most favored their natural, devil-given claws and teeth, preferring their kills up close and passionate.

Not appreciating my attention, many flared their wings and hissed at me —like vultures over roadkill when you tried to chase them away. I narrowed my eyes and slowly lifted my hand to point my finger at them. They screamed and fled, ducking out of sight. A faint smile tugged at my cheeks.

Pussies.

The night sky was a dark, wine-colored red, even tinting the wisps of clouds drifting by—courtesy of the magical barrier now surrounding Castle Dracula that prevented anyone from escaping until Dracula was dead. The moon was pregnant and full, hanging heavily in the sky like a bulging droplet of blood.

The Blood Moon. The main reason we—and by *we*, I meant Samael— had been able to set up the barrier and this secret invasion of Castle Dracula so that we could assassinate the Sultan of Suck.

All without him knowing.

Which, judging by the piano music and the fact that the doors had opened on their own, had officially gone to shit. Samael cleared his throat beside me. I slowly turned to look at this unknown entity, basically a stranger to me.

Samael was quite tall with broad, stocky shoulders—almost like a blacksmith. Even standing motionless in a place where we were vastly outnumbered, his aura oozed of calm, solid authority, reminding me of a military commander of some kind—one who had seen a battle go to hell and had single-handedly brought his terrified, wounded men back home, convincing them to sing a ballad of victory like they were heroes. All while the commander nodded along with a charismatic grin, wielding a cigar, an empty flask, and minimal personal casualties. If you looked closely enough, you might even catch him pinching the nurse's ass on his way to refill his flask.

And he was the kind of man who would earn only a sultry, smoky, encouraging smile in response to that pinch.

We've all met a person like this. Charisma exudes from their every pore —the world giving them the latitude to say the most outlandish things and earn only a bemused smirk or shake of the head. His long dark hair brushed just past his shoulders and his angular face was solid and dangerous—like carved granite. To be entirely blunt, he was beautiful, and I'd caught myself admiring him several times when he wasn't looking. Not that I was personally interested in him, but he had one of those mesmerizing looks that couldn't help but draw attention. A man in the prime of his life.

Or an angel in the prime of his fall.

I only knew a handful of things about him.

He was a Greater Demon.

He was incredibly powerful.

And he was my Godfather—because my parents had been insane.

Samael had arranged for this little field trip with his Goddaughter by setting up Roland—using the man's grief over my alleged death—to open this otherwise impossible access to Castle Dracula so that we could kill our first Master.

I'd only learned about these Masters within the last few days—a group of entitled, spoiled children ejected from the godly loins of some of the most powerful super-supernatural entities mankind knew. These children had formed a club, deciding that they'd had enough of listening to their parents and thought they could do a better job. So they'd whipped out their crayons and scribbled out a plan to take over the world—desiring to enslave the puny creatures inhabiting its surface—and kick their parents to the curb.

The problem was that they had grown up since those early days, and rather than putting their childish fancies away, they had dusted off their manifesto and gotten to work.

They were an elusive bunch—the most secret of secret societies. The infamous Count Dracula was the only one I knew of. Correction—the only one I'd been *told* was a Master.

But demons had a *friends-with-benefits* relationship with the truth. It was just their nature. Even though I'd learned that my blood was powerful enough to exchange with another person to form a magical Blood Bond—a tie that allegedly prevented the other person from betraying me—I wasn't fully invested in this family road trip. I was just traveling in the same direction as my Godfather.

If I focused intently, I could see the Blood Bond that connected Samael to me, and it was significantly thicker and stronger than any I shared with my other friends. Even still, I wasn't quite sure what to make of it.

He was way too excited about our budding relationship. He'd known about being my Godfather pretty much since my birth, but I'd only found out about it less than an hour ago and definitely had mixed feelings.

Samael, on the other hand, had been excited for quite some time, explaining that the only reason he had hunted and pursued me over the past few years was to teach me how to be strong, and to make sure I had what it took to fight the Masters.

So he was already starting off on the wrong foot. I was absolutely *done* proving to anyone what I was or wasn't capable of.

Godfather, I thought to myself. I'd called him *Godless* when he'd tried to get too chipper a few minutes ago. The irony of it all—if not for the macabre scenery—was not lost on me. A Greater Demon—an angel who had chosen not to follow his daddy, God—was excited to be my Godfather.

Which really made me begin to doubt my mother's sanity. I mean, who chose a Greater *Demon* to be a *God*-father? It was kind of in the freaking name. Maybe the hospital had been experimenting with some new pain meds when she had me.

Because all these obviously rational thoughts contradicted the Blood Bond connecting us. And he'd given me the *choice* to come here—even kneeling at my feet less than an hour ago, giving me the option to kill him if I thought he was lying. In a crazy, broken-home kind of way, his actions over the past few years had checked out.

Which left me sitting on the fence, debating which way to lean.

I felt him watching me, so I turned to face him. "Why did you really choose to work for my mother? Agreeing to become my Godfather?" I asked, not buying his earlier answers.

This strong, charismatic, authoritative man...bit his lip, looking extremely uncomfortable. "You wouldn't believe me," he finally said.

I narrowed my eyes. "True. And you're still going to tell me."

He sighed wearily. "First Corinthians, chapter thirteen."

I grabbed him by the collar and slammed him up against the door, banging his head against the wood and very seriously considering choking him to death. "Don't you dare joke about my mother like that. She loved Titus, not you."

Because that was the passage about unconditional love.

Despite my aggression, Samael nodded patiently. "Entirely true." When I still didn't let go, he jerked his chin towards the castle. "We have more important things to worry about inside, Callie..."

I grunted, letting him go forcefully. "We're not finished with this conversation, Sammy," I finally muttered.

He beamed excitedly, despite my obvious displeasure. "Nicknames. Alright, Call—" He cut off abruptly, scratching at his jaw, obviously unable to come up with a nickname since my real name had already been shortened.

Excalibur had become *Callie*.

Because I'd learned that when my mom wasn't auditioning the worst of the worst to be my Godfather, she'd been bonding a piece of Excalibur into my very soul. The Name. Thankfully, it no longer resided inside of me, having been transferred to an old leather sheath locked away with Pandora in Nate Temple's Armory.

But once I finished my date with Dracula, I was supposed to personally deliver the sheath to...well, *someone* in St. Louis. I wasn't even sure who. I'd been on such a wild excursion in Kansas City over the last few days that I hadn't even bothered asking Nate about it. I'd had enough on my plate. And why worry about the little things when probable death had been on my calendar?

I walked past Samael to enter Castle Dracula, shivering at the thought that I was walking into the mouth of a Beast.

Because that was exactly what we were doing. Much like Nate Temple's mansion in St. Louis, Castle Dracula harbored a Beast—a celestial entity of some kind that had successfully bonded with the sprawling castle so that it was actually a living, sentient being.

The humans who had been able to successfully bond with Beasts had been known as Makers—and Makers were to wizards what wizards were to non-magical humans. Their thoughts were literally magic—they could *think* something and make it become *reality*. No middle steps.

If a wizard wanted a fireball thrown at you, they had to draw heat from their surroundings, ignite it, and then draw more energy from the air to get the necessary propulsion to throw it at you. Not hard, but several steps.

If a Maker wanted a fireball thrown at you...ya' just became a flamer, bro. Period.

Because Makers were empowered—or assisted by—the Beasts clutching their souls like parasites.

Except sometimes Beasts chose locations over people. Ever heard about the Bermuda Triangle? Beast. Volcanoes that erupt out of nowhere? Beast. Certain places around the world that were famous for giving visitors some extremely strong sensation—whether it be fear, bliss, romance, et cetera? Beast, Beast, Beast, Beast-cetera.

Nate Temple's mansion was possessed by a Beast named Falco—not needing a Maker to keep it in line.

Castle Dracula was no different.

So as I stepped through those doors, I was—quite literally—walking into a set of open jaws. And I was pretty sure I could feel the Beast inhaling my scent with a purr of anticipation.

The only way out was to find the Beast's gag reflex.

According to Samael, there was a weapon deep within the center of Castle Dracula, and it was the only thing capable of ending the Master.

Dracula's Bane.

Ripping out Dracula's tonsils was pretty much our only goal on this field trip. Otherwise it was just an elaborate, $6.99, suicide-mission-special.

2

We entered a marble hallway that was at least thirty paces wide, the ceiling about fifty feet over our heads—not as high as the roof I had seen from outside, letting me know there were more levels above us.

I had a feeling that was going to become a theme, because I'd gotten a chance in the courtyard to look out over the walled estate. Now, I wasn't a distance-ologist or anything, but the enclosed place seemed to stretch across *miles* of rocky hilltops. It was easily the size of many small towns I had traveled through in Missouri, complete with parks, dozens of cobbled streets, vibrant gardens, an observatory, a labyrinth, a small lake, cemeteries, and towers—lots and lots of towers. I'd seen a handful of stone staircases designed to look like serpents that encircled towers the size of small skyscrapers. Some of the structures were detached from the castle proper, broken up by the outdoor areas, but most were interconnected in a tiered, sprawling monstrosity of elegant spires, titanic stairways, jagged cliffs, stone keeps, and bridges as wide as small highways that looked engineered to withstand the weight of multiple armored tanks.

I knew the interior of the castle would take just as much getting used to, anticipating that most rooms, or sections, of the castle would be as large as department stores. The scope of construction—especially for the time period when it had been built—blew my mind. It was astonishing to consider something similar being built *today*. It would have taken hundreds and hundreds of years without modern-day, heavy equipment.

Of course, I was entirely certain that Dracula had cheated, using his Beast to bring the castle to life.

If I hadn't taken the time to study the castle from the outside, I might have passed out upon setting foot in the marble hallway.

Even though this room had no windows, long, heavy drapes hung down from the ceiling nearest the walls, stretching all the way to the floor like smears of blood. A ten-foot-wide, spongy, violet carpet stretched across the full-length of the room, starting where we now stood and ending at a set of black double doors.

Fun fact—according to *Drac Daily*, streams of blood built into the floors were making a comeback in the upper echelons of interior decorating. Or maybe he just wanted easy access to his drink of choice—like a professional football player having fountains of Gatorade throughout his home—because scarlet streams of flowing blood lined either side of the purple-carpeted path, emitting an inviting, bubbling, gurgling sound. They looked deep enough to wade in and too wide to jump across. Something about it really set the mood for me, making me feel welcome.

Other than marble columns the size of Redwoods interspersed throughout the room supporting the ceiling, the area was entirely empty. I turned to Samael only to find him smiling absently, nodding his approval at the design. Or maybe at the piano music playing in the distance.

I grunted imperiously and began walking down the purple carpet between the two streams of blood. With no other indication of where to go, and not seeing any doors but those at the far end of the hall, I made my way onward, ignoring the sensation of the castle's sentient Beast taking stock of my pulse, my aura, and whatever else it was checking.

Because I definitely felt like I was being watched by a predator.

"Be on your guard," Samael warned, eyes alert. I rolled my eyes at the understatement of the year. This wasn't my first rodeo. I had so many questions I had wanted to ask Samael, but the fact that the doors to the Castle had opened of their own accord almost as soon as we had arrived made it pretty obvious that we were expected and didn't have time for a chat.

"What can we expect?" I asked, hoping he had some inkling on what we would be dealing with here.

He shook his head in answer. "Anything."

I grunted. I had my new Horseman's Mask of Despair in the pocket of my Darling and Dear jacket, but I kept my hand rested on the hilt of the katana tucked into a loop on the white ninja outfit I wore.

The bloody Cross Pattée covering my chest was the opposite of subtle, and recalling that I had drawn it with vampire blood made me suddenly wary that I might accidentally offend our host. That would just be terrible.

In addition to the Mask, jacket, and Silver katana, I had my Darling and Dear ass-kicking boots and the Seal of Solomon on my finger; my only other armor or weapon was my dazzling smile and my baby blues.

The über-resistant Darling and Dear threads would be helpful, but unless Dracula had a few demon hookers lounging around, my Seal of Solomon—able to imprison said *filles de joie* and sulfur strumpets—wouldn't be worth a... brass nail. Heh.

I looked over at Samael. "Have any more of the Omega—"

His finger was suddenly pressed over my lips and his face was pale, his eyes wide with alarm. "Not here," he whispered. "It's best to assume we're being watched from here on out. Consider your words and actions very carefully. In the land of the blind, the one-eyed man is king," he said, reciting the parable from the Bible. "Or queen," he added with a faint smile.

I frowned, not really sure how that tied into anything.

"All those questions you want answered will have to wait." He smiled grimly. "If we die, answers to your questions will do you no good. We have an expectant audience. And we have parts we must play, whether we want to or not."

I nodded, feeling like a rookie Shepherd all of a sudden—like it was my first time on a hunt with Roland and I'd just knocked over a vase in a house full of shifters. Of course we were being watched. We were inside a damned living Beast. Samael finally withdrew his finger and we continued onward to the tall, black, double doors—relatively small compared to everything else we had seen so far. They were only ten-feet-tall.

Samael pulled open the doors and I already had my katana out, ready for an assault.

Instead, we found a normal-sized, warm, cozy corridor. Paintings of forests hung from the walls, and a few chairs and side tables hugged the walls to form quaint seating areas—complete with tiny lamps that cast a soothing glow throughout the small hallway. A bouquet of what looked like two-dozen

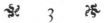

How were we supposed to kill the oldest vampire in the world at a formal dinner party? What if it was a freaking monster's ball? He obviously had at least one or two friends living here with him. This dinner could be a slaughter like that Red Wedding episode in Game of Thrones.

I leaned back with a nervous sigh, controlling my rising panic. I'd already been through so much tonight before coming here. Roland. War in the streets of Kansas City. Betrayal. Death. I was kind of all tapped-out on surprises.

I'd put on my fucking Horseman's Mask for the first time, for crying out loud. If I was being honest, I was a little miffed that I hadn't heard Heavenly trumpets, an angelic chorus, or seen cherubic backup dancers frolicking across the Heavens. Even a drum solo would have sufficed. I'd hoped to have some epic entrance music for such a monumental moment.

Instead, the Horseman of Despair had donned her Mask for the first time in utter silence.

Thinking about it in those words, a small smile crept across my cheeks. It was...fitting, I guess.

As eager as I was to put the Mask on, storm out of the room, and go rip Dracula to shreds at his own party, I remained sitting on the divan. Dracula already knew we were here and he hadn't sent an army after us. Instead, he'd tailored some evening clothes for us and invited us to dinner. I closed my eyes, and focused on the totem I used for meditation, centering myself.

Dracula wanted something from us.

I carefully considered my steps for the figurative dance ahead. There were a handful of different ways to approach it. We were obviously about to come face-to-face with Count Dracula—the world's first vampire. The secret leader of the entire Sanguine Council.

He should have no idea of what had transpired in Kansas City, so what kind of opportunities and advantages did that give us? If anything, he'd know I was a wizard, but he wouldn't know about my Horseman's Mask. I also had a Greater Demon on my side, and I'd seen Samael flex before. He was probably the scariest monster I'd seen in person. Dracula was no chump, but I couldn't imagine him being stronger than one of Heaven's Mightiest Rejects and a Horseman.

I knew he also had his Beast, that he was a Master, and that he collected rare magical items, so I didn't anticipate this being a simple, linear fight—which was why we had hoped to sneak in and assassinate him.

I spent a few more minutes going over any other pertinent information I could think of before I made my decision. I opened my eyes, feeling utterly calm. I scooped up the bottle of wine in one hand and the dress in the other before opening the door to the hallway.

Only to find a freaking skeleton waiting for me.

I gasped at the unexpected host, startled to realize that I was holding the wine bottle overhead—ready to react like someone had dared to switch off *Jessie's Girl* in the middle of the chorus at my local bar back in Kansas City.

The skeleton didn't react in the slightest. It just watched me. Without eyeballs, it was hard to tell, but those eye sockets were pointed my way. It didn't advance or speak. In fact, the skeleton almost seemed sophisticated. Docile. Subservient. It was about an inch shorter than me and wore calf-high leather boots—folded back down at the top like those worn by pirates. Based on the boots, I took a gamble and decided he was male—since there was no skeletal equivalent to a man's pride and joy, despite what many would have you believe.

A shredded red fabric hung down his chest, ending in a point over his sternum. It reminded me of a train robber's bandana from the Wild West era, although the fabric was much longer, bunching up around the shoulders almost like a scarf.

His bones were the color of aged ivory, and they were pitted with dark stains. I blinked as I suddenly noticed that the ligaments connecting his bones together consisted of smoldering black and red embers that occasionally burped up an errant spark or two like a campfire. Luckily for him, they didn't catch his scarf ablaze.

It made me think of the embers and sparks I had seen on the bridge connecting Kansas City to Castle Dracula—the place Pandora had been so terrified of. Samael had said the place went by many names—Purgatory, Neverwas, the Night Currents. And it looked like this pirate-train-robber had been born there.

Not seeing Samael, I side-stepped over to the door leading to his dressing room, keeping one eye on the skeleton to make sure he didn't jump my bones.

Heh.

He just watched me patiently, slowly pivoting his neck. I don't know if it would have been creepier to have him talk to me in a charming British accent or maintain his chosen silence. Seeing that Samael's dressing room was empty, I cursed under my breath and glared at the skeleton dude.

"Where is my companion?"

He stared at me, his ligaments crackling softly, ever-burning. And then he shrugged.

"Speak or I walk," I demanded. "And I'm keeping the wine."

"You can't leave," the skeleton rasped dustily. "No one can leave."

I narrowed my eyes. "First of all, I don't think I like your tone. Second of all—" and without any warning, I cracked him across the jaw with the bottle of wine. His skull spun around 180 degrees with a *rat-a-tat-tat* sound. I was momentarily surprised that the bottle of wine hadn't shattered. "Abracadabra," I muttered.

The skeleton gasped dustily, lifting his bony hands to realign his skull. I used the opportunity to drape the red dress down over his head and outstretched arms. It was a struggle, but I managed to wrestle it on before sweeping his legs out from under him, knocking him down to the floor on his tailbone.

I shoved the bottle of wine into my jacket pocket and grabbed him by both boots. Then I began dragging him towards the sound of the piano. I back-kicked the doors open—glad they hadn't needed to be pulled open or I might have embarrassed myself—and darted into the room, dragging the gasping skeleton behind me. The volume of the music let me know I'd found the right place, but I didn't bother checking out the room.

I would only have one chance to make a first impression.

Instead of elegantly descending a set of steps before an adoring crowd in my exquisite red dress, I executed an Olympic skeleton throw in my ninja gear. I slowly began to spin, swinging the skeleton through the air in two complete rotations to build up some momentum. At the apex of my third turn—aiming directly for the piano—I released the poor skeleton's boots, hurling him into the air. I crouched slightly to regain my balance, gripping the neck of the wine bottle as I watched the dress-clad skeleton sail across the room, emitting a dusty wheeze and a trail of sparks. Then I leaned back and pitched the bottle of wine at my target.

It struck him in the back of the head—pure luck—with a solid *crack*, and exploded in a shower of glass and wine. The blow was hard enough to knock his skull clean off his neck and up high into the air where it ricocheted off the wall and towards the ceiling.

But the body in the red dress…

Sailed straight into the man seated at the glossy black piano.

Or, it *would have* crashed into him if he hadn't transformed into a cloud of red mist at the last possible second.

The skeleton slammed into the piano vertebrae first, sending several random bones whipping into the air. He tried using his hands to catch his balance, which resulted in an impressive, partial glissando as his frictionless fingers slid over the keys. But the virginal pianist's grand debut ended prematurely when the open lid of the piano crashed down, pinning his upper body inside with a shower of sparks.

The ricocheting skull struck the lid of the piano and then bounced away towards the keyboard. The struggling, cross-dressing skeleton lashed out to try and catch it, but missed twice—hitting the keys instead—before his third and fourth attempt pinned the skull against the far corner—resulting in the famous *dun-dun-dun-duuun* jingle.

I burst out laughing, unable to believe the odds.

The skeleton managed to free himself from the piano as my laughter slowly faded. I sighed, shaking my head.

"Where, oh where, did my pianist go?" I taunted, locking onto the crimson mist.

ally eaten a real meal. It felt like years ago. I pointedly shifted the plate to the side anyway. "Where is my companion?" I asked, lifting my eyes back to Dracula.

Dracula just smiled at me, having somewhat regained his composure. "Perhaps he's taking a tour. It is an impressive castle, is it not?"

I narrowed my eyes, allowing a bit of magic to visibly crackle down my arms.

"Oh, don't be like that," Dracula encouraged pleasantly. "Eat. My wolves caught that fresh this afternoon."

I pursed my lips, staring back at him. It was no accident that he'd humble-bragged about having wolves as pets. He had an army of skeletons, so why wouldn't he have werewolves? His grin stretched wider as if he could read my thoughts—that I was analyzing his every word. He was probably having the time of his life. He didn't get many visitors—only food.

And keeping his existence a secret made it practically impossible to socialize.

He might act like he knew everything and held all the cards, but he didn't know about my Horseman's Mask. He only knew that I was powerful. Anything that had happened in the last year in Kansas City was likely news to him because Samael and Roland hadn't let any specific information about their plan get out—not wanting Dracula to get wind of the assassination attempt. That had been the entire purpose of their plan, after all. They hadn't even told their own vampires, not wanting anyone to leak the plan to the Sanguine Council, who would have leaked it to him.

But how aware was he of the world at large? If he ran the Sanguine Council, I was betting he had a fair idea of the power players in the world. Did he know about Nate Temple? Or about me and my allies? Why wasn't he even slightly concerned that we had succeeded in invading his sanctum sanctorum —the place he felt safest in the entire world?

The only thing Dracula could know was that I was either powerful or stupid. Maybe both. That was it. There was every chance he had no idea who I was, as a matter of fact. I'd been gone for a year, after all, shortly after I built the reputation as the White Rose. I was old news, presumed dead.

Did he know Samael? The demon had been locked up inside my ring for quite some time, but both men had been around for a while.

"You aren't a vampire," Dracula said suddenly, sounding almost surprised. And...disappointed, for some reason. "You look familiar, yet I do not know your name," he continued, since my silence made it obvious that I hadn't intended to respond.

So he *hadn't* known I was coming. Thinking back on the red dress, I suddenly had a nauseating thought. It had likely belonged to one of his old victims. I was doubly glad I hadn't tried it on, now. I thought about his question and decided that it wasn't really a necessary secret to keep. "Callie Penrose."

He scratched his jaw, studying me. "I've never heard of you." Which was kind of strange. I'd had a few run-ins with the Sanguine Council, so he should have heard at least something about me from them. Maybe he wasn't as all-knowing as I had feared. "What exactly did you intend in coming here?"

"You and I have unfinished business. A date, you could say."

He smiled, flashing brilliantly white teeth. "My dear, we don't have *any* business. There is nothing to finish if we've never started."

"Sure we do. My companion is missing, remember?" I repeated in a darker tone.

On cue, Samael suddenly slipped into the room, clad in his tuxedo. And from a door directly behind Dracula. Everyone was so transfixed on me that they didn't seem to have noticed. I didn't look, keeping my eyes locked on Dracula. Was Samael going to exterminate the vampire before we even had a chance to go sightseeing? Or...

Samael walked up and placed a hand on Dracula's shoulder. "She looks familiar because you knew her parents."

I heard a faint ringing in my ears as the blood rushed to my head. Samael...had betrayed me. Motherfucker. We hadn't even been here ten minutes! Despite all the contrary evidence and our Blood Bond, I had known deep down that I would never be able to trust him. Even though I was young by most standards, I was old enough to have learned that magic always had a back door, and that our elders loved exploiting them.

And if anyone would know a way around a Blood Bond, it would definitely be one of the a-holes who once broke a sacred bond with God. What confused me was why Samael would go through such an elaborate ruse to get me here if he worked for—or with—Dracula? Surely, he could have found a simpler way.

There was something else going on here.

Dracula didn't look remotely surprised by Samael's proximity or affectionate touch. He did look taken aback by Samael's comment. "Pardon?"

"She is the daughter of Constance and Titus," Samael explained, not meeting my eyes. "The same Constance who imprisoned me for years."

"WHAT?" Dracula snarled, his face darkening as he clenched his jaws. "That's...*impossible!*"

"You...knew my parents?" I asked Dracula, incredulous.

He just glared back at me for a few moments. Then he rounded on

Samael, hissing. "You could have mentioned her at any point in the last year, demon."

Samael shrugged easily, still ignoring my glare. "I put a year of effort into getting Roland Haviar here, as we agreed. I thought this girl had died soon after I escaped the Seal of Solomon, but she showed up to interrupt my plans with Roland. After seeing her in action—how easily she defeated Roland—I believe she may even be *better* than our original plan." Dracula turned to appraise me thoughtfully, looking entirely too curious. "So I adapted, presuming you might be interested in such a serendipitous catch," he said in a low, crisp tone. "And remember this—you are not my master. We are *allies*. Equals at best."

Dracula grunted dismissively, but I could practically feel the tension in the air—neither man was pleased about their shared position of authority. Men always had to know who was alpha, otherwise they were totally help-less. "It looks more like you wasted a year and are trying to overcompensate for your failure," Dracula finally muttered. "She's not even a vampire. And Roland is still breathing. A nuisance I must deal with after..." he glanced over at me disgustedly, flicking a hand, "I tire of this one."

Samael reached over to pour himself a goblet of wine. "I believe I know a way around that," he said with a dark smile. "Did I mention that she was also Roland's student back when he was a Vatican Shepherd? In fact, she is the one who stopped your attack on Rome a few years ago—when you tried to cast the Shepherds into civil war. Perhaps fresh blood is exactly what we need."

I was too busy trying to figure out what nefarious plan they were talking about to be scared. Samael was a demon, and wouldn't do anything that didn't benefit himself in some way. So, was he playing both sides against the middle just for fun or had he already picked his side? Was I a pawn or a secret weapon?

Upon hearing about my history with Roland and the Sanguine Council, Dracula had grown entirely too interested. "Well..." he said thoughtfully. Then a slow smile stretched across his face. "Would you like to work with me, girl?"

I grunted. "I don't suck on command."

His smile evaporated. "So be it—"

"You lied to me, Sammy," I interrupted him, turning to Samael. "We should probably talk about that when the little guy goes down for his nap when the sun rises," I said, jerking a thumb at Dracula.

Samael sipped his wine, shrugging unconcernedly. "Demon," he admitted, implying that I should have known better and that I was an idiot for ever trusting him in the first place.

I nodded my agreement, lifting up my hand to inspect the Seal of Solomon in the light. "I almost forgot."

Samael's shoulders tightened infinitesimally, but he retained enough of his composure to smirk at me. "And there is no sunlight here. Of course."

Motherfucker.

I turned back to Dracula, disappointed to find him so carefully composed after my blatant disrespect. It was also apparent that my attitude had succeeded in turning him away from Samael's suggestion—that I was a better candidate than Roland for their grand plan, whatever that was.

I hadn't come here for games, though. I'd come here to kill this bastard, and for that, I needed him on edge. Before Samael convinced him to go along with whatever his scheme was.

I thought about how Dracula had reacted when Samael had mentioned my parents, and a wicked smile split my cheeks. Perfect. "My mother rejected you, didn't she? Turned you down for a Nephilim. Broke your little heart," I said, chuckling.

Dracula flashed his fangs at me. "Your mother managed to wound my Beast. Blinded her before narrowly escaping. My Beast has a long memory. Maybe you can talk with her...when I go down for my nap," he said, smirking icily. "Oh, that's right. I don't have to nap here at the seat of my power."

I kept my face composed, but my heart had skipped a beat. My mother had done the fuck *what* to his Beast? Good god.

"I can't say I'm surprised," I lied. "Your Beast doesn't seem very dangerous. Look at us, hanging out here like old friends. No one dying..." I trailed off meaningfully. "Maybe she can't *see* us."

Dracula snarled, and the air seemed to grow thicker as I felt the Beast focus on me, specifically, but...nothing else happened. Well, the skeletons grew agitated, their sharpened bones or grafted blades rasping as they rattled against their other bones. As the seconds continued to stretch on, I realized my theory was correct. Dracula...

Couldn't unleash his Beast on me—I was already inside. If I had been outside, threatening it directly, it could have hurt me. But attacking something within you was much more difficult. Maybe the Beast could make the floor drop out from under me or something, but that would put Dracula at risk, too. I wasn't sure if I was entirely correct, but I was close enough.

Or else the Beast would have killed me.

I lifted my arms, chuckling blatantly. "You're an empty legend, Dracula. A hollow hero. An empty nightmare. Your Beast keeps things *out*, but she's impotent to protect you from things already *inside*."

Silence rang out, and I even noticed Samael staring at me incredulously.

I leaned forward to speak in a loud, theatrical whisper. "And I'm deep inside you, Dracula..." I taunted mercilessly, mentally recalling everything his kind had ever done to bring me pain—murdering innocents, bringing terror to my city, almost breaking the Shepherds in Rome, and turning Roland into a vampire.

This man was behind it all.

My smile stretched wider. "Welcome to womanhood, Dracula. You're about to get fucked."

Seeing the unbridled rage on his face, I burst out laughing.

Other than my laughter, the room was eerily silent. An oppressive silence. The Beast had heard me, and she was imagining all the ways she would make me pay for my insolence.

"Bring it, Beast," I muttered, waving a hand.

Shadows suddenly danced around Dracula, sparks flaring out behind him. "I'll show you the power of my Beast," he snarled, lifting a lacy ruffled hand like a badass.

I squared my shoulders, ready for absolutely anything. My mother had banked everything on helping me become exponentially more powerful than her.

If she had been able to blind Dracula's Beast...I would skin it alive.

6

Samael ruined my fun, holding up a hand to stop Dracula from giving me the hug I knew he had wanted to deliver. Dracula visibly shuddered before rounding on Samael with a demanding glare.

"She's been a particular pain in my ass, and I would take great satisfaction from killing the daughter of my captor. But if I can hold my vengeance in check, so can you."

Dracula growled. "My Beast's vengeance trumps yours, devil." There was a hint of warning in his tone.

Samael grimaced but nodded. "I did not waste years of planning so you could get your rocks off in five minutes." Dracula's jaw tightened at that. "Even though she is not a vampire, I think I know a way to make this still work. Perhaps even better. To have your cake and eat it too."

His tone was cooperative but definitely not submissive. They weren't friends. I wondered if I could use that.

Dracula turned to him, looking guardedly pensive. "Oh?"

Samael nodded.

"And what do you propose?" Dracula asked, sounding curious. Samael leaned close, murmuring into his ear for a moment. Then he leaned back, waiting. Dracula looked like he'd just felt a questionably dangerous tummy rumble. Then he began shaking his head, smirking as if calling out Samael's bluff. "I should very much like to see this. I will play along."

The two turned to look at me as Samael spoke. "I'll need to get close."

"Step right up, Sammy," I said, allowing my magic to crackle down my arms and fists like an electric current. I was confident that I wouldn't like whatever Samael had suggested, but for Dracula to *doubt* it?

That made me expect something decidedly worse, and my imagination began to run wild with possible attacks he might use.

In all my scenarios, I hadn't expected a tag team.

Dracula's will suddenly struck me with a screaming, unceasing, gale force wind so that I had to lean forward in order to remain upright and keep my balance. I was so focused on not falling down that I failed to notice the skeletons suddenly swarming towards me. They hit me in an avalanche of bones, swarming over me to grab at my arms and legs, my hair and my jacket, gripping anything they could get their necromantic little digits on.

And Dracula's perpetual blast of force—like a vampiric leaf-blower on steroids—raged on, not affecting the skeletons in the slightest. Only me.

Panic overtook me as I visualized being buried alive beneath their collective mass—kind of like when you woke up in the middle of the night, freaking the hell out because your sheets were all tangled up, firmly restraining you as securely as a straightjacket.

I freaked the hell out.

My angelic wings of ephemeral smoke and fog suddenly erupted out from my back, somehow solid enough to slice a row of the skeletons entirely in half.

Then I spread my wings wide—grateful to see that Dracula's will slipped harmlessly through them like they were made of screen rather than them billowing out like a parachute. With a hoarse roar, I snapped them forward in a concussive *clap*, volleying his power back in some way that I didn't consciously understand.

But it worked.

The force doubled back on him with a *thump* that shattered glasses on the table, sending him skidding back into the piano as he gritted his teeth, glaring at me. The very walls suddenly began to quake, rattle, and roll as Dracula's Beast figuratively rolled up her sleeves to take a turn at exterminating the winged vermin causing her host harm.

My fight with her would take place solely on the magical spectrum since she didn't have a corporeal body, so I needed to conserve my power.

But keeping the skeletons at bay was consuming all my attention, their grabby hands preventing me from simply flying a safe distance away.

So I called upon my Silvers.

Silver blades erupted out from between the fingers of my fists so that each hand sported twin, feather-light claws as long as my forearm.

The White Rose was ready to wield her Silver thorns.

And I began tearing through the skeletal horde, slicing and spinning my way clear from those closest to me, regaining some room to move. I was thankful there wasn't much resistance. Their bones were so old that my claws ripped right through them—or maybe my Silvers were powerful enough for their density not to matter. Either way, they fell like reaped wheat all around me. I gained back enough room to use my wings, and abruptly slammed the left wing down like a shield as I used the right wing like a spear to impale a trio of skeletons.

As the skeletons fell, broke, or were sliced in two, the embers and sparks holding their bones together bloomed up into the air like a cyclone of fiery will-o'-the-wisps. Luckily, none of them burned me. I was screaming as I spun, bobbed, stabbed, tore and even stomped on my foes.

Their assault finally relented and I stood there panting, glaring at the heaps of dismantled femurs, tibias, and rib bones. I glanced down to see that a skull adorned one of the claws on either hand, and that they were silently screaming at me, their teeth rattling and clicking—still alive.

I lifted my head to look Dracula in the eyes as I kissed one of the skulls on the forehead. Then I slowly turned to look at Samael as I kissed the other skull on the forehead.

Then I let my Silver magic flow over each skull, encasing them in liquid metal. The skulls stopped trying to speak—perhaps unable to—and I lowered my hands to let them fall to the floor with heavy, metallic *clangs*.

Then I bent down and scooped up an errant rib bone. I hefted it in my palm. "Women, right?" I asked the two stupefied men, smiling. "God really dropped the ball on that decision, didn't he? Should have stuck with the dirt recipe."

I sensed movement in my peripheral vision and flung the rib bone like a throwing knife.

It sunk into the eye socket of a skeleton who had been attempting to sneak up on me. It also pinned him into the wall, shattering through the back of his skull. He struggled desperately to dislodge the rib of his fellow skeletal brother, hissing all the while.

I noticed the blood slaves meekly sweeping up the bones into neat piles and waving their hands over them. Sparks fell from their fingers to fall over the bones, and they suddenly began to twitch and move, rebuilding themselves into fully-functioning skeletons with new embers and sparks for ligaments. I narrowed my eyes. So the blood slaves were going to be a problem.

Because they were obviously necromantic field medics of some kind.

"Enough games," Dracula snarled. I felt the pressure in the air suddenly drop—not having even noticed it during my fight—its sudden absence felt like the ground had just fallen out from beneath my boots.

And Dracula's Beast grabbed me by the soul, somehow even pinning my wings to my back, proving that it was perfectly capable to dominate me on the physical plane as well as the magical.

I hissed and struggled, railing against the unseen appendages for any kind of weakness. Upon contact—or whatever this sensation could be called —I suddenly realized that I could feel the Beast itself. And it made my pulse skip a beat or ten.

It.

Was.

Immense.

Unbelievably immense. Like a force of nature. And some part of me realized that the Beast was as surprised as me—that I had somehow taken a peek beneath the curtain. I knew this because it suddenly grew incredibly warm as a tidal wave of rage surged up inside the Beast.

I took a wild guess and assumed it had verified my blood—the blood of Constance's descendant—the woman who had somehow taken the Beast's eyes. I struggled and fought harder, fearing it would simply engulf me and extinguish my soul like a pinched candle wick.

It wasn't just that it was powerful; it was that it was a power I couldn't even comprehend. Like I was a world-champion bodybuilder standing outside during a storm thinking I was strong enough to punch a tornado and knock it away from my house.

The two forms of strength weren't even comparable.

But that example was more believable than me trying to stand up against this Beast.

It made Falco look like a puny runt of the litter, where this was the matriarch of all Beasts everywhere.

I heard the two men arguing loudly, but couldn't make out their words as I strained against the Beast. "Enough!" Dracula finally commanded, sounding closer.

I gasped as the pressure abruptly eased, not having even realized it had been squeezing me so tightly that I hadn't been able to breathe. The Beast still held me in place, but it was no longer beating the hell out of my soul. My eyes abruptly felt like they were about to bug out of my face and my body was shaking. My Silver claws had simply snapped off and fallen to the floor. What the hell?

Samael was suddenly standing before me, studying me and my broken claws thoughtfully. He looked at me like an object, not an ounce of recognition in his eyes—not a sliver of compassion or camaraderie.

A scientist examining a lifeless object.

A stranger.

I wondered which Samael had been real. This one or the one who had entered Dracula's Castle with me. It sounded obvious—that this cruel Samael was the original, because he had obviously been working with Dracula the entire time. The part that didn't make sense was that he'd told Dracula that his goal had been to bring Roland here, but back in the church where I had fought Roland, Samael hadn't shown the slightest interest in the ex-Shepherd.

Samael had told me it had all been a setup to get *me* here, not Roland.

One of the two was a lie. Knowing he was a demon, I hadn't expected anything less—regardless of our Blood Bond. Maybe Dracula had a Blood Bond with Samael as well, and his was simply stronger than mine.

Ultimately, the motivations didn't really matter at the moment.

Samael lied so easily that it was impossible to know which lie was closest to the truth.

Samael stared at my arms and legs—the same spot I swore I could feel the furious Beast gripping me to hold me in place—even though there was no visible sign of my restraints.

I stared at Samael, my lips curling back. "Godless, dickless, spineless, powerless—"

He struck me across the jaw so strongly and casually that my vision winked out for a second. When it returned, stars spun across my field of sight. I hadn't fallen, thanks to the Beast holding me in place, which made the blow hurt more. Samael stared at me with zero emotional expression—no anger, no amusement. Just an emptiness. "It's time to play your part, girl. You will not enjoy it, but I will," he said, staring down at my unseen restraints again.

Dracula spoke up from across the room. "Go ahead."

I swabbed my tongue around my mouth, tonguing a tooth that felt slightly loose. Then I spit in his face, speckling it with blood and saliva.

He narrowed his eyes, and I felt a moment of vertigo as his eyes visibly darkened like they were trying to pull me into a void of nothingness. I averted my eyes to stare at his nose instead.

He chuckled derisively. "Embrace the Beast, daughter of Solomon."

And he placed his palm on my forehead. My skin crackled and hissed.

I screamed as fire ripped through me like a trail of lit gasoline from forehead to toes. It burned and ravaged and...cleansed.

Cleansed me of all power. I wasn't sure how I knew this through the pain, but I was certain of it. My powers were gone, burnt away. The fire slowly faded as it smoldered and cooled, and the Beast's grip slowly evaporated with a satisfied purr—like it had just consumed a large meal and was going down for a nap.

I fell to the ground, unable to support my own weight.

7

My arm and fingers shook as I weakly reached out to grab one of my broken Silver claws less than a foot away, and it took every ounce of mental and physical strength I could muster to get them working in concert, even if it was slightly arthritic and at a glacial speed. Like those dreams where you ran as fast as you possibly could—even faster than physically possible—only to find that the monster chasing you was only walking, laughing wickedly as he somehow managed to close the distance.

That you simply could not move fast enough to escape his leisurely stroll, even though you were putting absolutely everything you had into it.

Samael chuckled, kicking the Silver claw out of reach—waiting until I was about an inch away from contact to do so, the bastard.

His laugh made me imagine a sadistic kid with a magnifying glass after discovering an ant hill.

I reached within me, trying to call up my Silvers...and failed.

I tried my wizard's magic, and sensed only smoke from the internal inferno that had blazed through me.

I even considered snatching at my Horseman's Mask but I knew I would never reach it before Samael stopped me. I needed a minute to catch my breath before trying that.

I tried calling upon my wings to at least fly back from my enemies, anything to get away...

And I felt only the physical silence of an abandoned church.

I was, more or less, a Regular, with no magic to speak of.

Dracula grunted in satisfaction, staring down at me. I hadn't realized he'd approached. I glared up at him, struggling to get my muscles to obey so that I could at least stand. "Incredible," he mused, staring at my forehead as I glared at him. "The Mark of the Beast. I thought you were boasting! It has been some time since I've seen true devil-work. My resident demon prefers gossip to actual work."

Samael grunted knowingly. "I'm surprised you keep her around. I've always hated her, and that's saying something." He smiled faintly. "I could take her off your hands—"

"You will do no such thing. Her gossip falls on deaf ears, and I must admit, she is occasionally useful. Enough to grant her continued existence."

"As you wish," Samael said, not sounding best pleased.

"While our guest is recovering, tell me what you did and why. What do you plan to do.." Dracula asked Samael, his voice trailing off as the two of them walked away to speak in private—too quietly for me to hear.

As much as I wanted to eavesdrop on their talk, getting back on my feet was more important. I groaned as I managed to prop myself up on my elbows. Then I actually sat up, supporting my weight with my hands. The effort left me panting and dizzy, but I pressed on. Even though my body was weak, I didn't necessarily *hurt*—even on my forehead where Samael had touched me with the Mark of the Beast.

I knew that phrase was referenced in the Book of Revelations in the Bible; however, I didn't understand how it had taken my powers away.

The Mark of the Beast was a brand to be given to all mankind who were left behind in the End Days, like a farmer branding his cattle to prove ownership.

Except you wouldn't be owned by any farmer. You would be owned by the Devil—or one of his minions.

And the Mark was a number—666.

So...

What did that have to do with my various powers?

I knew one thing, though. My Godfather was the worst kind of asshole.

I grunted, climbing awkwardly to my feet. The blood rushed to my head and I had to grip the table with my hands to steady my balance. I waited until my vision steadied before loudly clearing my throat, interrupting them as rudely as I could manage. "What did you do to me?" I demanded.

Dracula turned to smile at me, not bothered by my interruption in the slightest. Worse, he looked eager. "Samael was quite clever. He was just telling me how he used devilry to give you the Mark of the Beast, forming a conduit with Sanguina that I hadn't considered possible." Seeing the confusion on my face, he pointed up at the ceiling. "Sanguina is the name of Castle Dracula's Beast."

I glanced pointedly at the bloody Cross Pattée covering my chest. "Even though my outfit says otherwise, I'm not really up-to-date on the churchy stuff. The Mark of the Beast is from Revelations, so how would that take away my powers or tie me to...Sanguina?" I said, testing out the name. I was surprised that I didn't feel her freak the hell out when I said it. I didn't feel her at all, as a matter of fact. That couldn't be good. "Shouldn't it make me some kind of zombie or servant of Hell?" I asked, genuinely confused.

Dracula and Samael were both nodding, although Samael's grin was smug and he looked as if a great weight had been lifted from his shoulders. As if he had finally gotten his revenge against me for the crimes of my mother, finally able to taste freedom after his long prison sentence within the Seal of Solomon.

Dracula motioned for Samael to explain, chuckling and shaking his head, looking thoroughly impressed by what Samael had done.

Samael turned his grin my way. "I was able to bond your powers to Sanguina because your mother took her eyes, and you share your mother's blood. And since Sanguina is a *Beast*, the Mark of the *Beast* was a close enough conduit to bridge the gap," he explained.

That...actually made sense. Damn it.

"Tit-for-tat," he continued. "I'll admit a small personal win as well—your mother bonded me in chains, and now I've bonded you in chains." I narrowed my eyes, but didn't say anything. "The Mark of the Beast is so much more than a mere bond of servitude to Hell. If I hadn't been here in the heart of Dracula's Beast, it never would have been possible. I wish I had thought of the connection sooner," he admitted.

Dracula interrupted. "Is this something any demon could do?" he asked, suddenly looking concerned.

Samael snorted. "All demons know how to *draw* it, but only Greater

Demons are strong enough to *power* it. An army of demons could doodle this all over your castle, and it would have the same effect as them drawing stick figures."

Dracula looked immensely relieved.

I cut in, not caring about Professor Samael's *Demonology 101* lesson. "Since Dracula looks like he's about to fanboy so hard that he's dangerously close to dry-humping your leg, I'm guessing you already have a plan for when I tell you that I want my powers back. Right now."

Dracula's eyes narrowed slightly at my assessment, but Samael simply nodded. "If you want your powers back, you will have to make a trade with Sanguina."

Dracula cleared his throat. "That was one of my questions, too," he told me. "Those inhabiting my castle are bonded to me by blood, and in effect, bonded to Sanguina. Their bond to me is the only thing keeping them safe from Sanguina's...appetite."

I nodded slowly, working that out in my mind. "Sanguina won't eat those bonded to you. And what Samael did to me is similar enough in effect, bonding me to her indirectly through this Mark. I'm assuming I can't just wipe it off..."

Samael laughed harshly. "Go ahead and try. It won't feel pleasant."

So I did. I reached up and wiped my forehead with my sleeve.

And fucking collapsed like a sack of potatoes, hissing as if I'd scraped a raw wound.

Dracula's eyes widened, and Samael nodded satisfactorily. "Only a Greater Demon can remove it," he said in a lecturing tone as I climbed back to my feet.

"Right," I said, knowing that I would not be trying that again.

Samael cleared his throat. "Now. The difference with your relationship with Sanguina is that I gave her a taste of your powers, and she now knows you are the daughter of the one who took her eyes. She is *very* hungry to eat you, Callie. If I hadn't put her to sleep, you would already be dead. With you, there is no buffer of protection like the inhabitants of this castle can claim. In three days, she will wake, and you shall die."

"Unless," Dracula said, holding up a finger, "you give her something else she desires. Over the years, I have gifted magical ruby amulets from my treasury to certain residents of my castle as a token of gratitude to thank them for one thing or another," he said, gesturing vaguely with his hand. "There are about forty of them in total, and Sanguina has always wanted to eat those residents more than the others—to see if she could taste the extra dash of loyalty in their blood." He frowned and turned to look at Samael. "How many does she need again?" he asked.

"Six," Samael replied dryly before taking a sip of his wine.

Which was interesting. 666 was the Mark of the Beast but...I was also the Sixth Horseman.

Coincidence?

Dracula snapped his fingers. "Right. You could find and kill any six of these forty esteemed residents, and dip their amulets in their blood. The amulets have the ability to absorb their blood and essence, you see. Then, when you are ready to feed them to Sanguina, simply shatter them on the floor. Each shattered necklace will result in some of your powers returning. When all six have been broken, I will call Sanguina off."

Forty options and I had to pick six. What kind of *esteemed residents* were we talking about? Frankenstein? The original Renfield? I'd read up on Dracula over the years, but it had primarily been via Bram Stoker. And, thinking that Dracula had died at the end, I hadn't really delved much further into his specific story. Who had he been friends with?

And...could I kill *any* of them without my powers?

I studied the two men, thinking furiously. "Let me get this straight. You're going to just let me walk around the castle to feed six of your most valued residents to your dog so that your dog doesn't eat *me*?" I asked, trying to comprehend why the hell anyone—especially Dracula—would want such a thing done. I even wondered if I had misheard him.

Dracula nodded. "If you survive that long, you will join me for dinner at the end of the three days. At which point, I'm sure you will try to kill me since you will have all your magic back, and I will be forced to swat you down like a child. Afterwards, you will serve me for eternity, whether you want to or not." He leaned forward, smiling darkly. "Or you can reconsider your earlier answer about working with me. We can skip all of the games and you can begin serving me right now."

I narrowed my eyes, not liking the sound of that one bit. Especially after hearing how much he valued his current residents. "I'd prefer the chance to fight you on even ground, since you so bravely took away my weapons before flexing," I said, taunting him.

He smiled good-naturedly. "So be it. I will arrange for a guide to show you around, otherwise you will never even *find* your six targets in the three days Samael has given you. Do with the guide what you will. I have no further use for him. I also won't tell any of my people about your little visit or you wouldn't last an hour. But if they sense you..." he trailed off, shrugging with an anticipatory grin.

"How considerate," I muttered.

He smiled politely. "You're welcome. Don't be too picky on your targets. Your time is limited and there is a lot of ground to explore." He rubbed his hands together excitedly. "Samael and I will be rather busy over the next three days, but I truly look forward to our dinner. You can tell me all about your adventures before we begin working together!"

Then he gave me a mocking bow, and motioned for Samael to follow him towards the door in the back of the room—the same one Samael had initially entered from. Samael hesitated after a few steps, and then cleared his throat pointedly.

Dracula slowed, turning to him. "Yes?"

"You forgot to mention that each shattered necklace will bring Sanguina up from her slumber. That she will fully wake when all six are broken. What if Miss Penrose is ambitious and finishes early? I warned you that she is rather competent."

My stomach lurched, even though I kept my face blank.

Dracula considered the question, scratching at his chin. "Well, I'm not going to change our dinner reservation. You and I have much work to do over the next three days, Samael. Business before pleasure, I always say."

Samael nodded his agreement. Neither of them bothered looking at me. "So what happens if Sanguina wakes early and we are too busy working?"

Dracula thought about it and finally nodded. "I see what you mean." He turned to me, dipping his chin again. "It seems your choice is to either dine with me in three days, or be *dined upon* if you are too...*ambitious*. I'll leave the decision up to you. But we could do great things together, Miss Penrose."

To summarize, it would be suicide to get all my powers back as fast as possible and go exploring. Like I needed to do to find Dracula's Bane—the only weapon that could permanently kill him, apparently.

At least, if Samael hadn't been lying about that as well.

Unless I wanted to meet the puppy who thought I was her favorite new chew toy. Despite telling me that he would call off Sanguina if I killed six of his residents, the caveat was that I had to time my breaking of the amulets to happen right before our dinner—or else Sanguina would kill me since he would be too *busy* to stop her.

I folded my arms across my chest. "It would be really convenient if you told me where the heart of your castle is. I need to pick something up really quick before dinner. It's a stake knife, you see..."

Dracula chuckled. "Hilarious."

"No," I said, shaking my head. "Hell-arious. But you won't get the joke until I drive the point home. You'll see. It's all about the timing. But first, I'm going to make you tell me all about your secret club, the Masters."

He stared at me for a long moment, and then let out a deep laugh, shaking his head as he glanced at Samael as if to ask if this was really happening. Samael just sighed and gave him a nod. Dracula turned back to me. "Even with all your powers, you wouldn't stand a chance against me and my Beast. Her very thoughts have killed even the strongest of men. It was a game we played many times in our youth. I'll even take you to see her in person after our dinner. You can physically meet her, you know. She is not just an unseen entity in the walls. She is *alive...*"

I suppressed a shudder, masking my fear with snark. "Only one way to find out, Johnny B. Suckit. Now, where is our dinner date?"

"Right here," he said, holding out his arms. "I'll have the Clock Tower toll...six times," he said, chuckling at how clever he thought he was to match numbers together, "to give you a one-hour warning before it is time for our dinner. Tardiness is incredibly rude, after all."

"Incredibly," I said dryly, but all I could visualize was that purple vampire guy—the Count—from Sesame Street. *Six, I give you six chimes! Ah, ah, ah!*

Count Dracula dipped his head one last time and turned to leave, already talking to Samael over his shoulder. "Let us go celebrate your good service with some wine, shall we..."

Their conversation was cut off as the door closed behind them.

8

The rest of the skeletons and blood slaves in the room simply left through side doors, leaving me entirely alone—which was about the strangest thing imaginable. How calmly everyone was acting.

I reached out to the table and dislodged my katana, staring at it in silence for a long time.

A human—even well-trained—stood very, very, long odds to find and kill six powerful monsters in only seventy-two hours. Especially when Dracula had hordes of monsters walking around as guards. I wasn't simply dueling six monsters in a fair fight.

I was sneaking through their camp to assassinate six of their commanders before the rest of the army woke up and caught me. Even though Dracula wasn't going to warn them about me, I was pretty sure they would come after me if they saw me sneaking around.

And I had to do it all without magic.

Considering the size of Castle Dracula, it wasn't like they were all lined up for me. They could be anywhere. And could be anyone.

I still had the Mask of Despair in my pocket, but Samael hadn't said anything about that. It was unlikely he would have forgotten such an obvious thing...so why had he not mentioned it? Maybe the Mark of the Beast was strong enough to block even that? He *had* burned me on the forehead—the same place where Despair was magically branded into my flesh.

Had he broken my Horseman power somehow? I desperately wanted to check my pocket to make sure the Horseman Mask wasn't destroyed, but I didn't want to give away my only potential magic until I found a safe place to do so.

In a strange way, this was all a very anti-climactic turn of events from the all-out-brawl I had anticipated.

Yet it was also so much worse than I could have imagined.

I heard a sudden rattling sound beside me and instinctively swung my katana without looking. My blade easily decapitated the skeleton standing beside me. His head fell towards me and I caught it in my other hand by pure reflex.

It was the dude I had put in the red dress. The only reason I knew that was because he still wore his kinky pirate boots and the large red bandana, and all the other skeletons I'd seen were naked with weapons for limbs. His skull stared up at me from my hand. "Would you please stop knocking my head off?" he asked in probably the politest tone I'd ever heard.

I winced, both at the concept of holding his talking skull in my hand, and in slight guilt at my repeat offenses. The headless body of the skeleton walked up to me, bending at the waist in a silent request for me to return the merchandise.

I thought about it. The skeleton could obviously still talk without his body. Maybe I could use him for answers on where my guests lived, holding the skull hostage.

Which would mean carrying around a skull to have easy access to answers. Like my own personal assistant—Siri.

Skulli.

I realized I was internally humming the X-Files theme song in my head and snapped out of it.

Finally, I shook my head. Lugging around a talking skull was just really freaking strange, and I didn't have a bag or anything to carry it so it would only get in my way during a fight. Or it would say something at the worst possible moment, like while I was trying to stealthily assassinate one of my targets.

"You're thinking about keeping my skull, aren't you?" he asked, gloomily.

I shook my head a little too quickly. "No. Of course not. That would be creepy."

Somehow, he managed a doubtful look by raising a ridge-bone over his eye—the same place an eyebrow would be on a human face. Or I could have just imagined it. "You *were* considering it," he muttered unhappily.

"No. Really. It's not like you could help me or anything—"

"I could help immensely. I know the castle like the back of my hand."

"But you won't, of course. You work for Drac—"

"My Master has given me to you. I am yours."

"Oh! You're the *guide*!" I blurted, having forgotten about Dracula's mention of giving me one. He wobbled in my hands—a nodding gesture. I stared down at him for a few moments, wondering how I felt about having Dracula's henchman lurking around me for the next three days. "Then I could just plop your head back on and you can point me in the right direction, so I wouldn't need to keep your skull. If I had been considering it, of course."

"There is every chance I would betray you or attack you when you let your guard down. I am a dastardly fiend."

I dropped the skull on the floor, preparing to stomp on him. "I knew it! Not so tough now, are we?" I crowed.

"That was a joke," he said dejectedly, staring up at me. "I am no danger. I haven't even earned the right to arm myself." I hesitated, lowering my boot with a frown. His skull hopped back upright somehow, and he swiveled to direct his gaze at the boots and bandana skeleton body still waiting patiently beside me. "My arms. I haven't earned the right to sharpen them to blades, let alone to dip them in the Eternal Metal."

I stared at the skeleton's arms, shaking my head. He hadn't earned the right to sharpen his appendages into blades or to dip them into molten metal. The *right*.

"I am even less of a threat than you at the moment. We will probably both die in obscure, horrifying torment. Master Dracula obviously had no further use for me. I should have been armed fifty years ago. I am quite incompetent in combat."

I frowned in disbelief. "You're also one hell of a motivational speaker."

He shook his head. "No. I am quite uninspiring."

Jesus. I'd found Eeyore's skull. "You're telling me that your only value is your mind. Your head, essentially."

He nodded. "What little ingenuity I have is nullified by my severe incompetence in close combat—unlike my brothers. I am bluntly honest, but my memory is quite good. Perhaps that is why I'm useless in combat.

Brains over brawn. Many of my kind cannot even speak, let alone think. They just obey and fight."

Wow. He was really selling himself. "Alright. I'll just decapitate you if you cause problems. And I'll hide your head somewhere weird."

"Of course. I can show you some excellently strange places."

Yeah. This guy was going with me. I bent down to scoop him up. As I was shoving his skull back onto his vertebrae with a cringeworthy, crackling sound, I decided the gesture was intimate enough to require some kind of dialogue. "Don't you need one of the blood slaves to put yourself back together?"

The skeletons I had fought had needed magic to reanimate.

His skull snapped back into place with a faint pop and flare of sparks that didn't cause any burn damage despite plastering the back of my hand.

He jerked his neck and it spun in a full circle, accompanied by what sounded like a string of firecrackers. He finally let out a dusty sigh and returned my gaze. "I have never needed help to reanimate. I guess that is something I'm good at. Dying. Or not dying, technically."

"Any other helpful qualities?" I asked, trying not to sigh.

"I am remarkably cowardly."

I sighed, giving up. "Alright. What's your name?"

"Master Dracula doesn't name us. He uses his sheer will to command us."

I thought about it. When he'd struck the piano, he'd kind of slid down the keys like his bones were playing a xylophone. I kept my face blank as I looked up at him. "How about Xylo?" I asked, hoping he wouldn't get the reference. Xylo-bone.

He thought about it. "Xylo..." he mused, scratching at his chin. "I like this name very much. Can I truly keep it?"

I nodded slowly, his words making me feel guilty for how I had chosen it. "Um. That's what you generally do with names, yeah."

He lowered his gaze, repeating it a few times under his breath.

Perfect. Xylo-bone the Undying and the White Rose. Lookout Dracula.

"We should probably leave this area," he urged. "Patrols are more numerous here. Follow me," he said.

He led me towards a different door than the one Dracula and Samael had taken. I let him go first, not wanting to risk him setting me up for a trap.

Nothing happened, other than he led me into a much cozier hallway, almost like they angled towards the private living quarters of the place. Xylo led me down the hall in utter silence. We took three more doors and several additional turns in continued sheer quiet. I realized that if so many of his brothers couldn't talk, he probably wasn't used to conversation.

Xylo was naturally a mute. I'd have to break the ice.

"So, Xylo, you like balloons?" I asked, thinking of something happy.

He continued walking but managed to turn his head entirely backwards to look at me. "They are delightful. I found one once, but a werewolf popped it and kicked me down a well. It took me a few years to get back out. I lost the balloon down there."

I nodded wearily, not sure how to reply to that level of bullying. Maybe silence was preferable. Much better than talking to Eeyore.

9

The wind whipped at my hair, screaming and wailing all around me like the sounds of every soul that had ever been born here—and by born, I meant left their mortal restraints behind to decompose in the very soil of this cursed place where Dracula feasted on the poor, hapless creatures and bound their souls to his eternal service.

I'd told Xylo I needed a space far away from everything—somewhere I could somewhat peaceably gather my thoughts. Knowing I was currently in a house full of monsters, I would have been perfectly fine with knowing that the figurative torture and mutilation of innocents was happening two rooms away, rather than only one. Honestly, I hadn't expected him to know of anything even remotely resembling a suitable place.

Then he'd brought me up to the fucking roof of one of the towers. And it had a connecting bridge to another even *taller* tower. He'd assured me that the other tower was incredibly dangerous, but that it was locked with powerful magic and that hardly anyone ever used it.

Not entirely reassuring, but better than nothing.

I was hesitant to trust the skeleton as a result of his prior affiliations with Dracula, but something about the harmless, emo skeleton was kind of endearing—like having a stray puppy. And I had kicked his ass several times already when he'd shown me no signs of physical aggression. I'd just been reacting on the basic assumption that anyone here was an enemy, which was just common sense. Except he was nothing like his weaponized brothers. He was probably the mellowest being I'd ever met. He just didn't care about anything or anyone strongly enough to want to fight for it—even Dracula. For better or for worse, I would use him—and keep a close eye on him for any sign of betrayal.

I sat down on the stone railing of the bridge, directly in the center of the two towers, dangling my feet over the abyss. I pulled out my silver butterfly charm—a magically concealed form for my Horseman Mask—and held it in my fist, doing nothing with it other than establishing direct contact with it. That was important to me.

The bridge reminded me of another I'd once visited. It had also hung over a vast, seemingly eternal space and either end had held dangers for puny little humans who thought they could play with vastly superior beings.

I'd fought Samael there. He'd killed Cain. The only reason Cain had been brought back to life was due to us both passing the test from Solomon's Temple.

Regardless, I was experiencing some deep feelings right about now. I had already been in a dark place, having just come off a fight with Roland where I'd fully intended to kill him, only to find out that we had all been pawns in a game orchestrated by beings much stronger than any of us—namely, Samael and his associates.

Xuanwu—the Black Tortoise.

Qinglong—the Azure Dragon.

And the Unholy Trinity—as they'd called themselves—had apparently set all of that up as a favor to my mother. A promise they had made her to keep me safe in various ways—primarily, making Samael my Godfather and for us to come to Castle Dracula and bag-and-tag our first Master.

So, with Samael betraying me not even an hour into his alleged oath to fulfill my mother's wishes, was this another game? Was it a joke? On whom? My mother, me, or Dracula?

Was Samael one of these Masters?

And why had Dracula reacted so strangely when I mentioned the Masters? Had he been surprised I knew about them, or surprised that I cared to know the answers in light of my own troubles?

That Dracula had figuratively made me the unlucky sap tasked with kicking out all the guests still crashing at his house from the party last night —before the parental units came back home.

My method was simple—exsanguination.

Except...it made absolutely no sense. Why task me with killing his infernal fraternity brothers? Those most loyal.

I realized that I could spend the next few years trying to decide who had lied, to whom, and when, but that ultimately it didn't matter.

Rather than worrying about what anyone else thought—who they worked for, who they had promised what to—the only constant I could rely upon was what I was going to do about it.

What I wanted to do right now.

I needed to treat this as if everyone was working against me, and that if everyone but me ended up dead at the end...well, that was their fault for not filling me in on the details ahead of time. If they were on my side—really playing games against Dracula—then the only reason they wouldn't tell me anything beforehand was because they trusted me enough to be myself and do what I did best.

Kill monsters who did anything more felonious than jaywalking.

I had been thrown into the deep end of the pool without my floaties. Treading water as I debated which person had thrown me into the pool wouldn't help save me from drowning. Movement was life.

I would get answers after I reached shore—when I confronted Dracula.

Dracula...Vlad Dracul...Count Dracula. The Dragon. Whatever his name or origin really was. And his Beast, Sanguina—the source of his power. The creature that controlled everything as far as the eye could see.

The Castle Keep—as Xylo had called it—was where Dracula actually lived, and where I had first met the bastard and lost all my powers. It was the heart of the royal structure—what everyone imagined a castle would look like. Just a metric giga-fuck-ton bigger, more sinister, and scarier.

We had escaped through dozens of hallways, tunnels, rooms, and about fifty-bajillion stairs to finally reach two of the outermost towers, giving me the first chance to look back and get a clear view of the place.

The Castle Keep branched out into numerous towers of dark gray—almost black—stone connected together by battlements, bridges, and...probably a bunch of other really cool names that equated to architectural or engineering porn.

Xylo had gone on at length describing them to me, but I had zoned out.

All I needed to know was that the Castle Keep was the figurative *Pride Rock* from *The Lion King*.

And everything within the surrounding ring of titanic, moss-covered walls was called Castle Dracula—his kingdom.

Kind of confusing, really.

Sitting on my bridge, I focused on everything but the Keep. I stared out at the beautiful, seductive nightmare of a landscape. As horrifying as the place was, it also felt like I was looking at one of the Ancient Wonders of the World. The architecture of everything was exquisite, embellished, ornate, and built on a scale that only should have been possible in a movie or video game. Never in the real world.

Yet here I was.

And seeing it up close from hundreds of feet overhead, rather than from the Courtyard, was breathtaking. Ironically, it served to bring all the nightmares to life.

I stared outwards, trying to familiarize myself with the general layout of the area in front of the Castle Keep. I saw a giant observatory, the Clocktower Dracula had mentioned, a stadium that reminded me of the famous Coliseum in Rome, what looked like a replica of the U.S. Capitol building, several gardens of statues that looked like chessboards from this elevation, gargantuan fountains, dozens of cemeteries, and a hilly sprawl of wooded and floral gardens with fog-covered ponds that might even rival Central Park in New York City.

Nearest me was a collection of two and three-story buildings that resembled a decent-sized town, replete with darkened alleys, a few pubs, and even what appeared to be a brothel or inn featuring scantily clad women—sporting tails—barking out crude catcalls to those in the streets in an attempt to stroke up some business. Drunken singing and cursing drifted out from the open windows and door, so the women had either already tapped out their opportunities inside, or the prostitutes were trying to lure in new customers in order to spread their legs—their market share.

I spotted dozens of winged sentries scouting the perimeter of the outer walls, circling a few of the towers in what looked like a familiar routine to guard the Castle Keep. We were a good football field or two within the perimeter, so they didn't come anywhere near us.

I could even see vague glowing forms moving through some of the nearby cemeteries, packs of werewolves patrolling the woods, a handful of human-like creatures—maybe vampires—walking the streets, and dozens of the skeleton dudes standing in perfect circles just staring at each other.

Fucking weirdos.

Castle Dracula wasn't just a barracks for his vast and diverse army. It really was a home—a city. Remembering Nate Temple's Beast, Falco, and the crazy assortment of 'monsters' who often resided there...

It wasn't necessarily reassuring. Was Nate one bad day away from Falco becoming like this? Two bad days? Maybe that bad day had been weeks, months, or years ago, and no one knew it yet—perhaps not even Nate.

I dismissed the thought—knowing I couldn't do anything about it if I died in the next three days.

So, as I assessed the monsters going about their figurative day—even though Dracula had said the place was perpetual night—I remembered Dracula telling me that he wasn't notifying everyone that I was stalking the streets. No one was looking for me. If and when I raised enough hell, I was certain things would change, but for now, I had a semblance of safety.

If Dracula had wanted me dead, he could have simply locked me in the feast room and sent everyone to greet me. He could have also locked me up in a cell to imprison me.

Technically, thanks to the barrier around us that Samael had brought over from Kansas City, we were *all* prisoners here. None could leave until Dracula died.

Which meant I needed to find Dracula's Bane—as Samael had called it—in the belly of the currently sleeping Beast. Did that mean the Keep?

I went over it in my head a hundred times, trying to find some hidden clue or hint that Samael might have dropped.

That this was all some act, like he had said.

But the way he had hit me in the face...

The way he had cut off my power...

The way he had spoken about my mother...

He could have earned an award for best actor.

But something about the quest the two bastards had given me just didn't sit right. Another game rather than a direct confrontation. Try as I might, I couldn't think of a reason for them to go to such efforts unless either, or both, of them wanted something as a result of my quest.

I doubted the two men were discussing business. They were probably sitting in leather recliners, glad-handing each other about how incredibly clever they were. Maybe even having a double mani-pedi while they waited for our fateful dinner.

Despite Dracula's reassurance that he didn't intend to announce my arrival, that didn't mean that if I ran across some monsters that they were going to let me walk by. They just wouldn't be actively looking to maim and then murder me.

It also made me trust Xylo a little bit more. Dracula had no need to send a spy to befriend and betray me. That would ruin the fun of the trap he had already laid out. To watch his residents tear me limb from limb.

The way he had studied me across the table, though...

It was as if a part of him actually wanted me to succeed. That he wanted to face me. Because he was a recluse. Bored out of his mind hiding out in his castle. Everyone thought he was dead. He couldn't just go out and terrorize cities anymore. Well, he could, but he couldn't take credit for it. He secretly ran the world of vampires. Although impressive, it had a price.

Anonymity.

Right now he had a great board of directors in the Sanguine Council to handle all the day-to-day management. Dracula was the reclusive trust fund heir—and he was on house arrest.

One of the most feared, legendary creatures in human stories, and he couldn't revel in his reputation. I could understand that frustration. It sounded cool, but after a few months of riding your tricycle around your castle in your undies with a bottle of tequila while practicing your evil laugh, you realized you were pretty goddamned bored.

So what did my quest gain him?

The monsters below went about their duties.

The wind laughed at me.

Xylo studied me in silence.

And I continued to wonder...

❧ 10 ❧

The night sky hung overhead like an ominous blanket, seeming to somehow even dim the brilliance of the stars. The red moon added to the crimson haze in the air, but after spending the last few days in Kansas City, I'd apparently grown accustomed to Roland's barrier.

The only difference here was that the big, bad Master Vampire of this city was secretly the big, bad Master Vampire of *all* Master Vampires, working behind the curtains like the vampire of Oz, and the city itself was the birthplace of countless legends and tales—even if the most notable had been sold as fiction thanks to Bram Stoker.

But...was it?

How accurate was that story? About Jonathan Harker coming to visit a wealthy nobleman at his personal estate, forced to stay within the castle for the duration of the meeting? Maybe that wasn't so much fiction, but fact.

It didn't really matter; I was just putting off what I was supposed to be doing here. I'd done plenty of that already, and I had nothing to show for it.

Well...

Other than giving myself time to hold the Mask in my fist.

Which had been the entire point of it all.

"Mind standing over by the door, Xylo? I don't want the wind knocking you over the edge."

He stared at me blankly. "The wind goes right through me." He used his bone fingers to play a little ditty down his rib bones—literally tickling the ivories—and then held up his arms to prove that the wind had no effect on him. The only indication that it was windy was that the red bundle of fabric around his neck and shoulders that was both scarf and bandana whipped around, but he didn't appear to notice it. I'd seen something similar when Dracula hit me with the power of his will—none of the skeletons had been affected in the slightest.

I sighed. "I need you to keep an eye out for trouble," I said instead.

He stared back at me—and that drawn-out, eerie stillness from a walking, talking skeleton reminded me just how strange all of this really was. "Both of my eyes decayed long ago," he finally said, poking a bony digit two-knuckles-deep into his ocular cavity.

My stomach made a strange wriggling sensation at the imagined organs that should have been inside. "I was trying to be polite. I just need some privacy and I want you to make sure no one disturbs me or sneaks up on us."

He cocked his head, withdrawing his finger from his eye socket. "Polite? To me?" he asked, not seeming to understand. "How peculiar..." he said to himself, already turning to walk away from me. Was that because he didn't understand what *polite* meant or because he didn't know why I would bother being polite to *him*?

He stopped to stand before the supposedly dangerous, locked magical door that he'd told me hardly anyone ever used, and clenched his fists in an aggressive pantomime of menace. The only menacing thing about him was his scarf whipping in the wind, like he was some dead pirate king protecting his buried treasure. He'd already admitted he had zero combat ability, so it was comical to see him acting as if he would be able to stop one of the monsters if they happened to stumble onto the fiftieth floor of this specific tower for a smoke break on the bridge. We hadn't seen anyone at all in the tower we had climbed, so I wasn't too concerned about an attack. I'd also checked the nearby rooftops and spires for gargoyles, but the rooftops surrounding us were quiet and empty.

Xylo had been true to his word. It was a nice, quiet spot.

Having already tried—and failed—to tap into my powers back in the...

I decided to dub it the Feast Hall. It was the location for my future fight with Dracula, so I couldn't just call it the *dining room*.

Having failed to call up any of my old powers there, I tried again now, hoping to find that Samael had been putting on a show, lying to Dracula about what he'd done with the Mark of the Beast.

Perhaps he had left me my wizard's magic or something.

But I let out an annoyed sigh after only a few moments of trying to access my toolbox of powers. Samael hadn't been lying.

I couldn't use my wizard's magic. Even worse, I could still sense it—like staring through a glass display case at a priceless Hermes bag. Inches away, but it might as well have been a million miles.

I still couldn't call up my Silvers to make my claws.

I tried to tap into the Silvers to get that strange time-distorted perception of my surroundings. Fail.

I even tried calling up the Spear of Destiny—the Spear that had pierced Jesus' side on the Cross. It was healing somewhere within my soul, and Archangel Michael had called me the sheath prophesied to keep it safe.

You know, like keeping it away from Castle Dracula, for example.

It was unresponsive, but that could have been entirely unrelated. I'd never been consistently successful at calling it up. I'd gotten better, but when I needed to whip it out the most, it stubbornly refused. Maybe I needed some Holy Viagra—the little Pearly Pill.

Unlike a three-year-old boy who had just discovered his penis and wanted to whip it out at every opportunity to show the world his built-in sword and watch them bask in the radiance of his mighty blade, I had no penis saber to wield.

I see your Schwartz is as big as mine, the old movie quote popped into my head, unbidden.

Penultimately, I tried calling upon my Angel wings and gauntlets—something that was literally part of *me* thanks to an angelic blood transfusion I'd inadvertently been subjected to. Other than a faint warming sensation forming across my shoulder blades, nothing happened. I kept at it until I started to feel a tension headache forming.

Which left me my last resort. The Horseman Mask clutched in my fist.

The Mask of Despair. The Sixth Horseman of the Apocalypse.

Although my first use of it earlier tonight had been incredible, it had also powered down very rapidly. Probably because we hadn't officially bonded with each other yet. Relationships took time to build.

Those who just slapped them on and hoped for the best risked damaging the Masks, or even themselves. Like Nate Temple, the Fifth Horseman of the Apocalypse, had done with his Mask of Hope. I hadn't wanted to risk any of that, but if it ended up being my only chance at escaping Castle Dracula...

Basically, my most tried and true methods of power had failed, and my only immediate armor was the most tentative power I had access to. I wasn't holding out much hope.

Or maybe Xylo's emo aura was infecting me.

I made one last sweep of the surrounding area to make sure we were still alone before I unclenched my fist. The butterfly charm was only an illusion —a safeguard so that I wasn't literally lugging around a Mask all the time. I'd chosen the butterfly charm for personal reasons, and with a thought, I would be able to reveal the Horseman Mask.

But I didn't do that yet. The reason I'd been holding it this whole time was in hopes that it would reestablish our bond. You didn't rev an engine— or a woman—cold, gentlemen.

That approach—with either example—was just asking for an explosion of shrapnel in a wide blast radius.

I stared down at the silver charm, my pulse quickening. Could Samael have really made such a glaring mistake? Taking away my old reliable powers but leaving me the equivalent of a nuclear bomb?

If so, maybe I could drift through the castle in my mist form—an ability the Mask seemed to have—find Dracula, kill him, and then take my time with regaining my powers from Sanguina. At least it would save me the trouble of having to fight Dracula and Sanguina back-to-back.

Then again, I'd seen Dracula shift into a red mist, so maybe that option was out.

My brief interaction with the Mask had taught me a lot—it had forced me to confront a lot of internal self-doubts and concerns. Despair was manipulative, tricky, and deceitful, so I closed my eyes to focus. I took six deep breaths—for luck, since I was the Sixth Horseman—and focused on the power hidden within the butterfly charm.

Despair was the antithesis of Hope, and Despair was a dicey landscape to traverse. It was a darker, subtler, more introspective power. A blade that could cut both ways. It was self-doubt, self-pity, and any other negative thought that ever whispered in your ears that you were not strong enough, not good enough...

That was Despair.

Learning how to bond with such a depressing power without letting it roll over me had taken a lot of meditation to discern. I had related it to a battle on two fronts:

Firstly, I faced an army of negative thoughts striking the outer walls of my mental defenses like battering rams. Waves of self-doubt and criticism. Except they were all vague, generic lies.

You'll never be good enough, strong enough. No one could ever love you. Claire is so much prettier than you'll ever be.

They were an army of infantry with no real finesse, but they made up for it in numbers. The only way to survive them was to counter the flood of vague lies with opposing vague lies.

I can do anything. I will win the lottery. Everyone thinks I'm gorgeous.

Each outlandishly encouraging thought you could drum up became a miniature Tony Robbins ready to fire the-power-of-positive-thinking arrows into the advancing horde.

The second, more dangerous, front Despair attacked on was internal.

Because everyone had Despair inside of them, and it had to be accepted and admitted. While the army of lies was attacking the castle walls, an elite special forces team of legitimate self-doubt and personal failings had already infiltrated your castle and were slowly poisoning your meals, taking immense pleasure in your slow, painful demise.

Those stealthy, elusive assassins had been tricky for me to analyze. Battling them head-on was difficult because those agents of despair attacked with the truth.

Remember when your boyfriend broke up with you in sixth grade? When you flunked that test freshman year? When you lost that promotion at your job? How you always get pimples before a date?

They were relentless, and truthful, and they cut to the bone.

I had to accept these failures as one-time occurrences, not the deciding prophecy of my life.

I did all of that now, staring down at the butterfly charm.

And in return...

It did a whole lot of nothing.

I let out a breath, ironically feeling despair as the Mask of Despair failed to respond to me. I couldn't even make it turn into the actual Horseman Mask, which wasn't even really using its power. That was a very bad sign. Damn.

Even though it didn't react, I could sense that there was still power inside it. Just that I was blocked from accessing it. Like my wizard's magic. Damn, damn, damn.

I turned to find Xylo glancing back at me—turning only his skull so that his body still faced the door—letting me know that I'd cursed out loud. I motioned him over to join me. It was looking like I had to pick door number one, kill them without the help of my magic, and then collect their blood in their ruby amulet to at least get *some* of my power back.

And then use that power to kill five more.

Then Sanguina.

And finally, Dracula.

I hoped Xylo had a good map of the place and a dossier on each inhabitant so that I could pick an easy foe first. Xylo reached me, hesitating a few paces away, and his eyes were riveted on my clenched fist that concealed the butterfly charm. "No luck?" he asked in a careful tone. I hadn't told him exactly what I had been trying—what I held in my fist. I'd just told him I might have a backup power I could use.

I shook my head. "No," I sighed, studying him thoughtfully as I searched for any signs he may have ulterior motives—like obtaining my Mask. The embers and sparks holding his bones together occasionally flared and smoldered—lines of red and yellow light spiderwebbing across the surface of the coal-like substance. The sparks didn't seem to bother him in the slightest, and I was still surprised to find that they didn't burn if they touched my own skin. "Still willing to help me? It seems Samael was telling the truth back there," I told him, wanting to be honest.

Even though he was undying, and that Dracula had given him to me to do with as I will, I didn't think honesty was part of Baron Blood-Junkie's character. If I failed—died horribly—and Dracula believed Xylo had broken some unspoken rule, Xylo might suffer greatly.

Because he could torture an undying person for as long as he wanted.

Xylo stared down at my fist for a few more moments before looking up at me. "Nothing has really changed. If you don't mind me asking..." He trailed off, waiting for my answer. I nodded. "What were you trying to do? I...feel something in your hand, and I haven't felt anything for a very, *very* long time."

I hesitated, not sure how much I was willing to trust him. Maybe Dracula really had put him here to steal my Horseman's Mask.

I wished I had a way to establish a Blood Bond between us. It would be the perfect test to see whose bond was stronger—Dracula's or mine. But I hadn't been able to see bonds since my other powers had been taken. I'd already checked as Xylo led me through the tower.

Xylo didn't even have blood for me to bond with, and he also had no method for digesting my blood, essentially nullifying that option even if I had that power remaining. Maybe I could rub some of my blood on his lips or something, but I wouldn't be able to know if it worked or not.

I shook my head. "It's nothing—*gah!*" I gasped as the freaking butterfly charm suddenly *bit* me, causing me to reflexively unclench my grip on the charm and yank my hand away as if it had become a hot coal.

It hit the ground with a surprisingly deep *clink* sound, and it didn't even bounce, strangely enough. It just landed entirely flat like it had struck a magnet. I felt a rumbling sensation in the stones beneath my boots and knew that Dracula's Beast had somehow sensed it, momentarily stirring from her deep slumber.

Shit.

11

I waited for the bridge to suddenly give out from beneath us.

But...nothing happened. The rumbling sensation faded almost as abruptly as it appeared, hopefully meaning that Sanguina had gone back to sleep. I let out a breath of relief and stared down at my palm, expecting to see singed skin, but my flesh wasn't even flushed, let alone bleeding. It hadn't actually bit me.

So...what the hell *had* it done?

I looked up to find that Xylo stood unnaturally still, staring down at the small charm with his jaws hanging open. "What..." he whispered, unable to peel his attention away from the butterfly charm.

I hurriedly tried to avert his interest, wanting to finish what I had tried to say before it bit me. "It's nothing..." I said lamely, my hand drifting to my katana as I realized I was already too late, because Xylo was crouching down over it, seemingly unable to hear me. He didn't look greedy or suddenly evil —like he would look if he was trying to take it for himself. He looked genuinely awed, entirely enthralled by the small charm. But I remembered what Nate Temple had once told me about other people trying to touch his Horseman's Mask and getting the living hell zapped out of them.

I couldn't risk sounding too desperate. Otherwise he might consider trying to keep it for himself, and I would be forced to cut his arm off so I could get it back before he made a run for it. "Xylo—" I urged, but I wasn't fast enough. His skeletal claw carefully scooped up the Mask of Despair, cupping it like it was some priceless piece of ancient glass.

And it didn't zap him like it should have. Maybe because he was already dead and his bones weren't affected by electricity, just like they weren't affected by wind.

He stared down at it in utter silence, entranced. I very carefully squeezed the hilt of my Silver-powered katana in case he did anything even remotely too fast for my taste. Homeboy was going to lose an appendage again if he even *rattled* unexpectedly.

I silently chastised myself for not taking the damned skull rather than letting him traipse around on his own two feet. Boots. Whatever.

"This...echoes," he whispered dryly, talking more to himself. I frowned, wondering what he meant. It hadn't zapped him, and it hadn't changed into the actual Horseman's Mask, so what was he talking about? He reached in to poke it with a finger from his other hand. "If I just—"

Shadows instantly erupted out from the butterfly charm, as thick and dark as smoke from an oil fire, enshrouding Xylo so entirely that I could no longer see him through it. My pulse suddenly ratcheted up about a million miles per hour as horror swamped me. What had he done to my Mask? Had Dracula summoned him back, having completed his mission to steal my last power?

Oh, god.

I heard a faint, dismissive cough from within the cloud, and then embers and sparks began to penetrate the smog, brilliant and blinding as they poured over the ground around Xylo, splashing down like hailstones of smoldering coals to bounce and skip over the stone bridge. And the shadow slowly began to fade away as if it was being sucked up by a fan in the direct center of the cloud. Xylo.

Were his embers and sparks countering the shadowy cloud? Eating the cloud? Or absorbing it? Was the dark cloud my Horseman's power? Had he just drained the power from the Mask?

Xylo emerged from the shadow, slowly climbing back upright. The smoke visibly pooled in his eye sockets, even as the rest of the shadowy cloud was devoured by the embers and sparks holding his bones together.

Before I could demand he hand over the charm, I gasped as a current of raw energy suddenly bloomed within me—like I had just taken the perfect power nap.

I hadn't even realized I'd been tired. The energy crackled throughout my body, searching out any crevice or crack, any weary muscle or aching joint, relaxing muscles that I hadn't even known were in knots. Injuries and bruises earned from my fight with Roland faded away. I let out a shuddering breath, unable to speak as the energy seemed to even zip through my internal organs. My breathing suddenly felt easier, my stomach abruptly calmer and not hungry, my eyesight momentarily sharper. My tongue tingled and my skin flushed with prickling warmth as blood flooded through my body.

It was an exaggerated form of when I had once tried a pre-workout drink.

After moments or minutes, I wasn't sure, I finally settled back on my heels and lowered my arms—not even realizing I'd been standing on the balls of my feet with my hands to the heavens as if I'd just high-fived God in an exultant yet subconscious prayer stretch after a godly yoga session.

Goga session.

Xylo was staring at me, looking just as startled and content as I felt.

Except the last of the dark cloud—smoke as black and shadowy as the depths of a deep, underground cave—now pooled within his eye sockets, ever-shifting and roiling like the steam over a cauldron of witch's brew. He still held the charm in his hand but seemed to have forgotten it as he stared at me instead.

"I...feel you," he said faintly, sounding as if he'd been exceedingly careful in choosing his words.

I stared back, stunned to find that I was slowly nodding as I realized I felt something similar from him. In fact, I could almost feel the charm in his hand—not physically, but more as if some deep intuition confirmed that he was holding it. I even felt confident that I could turn around and accurately guess which hand he held it in—no matter how many times he might try switching them back and forth—like a disembodied extension of myself.

The most amazing part was that I was touching magic again. Even though it was a strange and scary and exciting flavor of magic that I couldn't explain, I was touching magic again. Even that small touch was enough to strengthen my confidence, my resolve for the tasks ahead.

I studied Xylo, noticing that my perception of him went far beyond the mere physical.

His mind was a dark, twisted bramble of thorns—a maze with a center that kept getting farther away the harder he tried to find it.

He might not physically feel pain, but what resided inside him was incredibly superior to anything that might be done to his physical form. Even attempting to *comprehend* that swamping darkness inside him...the magnitude of it threatened to consume me utterly.

Despite the metaphor not quite fitting the situation, the only way I could think to describe it was a bone-deep pain infesting his very marrow. Except I knew for a fact that he didn't understand it—not knowing what had caused it, where it had come from, or why he felt it—and that he had simply chosen to accept it as the natural order of his existence.

He no longer cared to question it.

I blinked away tears, my breathing shallow as I stared at him staring at me. I was confident that his inner pain wasn't some deeply buried guilt. I was also entirely certain that it wasn't him purposefully holding back some secret. He truly didn't know what it was that made him feel this way, and he no longer cared to find an explanation, let alone a solution.

He was familiar—old friends—with his sorrow and held only a bleak acceptance of his fate. He didn't even see it as a sorrow anymore. It was just the way things were. Period.

And it suddenly clicked in my mind. His morose, defeated demeanor. His lack of self-confidence. It all stemmed from this darkness within, this unanswered question.

And that despair had somehow opened him up to my Mask.

Despite his lack of confidence and swagger, I sensed an alarmingly deep well of power within Xylo—maybe even the source of his embers and sparks. But it was elusive, entirely foreign to me, and I didn't know what to make of it. The power wasn't necessarily evil, but it definitely wasn't nice either. It just *was*.

Like a wolf having no sympathy for its prey. It wasn't that the wolf didn't care for the dead rabbit's family, it was that it didn't have the capacity to entertain such an abstract thought of anything beyond the immediate solution to its own hunger.

Eating meant surviving.

And that fresh spurt of rabbit's blood hitting the wolf's tongue after a merry chase through the forest was undeniably rewarding—the sweet, savory taste of victory.

Whatever this power was, it was simply a tool Xylo had access to. The unsympathetic nature of that power wasn't a reflection of Xylo's character any more than my own powers were a reflection of mine. My mind controlled my magic, the magic didn't control my mind—because Roland had taught me the dangers in letting passions rule your objectivity.

To further prove the point, I didn't think Xylo was even aware of the potential of the power within—at least that he didn't know how to use it in any beneficial manner. Dracula never would have allowed it—and probably should have killed him for even having it.

Which begged the question...

Why had Dracula handed Xylo over to me with even less concern than he would have shown for his collection of last season's vampire capes? Maybe he didn't know? Or...

Maybe my Horseman's Mask had woken it up or activated it. Maybe it *was* the magic of Despair fusing itself to his bones. With rising panic, I probed deeper, and it only took me a moment to verify that this wasn't the case—that he hadn't drained my Mask or stolen its power. I could still sense the power from the charm, and Xylo's power—although similar to the Mask —had a different aura, I guess you could say.

I still let out a sigh of relief.

Even though I didn't share Xylo's naturally defeatist attitude, I felt a kindred spirit in Xylo. A bond or camaraderie between us.

He cocked his head suddenly—his only movement in minutes. "What is this bizarre feeling?" he asked, sounding decidedly uneasy and not best pleased.

I laughed, unable to help myself. He was reading me just as I was reading him. "Joy. You're picking up on my relief and joy, Xylo."

He mouthed the words as if trying to digest the alien emotions. Finally, he shook his head, choosing to accept it rather than question it.

His go-to coping mechanism.

A new thought hit me, and I abruptly closed my eyes, holding up a finger for him to give me a moment of silence. I focused on the new shared sensations between us.

And my legs almost buckled in disbelief.

12

I was able to visibly see the strange yet powerful bond between us, much like the Blood Bonds I had shared with a few others recently. Except... this was also entirely different than those. Bony spines as numerous as a blackberry bramble connected us in place of the cord of light. Branches, roots, and vines consisting of aged ivory tendrils connected us in dozens of places, the bone cracked and dry.

Despite the brittle appearance, I knew they were incredibly resilient. Still...

"Would you mind drinking my blood, Xylo?" I asked without opening my eyes. Because as I studied him closer, I saw a pulsing black cord of anti-light stretching out from behind him, fat and sluggish. Our multiple bonds severely outnumbered that black one, but it looked so sluggish and deliriously happy that I wanted to kill it with figurative salt and fire.

Dracula's Blood Bond. I just knew it.

I opened my eyes to look at Xylo.

The smoke now living in his eye-sockets shifted back and forth as he stared back at me. I actually preferred it to the empty socket and interior of the skull look. "I can try," Xylo said uncertainly, knowing he had no way to actually consume my blood.

Maybe I could just draw a smiley face on his forehead with my blood.

I drew my katana a few inches and sliced my palm open on the base of the blade. Then I walked over to Xylo and lifted my fist above his head. "Open wide and swallow," I said. "If you remember how."

He tilted his head back and spread his bony mouth open. My blood dripped freely over his teeth and jaws, splashing down through his body and over his spine and rib bones. The blood immediately steamed where it came in contact with bone, and then the bones absorbed it—sucked it down like water poured on hot, dry sand.

Xylo shuddered violently with a rattling drum solo, groaning as he panted, his head still tilted back. I closed my eyes again, focusing on the bony roots between us and I watched in stunned disbelief as they grew stronger, thicker, and more vibrant. I also felt the wound on my palm grow very warm, but I didn't open my eyes to check.

More importantly, the fat, black, sluggish cord suddenly hissed and screamed in agony—just like I'd hoped when I'd thought of salt poured on a slug—writhing and whipping back and forth as it shriveled and shrank. Its whistling screams mirrored Xylo's sudden panting. I winced, hoping I hadn't caused him too much pain—

And realized that I could simply focus on him if I wanted to gauge his physical well-being. He was definitely uncomfortable, but I was relieved to see he wasn't in any unbearable agony.

The black cord of power abruptly popped, oozing black goop before it faded away to nothing.

Xylo let out a final, shuddering breath and I opened my eyes. I checked the wound on my palm to find it mostly healed, leaving only a faint pink line where the small cut had been. I grunted, looking up at Xylo.

He stared at me incredulously, the smoke in his eyes whipping back and forth as if battered by wild, shifting wind. He stared at me for about thirty seconds before I finally spoke, wondering if he was feeling something that I couldn't perceive.

"Are you...okay, Xylo?" I asked nervously.

He gave me a very slow nod. "Never better," he rasped, his voice raw.

I frowned. "It's just that you're staring at me, so I wanted to make sure you were okay..."

He nodded slowly. "I've never felt these things before. I was crying."

My heart cracked a little at his reaction to such a vital emotion—one he hadn't known existed—happiness.

"Oh," I said, embarrassed that I was intruding on his private cry. "That's okay, Xylo. I didn't see any tears so I thought you were waiting on me for something."

He shook his head. "That is how I cry. On the inside," he said, deadpan.

Wow.

Okay.

We had a long, dark road ahead of us before I would let him meet any of my friends—otherwise he might send them spiraling into depression via the bottom of a bottle of *Jose Cuervo*.

I shook my head, trying to wrap my own head around it all. I'd come up here looking to connect with my Horseman's Mask—and had instead found an ally. An ally who shared a strong affinity with Despair. I was doubly glad I hadn't chosen to just take his head, now.

"You should have this," Xylo said, holding out the butterfly charm. "It is not for me, but I think it tolerates me."

I smiled, nodding as I reached my hand out towards the charm, slightly relieved to hear him say he didn't want to keep it—because after seeing the reaction it had caused, I'll admit that doubt had entered my mind about who the real Horseman of Despair might be.

Despite the circuitous route I had taken, I had successfully found power of a sort up here. I felt excited. I now had a chance against Dracula and his guests. I could do this. I could win.

The butterfly charm shone in the crimson moonlight, my fingers almost touching it—

A stone monster suddenly dove down from the sky and struck Xylo like a meteoric hunting falcon, knocking him clear over the railing of the bridge and out into the empty air, taking my Horseman Mask with him.

My chances at survival fell with Xylo and my Mask. Three more thuds of stone striking stone sounded behind me, letting me know I had my own welcoming party to deal with.

I slowly turned, gritting my teeth and narrowing my eyes as my hand closed around the hilt of my katana. A trio of gargoyles with eyes of crimson fire stared back at me.

They knew not what they had just done.

But I was looking forward to showing them the error of their ways—that their remains would make perfect gravel for any infrastructure improvements that Dracula might have been considering.

As long as he did so before I killed him, too, of course.

❦ 13 ❦

I drew my katana, assessing my foes.

Their forms were solid, iron gray stone and they stood about a foot shorter than me. But they were two or three times wider and heavily sculpted with layers of dense muscle, like little Dracula had a field day in pottery class when he created them.

Gargoyles could come in pretty much any flavor of design, but most resembled some demented amalgam of beasts—mammal, reptile, or bird— upon a bipedal frame to create truly grotesque monstrosities. These gargoyles had the heads of mutant super-bats, complete with fiery eyes and pointed ears, but their bodies reminded me of substance-abusing dwarves— their short, stubby, and muscular frames weathered and pitted from eons of bad life decisions.

None of them held weapons, but their claws were at least six inches long, two inches thick at the base, and curled like a velociraptor—perfect for decapitating unwary wizards, for example. Those claws would allow them to grip ledges and perches much like a bird, locking them into place so they wouldn't fall.

Their hands and feet each had only three digits, but the tips of their talons sunk into the stone as they circled me, tearing into the bridge with bursts of sparks. My Darling and Dear jacket might have been able to fend those claws off, but if they struck my legs, I would instantly become a double-amputee—highly likely, given that I had no magic to shield myself.

Oh, and they were naked, showing off their dangly, awe-inspiring...man-ana sundaes. I narrowed my eyes, locking onto my obvious targets—their low-hanging fruit, as it were.

I would use my boots to put their cherries on top of their vaunted dessert dishes.

Their fiery, crimson eyes flickered menacingly, and they looked to hate me almost as much as I currently hated them. They'd just thrown my Mask and my brand-new sidekick off the bridge—all when I'd expected at least an hour of respite. Maybe Xylo's interaction with the Mask had flared up like a beacon, drawing their attention.

"Haven't you heard how rude it is to interrupt people when they are talking?" I demanded.

Rather than trade dialogue, they let out a simultaneous roar and thundered directly towards me—using their wings to make every third step a super-jump to cover more distance.

I stood motionless, timing the lead gargoyle's advance, and abruptly sprinted at him right as he started taking a super-jump. My abrupt motion allowed me to intercept him in mid-leap, before he could react, introducing his throat to my rising blade sooner than he'd anticipated.

His head fell to the stone, bouncing once before crumbling to gravel.

One of the other gargoyles slapped me in the lower back, grazing across my ass on the follow-through. My eyes bulged open as wide as saucers—more surprised than anything—as my girl-at-the-bar instincts kicked in.

Stop! Cherry time.

I spun, lunging out with my foot to kick him squarely in the groin. My foot hit him so hard that, not only did I put his cherries on top, my boot reduced his entire pelvic region to gravel. The force of the blow even surprised me. Especially when his stone banana broke completely *off* and fell to the ground.

He gasped and screamed, clutching at his ruined crotch with both claws, trying to keep any more of his genitals from falling.

The third gargoyle roared and struck me in my sword arm, batting the Silver blade out of my grip. I hissed angrily and jumped back a step in order to square off against my last opponent. But he didn't wait, already swiping one set of wicked claws at my right thigh. It hit me and I gasped in horror, having zero desire to see my leg resting on the ground like a drumstick beside his gargoyle wang.

But the pain I imagined from such a wound...

Never came.

I glanced down to see that my leg was perfectly intact. My pants were ripped where his claws had struck me, but my flesh only showed three red welts. We both stared at *that* for a few seconds, neither of us entirely sure what to make of it.

Then two more fucking gargoyles landed on the bridge, and these guys were the *A-Team*, each taller than the first trio, wielding dual axes and wearing what looked like capri pants. One look at them told me they were hardened killers and wouldn't be as easily defeated as the naked *Three Amigos*.

One had bird shit splattered on his forehead, so I subconsciously dubbed him *Shithead*. I spun back to the last surviving naked gargoyle and gave him a triple rabbit-punch to the throat. He flung his hands up, wheezing and gasping for air. I grabbed him by the wings and yanked downwards as I jumped up with my knee, driving it straight into his chin and snapping the lower half of his jaw clear off. He went limp and I quickly let go as he fell over the railing of the bridge like a bag of wet laundry.

I scooped up my katana and spun back to the axe-wielding gargoyles, hoping I could take them out fast enough that I could get off this damned bridge and find my way down to wherever Xylo had landed with my Mask.

So it caught me completely by surprise to see an ivory projectile suddenly shoot past me from over my shoulder to strike Shithead in the eye. He roared, swinging wildly with one of his axes hard enough to accidentally chop off his nameless buddy's wing. The amputated gargoyle instantly wailed in agony—revealing an orthodontist's wet dream of short, crooked nubs for teeth—as his severed wing crashed to the ground in a shower of gravel and dust.

And then *another* ivory projectile whipped past me to hit the amputated gargoyle directly in the tonsils, turning his wail into a choking cough as he gagged and struggled to breathe through the slightly curved—for her plea-sure—footlong throat-rocket. I instantly dubbed him *Deepthroat* as he collapsed to his knees, dropping both axes in the process. His fiery eyes flickered weakly as he looked torn about whether he should first dislodge the ivory missile from his throat or tourniquet his amputated wing stub.

I spun to look behind me, wondering what fresh new hell I was about to face—

And I gaped in disbelief, my gast entirely flabbered. If my brain had been an old PC—like my father had kept around the house for a decade too long —it would have fizzled and rebooted with a mild, melted plastic aroma and that haunting start-up music everyone kept in their memory banks for only the worst of their nightmares—right alongside the old dial-up-internet jingle.

Because Xylo was perched in a crouch atop the ledge, impersonating Frodo's bestie, Gollum—his bone face somehow managing to snarl night-marishly at the two gargoyles like they'd just stolen his precious ring. He also had his crimson cowl up like a hood, covering his head to show only his menacing look but still bunching around his shoulders like some kind of refugee, crazy-ass assassin. I finally understood what the ivory projectiles had been, because I watched in fascinated horror as Xylo deftly snapped off one of his own ribs before hurling it at the miserable gargoyles. The curved rib made a continuous *whoosh-whoosh* sound as it whipped past me like a boomerang before clocking Shithead in the ankles hard enough to knock him completely off his feet—so that he had the unique opportunity of falling face-first onto the stone bridge before he had the chance to use his wings.

Shithead also dropped one of his axes in his fall, and the heavy blade neatly sliced off Deepthroat's foot. His gagging turned into a hacking, high-pitched shriek and he decided it was time to put an end to friendly fire. He pounced on Shithead—Xylo's rib bone still lodged in his throat—and began pummeling Shithead's face with his fists, gravel ricocheting off the ground and ledge of the bridge like shrapnel.

Shithead finally went limp, and Deepthroat wasn't far behind him, collapsing onto his back for a quick breather.

Of course, his wing stub hit the ground first and he belted out a high-pitched keening sound before promptly passing out. I shook my head in disbelief, spinning back to Xylo.

"How in the *hell* did you make it all the way back up here so fast?" I demanded, wondering exactly what to make of his return. If his true purpose had been to steal my Mask, he wouldn't have come back to me.

His face slowly returned to normal—looking as if it took some mental effort or strain—and he shrugged bashfully, hopping down from the ledge to stand upright. "I climbed the tower," he said, pointing back at the tower we hadn't explored yet—the one he'd been guarding earlier—with the locked door.

I blinked at him a few times. "You just climbed the tower..." I repeated flatly.

He nodded, lowering his hood to settle back around his shoulders. The dark smoke in his eyes still shifted and swirled as if alive. "I figured you might need help since you no longer have your powers, so I did what I could. I felt them hitting you, so I came back as quickly as I knew how. Climbing the tower."

I shook my head, not certain I liked the sound of that. He'd felt the gargoyles hitting me? I hadn't felt him falling or hitting the ground, so it wasn't a shared feeling, thankfully. I glanced down at my leg again, wondering why I still had it. Then I slowly looked up at Xylo's bone leg. Then his neck where I'd decapitated him. All the damage I'd dealt him had only impacted his joints, not fracturing any of his bones.

Like his actual bones were impervious to damage.

Maybe...our strange bond had given me some of his resilience? Made me *stronger* somehow? That blow from the gargoyle should have at *least* shredded through my flesh. And I'd done some serious damage with my fists and feet.

Against *stone*.

I shook my head, realizing that we were still standing out in the open where we had just killed five gargoyles. We needed to get away from the bridge before reinforcements came to check on them. And I needed to go find my Horseman's Mask at the base of the bridge. "Let's go. We need to get out of sight quickly."

He nodded obediently. "Let me just go pick up my ribs."

He took two steps and then came to an abrupt halt with one boot still in the air. He slowly lowered it, grunting to himself as if surprised by a sudden thought. He stood still for a few moments and then cocked his head and raised his hand. His ribs suddenly ripped out of the distant gargoyles and hammered back into place on his own body, reattaching themselves with a flare of embers and sparks. I felt nothing, so the shared sensations were definitely only on his end. I shook my head in wonder but tried to keep the concern from my face as Xylo turned back to look at me—his face expressionless again. I approached and motioned for him to lead us away from the bridge, back to the first tower we had explored.

Instead, he grabbed my hand and pressed something cool into my palm.

I glanced down to see the butterfly charm.

Silence stretched between us and what felt like a lead blanket was abruptly removed from my shoulders.

"Thank you, Xylo," I whispered, relieved on multiple levels—that he had it in the first place, and that he was so casual about returning it.

He hadn't ever wanted it for himself—or Dracula.

He gave me an intent look—as if reading my thoughts—and shook his head. "I'm fairly certain that I should be thanking *you*. I've never felt so..." he trailed off, glancing down at his hands. The black smoke in his eye-sockets shifted and eddied wildly as if suddenly disturbed.

"Alive?" I suggested.

He considered that and finally shrugged. "Perhaps. It's rather confusing and loud. Is that what life feels like?"

I smiled crookedly, realizing that it was pretty damned accurate as definitions go. "Yeah."

I was pretty sure his strength had somehow made my skin tougher, and I was beyond grateful for it. Because that blow to my back—the one that had felt like someone swatting my ass—might have just proven fatal without Xylo's energy boost from our bond.

But it wasn't as tough as Xylo's bones. I still had welts, so I wasn't entirely immune to harm like he was.

I wasn't sure if this was a good development in the long run or not, but I was perfectly content focusing on the short run victories for the next few days.

"You're a pretty good shot, Xylo. A dead-eye, as a matter of fact."

He grunted, motioning for me to follow him into the tower. "I see better from a distance. If you can't fight up close, you fight from afar."

And he drummed his fingers across his ribs in a *knick-knack paddy-whack, give a dog a bone* beat, seeming to smile back at me mischievously. I laughed, shaking my head.

Yeah. He'd earned a drum solo.

14

Tendrils of thick mist curled and slithered through the graveyard, questing and searching aimlessly so that the tips of the tombstones resembled shark fins breaching the surface of the water in the ocean. Xylo and I were currently crouched down beneath that mist, and I grimaced distastefully as my fingers sunk into the moist, thick earth. The ground was pregnant with water—and probably the remains of those buried beneath our boots.

We remained absolutely silent as we watched the nearby patrol of...well, frogmen, I guess.

I wasn't entirely sure what they were, but they looked like humanoid, bipedal, warrior frogs. They carried algae-coated tridents in their webbed hands and wore whips at their hips that looked to be made of spare frog tongues—a coiled, gelatinous cord that glistened in the light of the crimson moon.

Xylo had informed me that not only did the whips stick to their targets like hot tar, but they could only be removed by a spoken word from one of the frogmen—some kind of magic. They were also acidic and could eat through flesh and armor upon contact.

Neither of us were sure what that might mean for me after our bond had strengthened my skin, but to be on the safe side, I made the executive decision to not let them hit me with their sticky tongue whips.

71

I counted twelve of the tall bastards walking around on their massive webbed feet—easy to audibly track due to the wet slapping sound they emitted with each step. They wore a strange scaled armor that Xylo warned was impervious to blades—only breakable by iron hooks—and wide, conical hats made from lily pads that looked like those old Asian straw hats worn by rice farmers for shade. Their golden, bulbous eyes seemed to glow from beneath the brims, and I found myself thinking of how accurately frogs could catch flies with a casual flick of their tongue.

I bet their whips were just as accurate.

I wondered if they were some creature from Fae or something Dracula had personally made. I had never heard of anything like them, and that typically put it into the Fae category in my personal experience. But this place was a brave new world to me.

Xylo wasn't sure of their origins either, telling me that Dracula simply called them *frogs*. Then again, Dracula called the werewolves *wolves*, and the vampires *children*. He wasn't very big on titles or anything, apparently.

Like they were all so far beneath him that he simply couldn't be bothered to learn their names or histories, let alone their flavor of creature. They existed only to serve him, and he let them crash on his couch as payment.

We were currently surrounded by several pairs of the glacially slow patrols, forcing us to hide in the cemetery just outside the Village—which was the actual name of the place, by the way—I had seen from the bridge. Since we didn't want to kill them and risk raising an alarm for all their buddies, we were pretty much stuck in the cemetery until we could be certain we were in the clear.

Which was just excellent since we had so much free time before we had to get to work.

I leaned closer to Xylo. "You should take off the red scarf. It's like waving a flag to point out our location," I breathed, annoyed at the delay.

The ridges above his smoky eye sockets bunched down with a faint grinding sound. "No. It is *mine*," he muttered louder than I would have wished. I was also surprised to see him—ironically—show a little backbone for once.

I studied him, keeping the frogmen in my peripheral vision. "Is it sentimental from your past?" I asked in what I hoped passed for an apologetic or sympathetic whisper.

His features gradually softened as he shook his head. "No. It is armor." I must have looked doubtful, because he gritted his teeth, looking annoyed. "It is resilient against blades and other weapons down here. It is dyed with the blood of one-thousand innocents," he said, matter-of-factly.

I blinked. Oh. "Wow...where did you get it?" I asked, doubting Dracula would have just given him something that had obviously taken a lot of work to create.

Then again, the blood of a thousand innocents soaking a cloth long enough to dye the fabric essentially made it a soiled dinner napkin that Dracula had never washed after using it for three meals a day, every day, for a year. Given that he was immortal, he might have hundreds of others just like it.

Xylo glanced over, relaxing his shoulders. I was surprised to see him get so worked up over my request. "Apologies. It's just...well, it's the only constant I've ever known. My oldest memory from my first day here. Dracula gave it to me as a welcoming gift when I awoke."

I nodded with an understanding smile. "It's okay. I didn't realize or I never would have suggested it. We'll just be extra careful," I told him, silently wondering exactly how Xylo's arrival here had worked. He said he'd *awoken* here...

So...where had he been before?

And how long ago had that been? None of the other skeletons had worn scarves, so why had Dracula given one to Xylo? Not wanting to alert the frogmen, I kept these questions to myself to ask him later.

Silence settled between us as we continued to watch the frogmen.

With nothing else to do, I scanned the horizon, recalling the last hour of our walk after descending the tower where we'd killed the gargoyles. I spotted the Coliseum-looking structure in the far distance and I wondered if we would get to see it up close—or if that was unwise. This wasn't a sight-seeing trip, after all.

A massive Clocktower rose in the distance, easily twenty stories tall and resembling a miniature Big Ben from London—but sculpted in the style of Notre Dame with sinister gargoyles and harsh spikes jutting out from around the face of the glowing silver clock itself. Dracula had said he'd have the Clocktower toll six times when dinner was ready.

I narrowed my eyes, shaking off the thought. I had a long way to go before worrying about dinner.

Instead, I replayed my conversation with Xylo as we'd left the tower with the dead gargoyles, feeling my shoulders grow tense as I remembered some of the things he'd told me.

Xylo had opened up quite a bit after I'd managed to break his bond with Dracula. Not that he'd suddenly begun talking crap on his old boss or anything—there had never been any animosity in his tone when he spoke of his hellish service to Dracula—because it was all he had ever known. He didn't have an example of anything better, so he didn't know enough to realize he was supposed to feel a certain way about his unique treatment.

Because Xylo quite literally knew nothing about who he had been before —his oldest memory was his first day here in Castle Dracula. All he knew was his time spent with Dracula as the outcast skeleton who couldn't fight worth a damn.

Essentially, he had been singled out from his brother skeletons as the joke of the castle. The court jester. Dracula had regularly given him impossible tasks or errands, only to watch him obviously fail and then hand him over to the werewolves as punishment.

So they could gnaw on his bones for a few days.

Or weeks.

He had only been allowed to put himself back together after the werewolves had finished with their fun.

Xylo had felt no pain in this because his bones really were nigh indestructible. In my opinion, the punishments were to see just how far Dracula could go before Xylo—who hadn't even been given a name—felt humiliation. Except Xylo couldn't feel humiliation, so the punishments had kept getting more creative.

It was also a standing order that anyone—for any reason—could use him as their punching bag and he was not permitted to defend himself.

He had told me all of this in a toneless summary. He hadn't sounded angry, judgmental, or even upset. It had been like listening to the weatherman on local cable.

It had been...disgusting.

And I had found myself beginning to personally hate Dracula rather than only looking at him as a bad monster who needed to be put down for the benefit of mankind.

Dracula was something much, much worse than a powerful monster or alleged member of the Masters.

He was a bully.

And if there was one type of person I couldn't tolerate, it was a bully. Especially those bullies who consciously knew that what they were doing was cruel—unlike children who might not comprehend the true impact of their actions.

I'm talking the seasoned bullies.

They were the enemy of all that was good in the world.

I had kept my judgment to myself, knowing it might be too much for a soul like Xylo to comprehend. He wasn't even remotely in touch with his feelings, and I was entirely certain that I didn't want the first emotion he internalized to be hate.

So I had focused on encouraging him, complimenting him on every little thing—like how incredible his throwing accuracy was, how wicked cool his hood had looked on the bridge, and how I knew an incredible pair of leather-smiths who could design a pair of boots specifically fitted for his unique feet. Because as we had walked, I had heard his feet sliding back and forth inside his boots, making his steps louder and clunkier than necessary.

At first, my compliments had made him truly uncomfortable, as if I had been lying to him or that I might have been mocking him.

But since we were now bonded and somehow shared—or could at least sense—each other's feelings, he had begun to silently watch me whenever I complimented him, trying to wrap his head around this strange woman who didn't call him a failure at every turn. But he couldn't deny I was speaking honestly, because he could *feel* my sincerity.

He hadn't exaggerated his navigational skills or knowledge of the castle layout. He truly was better than any guide I had ever met. He not only knew the ins and outs; he knew the *secret* ins and outs. He also knew the schedules of when areas were likely busy and who lived where. In my opinion, he was the undying embodiment of the memory of the castle itself.

We'd spent almost an hour sneaking about in order to give me a general lay of this area of the castle because he had said it was oftentimes smarter to flee than it was to confront an enemy.

Which was why we currently sat like frogs on a log rather than confronting the amphibian patrols circling us.

This area—the Village—was laid out in such a way that backup was always incredibly close and ready to tighten a noose around any sudden alerts. It was where the residents often went to unwind or cut loose after their shifts, so causing problems here would be like riding into Compton and throwing a rock at one of the houses just to see what happened.

Xylo had strongly emphasized that if we set off an alarm here and saw one or two additional guards pop up—even if we knew we could take the two new guards down—it was often a sleight of hand to give the fifty other guards circling the perimeter, just out of sight, time to box you in.

Long story short, Xylo told me that if we were seen, we should flee and regroup. And since he was a lifelong survivor of the bullies and thugs inhabiting Castle Dracula, I decided to trust his advice.

We already faced terrible odds trying to take out my targets. Because I was betting they had only earned Dracula's ruby amulet by being truly terrible or truly powerful—probably both. It wasn't like he handed them out to werewolves once they were potty-trained and learned not to piss on his rugs.

No. A gift from Dracula meant they had impressed him.

And having a better grasp on what kind of sadist Dracula was after hearing a handful of Xylo's stories, my mind was already racing with the levels of cruelty required to earn a gold star from the Sultan of Suck.

Which meant the winners were likely very powerful.

And with the Mark of the Beast on my forehead, I was pretty much a Regular without any powers.

My only advantage was my newly strengthened skin and my new Skeletal Dundee and his bone boomerangs. His rib-arangs.

We had already spent about an hour in this single area of Castle Dracula. And that had just been for stealth reconnaissance—teaching me how not to trip over my own two feet and ruin my chances entirely.

And there was a whole lot more to the place than just this area.

So I told Xylo I was willing to do whatever he recommended if it gained us even the slightest of advantages. If he thought I needed to run, hide, and regroup upon being seen by enemies, then that is what I would do. It wouldn't do us any good to also have armies of guards knowing exactly where we were because we hadn't practiced stealth.

I'd paid close attention so I could remember where the servants' stairs were—Xylo knew them so well because it was pretty much his usual circuit every day—corridors that weren't often used, paths between buildings, bridges, and any other number of things.

Then Xylo had spent another hour demanding that I lead the way through a certain area he had just detailed for me—to teach it back to him and prove I had been paying attention. I'd gotten everything right but the extra set of stairs in the back of the building. That was the best we'd had time for.

All while avoiding the creepy patrol of these frogmen.

Ultimately, they'd boxed us into the cemetery—without knowing we were even there, thankfully—and I felt confident that even Xylo would have been forced into the same trap if he had been the one leading us.

Surely, he couldn't have done better...

He smirked absently, probably reading my thoughts. Bastard.

"I did fine, Xylo," I muttered.

He grinned, nodding reassuringly.

But entirely too fast to look genuine.

❧ 15 ❧

I had rapidly come to the conclusion that without Xylo's knowledge, I would have likely walked into a trap within the first hour. I also wouldn't have had a personal shield and archer all rolled into one. And I would have been squishier without Xylo's bond protecting my skin. I'd bought all of that at the very small price of two dozen installments of positive reinforcement whenever Xylo began to discredit himself or get too morose.

Somehow, he did this in such a way that it didn't come across as needy. He sought no affection or attention. It was simply all that he'd been told his entire undead-life—like he was a record stuck on repeat to recite those self-defeating comments over and over again. Dracula had seen that Xylo was different, not very useful, and had decided his only benefit was as a servant.

And Dracula relished in constantly berating him for his failures and never honoring him for his virtues.

You could tell a lot about a person from how they treated those hierarchically beneath them. How a boss treated his employees, how a host treated the cooks, how a wealthy person treated those less fortunate, how a master treated a minion, and even how a pastor treated his congregation.

With one added caveat.

Not only how masters treated their minions in general, but how they treated them *when no one was watching.*

That was vital. Everyone acted better when they were being observed. Good press, right?

But character was who you were in the dark when no one was there to tattle on you. Much like if you spied on toddlers playing together, you could hear all sorts of foreboding threats. *If you don't do this, I won't be your best friend anymore...*

Extortion and blackmail were learned at a very early age—it was the easiest way to get what you wanted, and as helpless as toddlers were in many ways, they were sharp enough to learn manipulation.

A more pious person would argue that this was proof of Original Sin.

Whether it was or wasn't was above my pay-grade. Knowing the result was all that really mattered for my immediate survival. And I was pretty sure I would need to get my Sunday Dress dirty to survive the next few days. The Confessional Booth was going to be a real doozy next week.

I could just imagine the discussion with Father David.

I made a new friend and bonded his bones to my soul. Yeah, he's undead, but I'm helping him build his self-confidence. That counts for something, right? How did I bond him? Oh, well I'm the sixth Horseman of the Apocalypse, of course. Hey, you're not supposed to laugh. Right, where was I? Yes, I had to kill six people last weekend. Where? I went on vacation with my godfather. No, I'd never met my victims before I killed them. Total strangers, don't worry. Why? Well, I wanted their jewelry.

I snapped myself out of the imagined scenario, focusing back on the matter at hand—at all the beautifully exciting confrontations that might result in my death over the next few days. About three seconds after considering a few nightmarish situations, I turned to look at Xylo instead.

His aged ivory bones drank in the crimson light of the moon and sky, making him look painted in blood—like he was a freshly de-skinned skeleton. He was nodding absently to himself, but I couldn't pick up on his thoughts, even though he seemed to have no problem reading mine.

Unfair. Looking into his mind was like shouting into an empty warehouse. There was just nothing happening in there right now. He was literally sitting there not thinking about anything at all—not even *consciously* trying to think of nothing like when I meditated. Because he had no emotions. It was chilling. I wasn't sure if that was just because he was a skeleton, but Dracula's treatment of him hadn't helped in the slightest.

Dracula wasn't the only source of Xylo's lack of self-confidence. I was pretty sure that it stemmed from not only being bad at all the things his friends were good at, but that he didn't know why he wasn't like everyone else. He was Rudolph the Red Nosed Reindeer—the *Before They Were Famous* edition.

Since he couldn't recall who he had been in his actual life, he didn't have any insights into why he was the only unique skeleton. He even told me that he'd never shared what he was good at with Dracula—like how he could hit the wings off a fly with his ribs, his seemingly impeccable memory, and that he could put himself back together all by himself—fearing it might mean something else was wrong with him.

Which worked in our favor, now, but Xylo's existence for the past... however long he'd been here had not been pleasant or even passively rewarding.

So, I'd broken the ice by explaining who I was, what I'd been through, and how I'd gotten here. I had also come clean about my butterfly charm— that it was a Horseman's Mask. He hadn't seemed remotely alarmed about me lugging around a Horseman's Mask, probably because he had no memory of what exactly that meant since he couldn't even remember his life from the real world. In fact, he actually seemed to open up quite a bit when I brought it up, looking excited about the topic—because he had a personal experience to relate it to—he'd bonded with it, after all. Even if his emotions were mostly nonexistent, when he'd picked up the Mask, he'd felt something all on his own for the first time in his conscious existence.

It didn't matter that he hadn't understood what the alien sensation was at the time or what he was supposed to do with it. All that mattered was that he finally had a memory of an emotion, now.

He'd mentioned feeling echoes. I hadn't wanted to press him on that yet, choosing to let him keep it to himself—to cherish his one emotion in private, perhaps even using it to build up his confidence in at least one steadfast absolute.

Even if it was Despair.

"Are you sure you want to go after the demon first?" he whispered suddenly, snapping me out of my thoughts. It was the third time he'd asked the same question. "There should be three amulets in this area near the Village," he suggested. "They are decidedly easier targets."

I nodded. "I think the demon might have some answers for me, and you said if Dracula's Bane is anywhere, it will be in the Infernal Armory near the Observatory," I whispered back at him, checking to make sure the frogs hadn't overheard us. Dracula had been concerned after Samael used the Mark of the Beast to lull the castle's Beast to sleep—like perhaps he needed to make sure his pet demon never learned of it. The Mark of the Beast was a Biblical Revelations event as far as I knew—a curse inflicted upon those who would be roped into serving the Devil during the End Days.

I still didn't really follow how in the world that had worked to bond me with Sanguina, but maybe this demon would know.

Also, she was apparently an enemy of Samael, so she might know some dirt on him or be willing to tell me some of his weaknesses—which I really needed to know since I was planning on holding him closely as I pressed my katana into his windpipe. Slowly.

So with him and Dracula both having strong feelings about this mystery demon, I wanted to introduce myself before either of them decided to pay her a visit. Because despite what Samael said about only Greater Demons having the strength to power the Mark of the Beast, she might know some way to rid myself of it. Or...

I could always make a deal for power. I shuddered at the thought, putting it on the back-burner. The integrity of my soul was important to me, but my soul was about to go on extended family medical leave if I failed here —whether by dying or being roped into working for Dracula.

Desperate times.

Not yet, though.

I had a little bit of experience battling demons, and I still had the Seal of Solomon in my pocket—something I had completely forgotten about in the chaos from the bridge. It was a demon trap—as long as I could get it to work —as long as it hadn't also been blocked from use by the Mark of the Beast. Even if brandishing the Seal of Solomon at the demon was just an empty threat, it was a pretty good one. Her fear of imprisonment might outweigh her current loyalty to Dracula.

Because here, she was probably treated like a queen and granted much respect or fear. Trading that in for an orange jumpsuit was a great big fall from grace, and not one she would likely choose to risk—unlike when she had originally chosen to fall from Heaven.

So yeah. I wanted to get to her first. Even if there were easier targets here. Because if Dracula or Samael paid her a visit before I did, I'd likely lose my only chance at obtaining helpful information. I wasn't sure if she would know anything worthwhile, but it was worth the risk if she shared even the tiniest advantage that I could later exploit against Samael or Dracula. Killing her first would also send a crystal-clear message to my dear, dear Godfather.

Not even demons were safe from the White Rose.

Even though it no longer hurt, I was very cognizant of the Mark of the Beast on my forehead—but I very wisely chose not to try touching it again. Samael had said it was so much more than a bond of servitude, but I didn't feel any bond or compulsion impacting my judgment.

Xylo nodded, but looked uneasy at my answer. Maybe he was scared of her. "Okay. To avoid heavily patrolled areas, we will need to take a shortcut through the Eternal Gardens," he murmured in a dry whisper, deftly tracing a rough sketch on the ground without a moment's hesitation, using rocks and twigs to quickly represent nearby points of interest. He'd shown me which main buildings to look out for so that even if I got lost—or we became separated—I would at least be able to avoid running into a guard-post or something. He'd also picked out rendezvous points that even I would be able to later find. One of those was the Clocktower that could be seen from pretty much everywhere.

Each section of Castle Dracula was guarded by different types of monster. When I'd pressed, Xylo had told me there were even Yeti on the opposite side of the grounds, but most of Dracula's guards were of the smaller more agile variety—werewolves, goblins, dwarves, gnomes, stregas, vampires, and creatures my size or smaller that relied upon numbers as opposed to one guard with boss-level power.

When it came to the actual monsters I would need to kill—those who wore the required amulet—Xylo had rattled off a handful of names, and I'd been both relieved and disappointed to find that I recognized none of them.

No Frankenstein or any of the stereotypical names that had slaughtered their way into so many movies and pop culture stories to become well-known by the world at large.

And...I wasn't quite sure how to feel about that. I'd anticipated having to fight and kill well-known legends like Frankenstein or Medusa or someone equally notorious. But it seemed that wasn't going to be the case. Which was very strange to me. We were talking about *Dracula*, and I didn't recognize *any* of the locals who lived here?

Which was another reason why I wanted to visit the demon first. At least I had some basis of common ground with a demon and maybe I could use my experience in killing a few of her pals to goad her into giving up some helpful information on Samael or Dracula.

I glanced up to see the frogmen finally strolling far enough away for us to make our escape. I urgently turned back to Xylo, jerking my chin to let him know we would need to move soon before someone else came by.

He nodded absently but didn't move, his eye-sockets scanning our surroundings warily. I was actually getting used to the whole skeleton thing. Even the smoky eyes.

Brush-happy girls had been wearing the smoky eye for years, and Xylo's version wasn't as scary as some of the botched jobs I'd seen.

Even young witchlings with their first cauldron and book of spells weren't as dangerous or frightening as a young girl with her first make-up kit.

I just hoped the smoke in Xylo's eyes wasn't some portent of doom.

I motioned for him to stand since he was still sitting on the ground, enshrouded in the mist so that he looked like a floating skull. "What's the demon's name?" I asked. "Maybe I've heard of her before."

Xylo stared out at the cemetery for a few more moments, not looking eager to get moving. Finally, he climbed to his feet with a faint rattling sound as his bones clinked against each other. "She does not use her name. Everyone just calls her the demon or demoness, and she is very dangerous, even in her current situation. While we are here, we could at least kill one of the nearby targets to get some of your powers—"

I shook my head firmly. "The demoness." I wondered why she didn't use her name here, since Samael obviously knew who she was. Did Dracula not let her since no one else seemed to have names?

Xylo nodded. "As you wish," he said in an obedient tone. Despite having failed to convince me to change my target, I didn't sense even a hint of annoyance or frustration in his voice. He was definitely the submissive in our *Fifty Shades of Bone* relationship.

I glanced down at my muddy hands and grimaced, realizing I had only the clothing I was wearing to wipe them off—my white ninja outfit from Xuanwu and Ryuu. The clothes would probably soon be speckled with blood, so there wasn't any logical justification to me cringing about getting my pretty pants dirty, but I couldn't help myself.

"What did you mean by her current situation?" I asked absently, scanning our surroundings to make sure we really were clear of patrols.

Xylo was quiet for a few moments. "It will make more sense if you see for yourself. I'm not entirely sure I understand it myself."

I nodded distractedly, trying to shake off the feeling that we were being watched. "Which way to these Gardens of Eternal Woe?"

He turned to me, looking confused. "Eternal Gardens," he corrected, pointing over my shoulder. Then he pointed in the opposite direction at a nearby body of water that looked like a swamp of sorts hugging up against the far side of the Village. "That is the Lake of Everlasting Woe."

I sighed. "Of course. My mistake."

What else would you name a lake?

16

Since he still hadn't made an effort to move, I began walking in the direction he'd indicated for the Eternal Gardens. I kept low, slipping from headstone to headstone, keeping alert for any other sentries. I heard Xylo's familiar shuffling gait behind me and wished I had some kind of rope or cord to tie his boots tighter so they would make less noise. I knew I was being paranoid, because it wasn't really that loud. More annoying than anything.

Our path brought us closer to the pub-like structure than I would have liked, but still far enough away to remain unobserved since the flickering braziers hanging from the awning near the entrance didn't cast light far enough to reveal us. But we were close enough to see and hear the same woman outside the entrance that I had spotted from up on the bridge hours ago. She was catcalling several male creatures in the street, suggesting nasty, sinful experiences that made even my cheeks flush red.

This hell harlot had a nastier mouth than any seaman I'd ever heard about, and she had absolutely no shame as she continued hounding for a pounding to anyone who would listen.

But the men hurried on by, not even bothering to acknowledge her. She seamlessly changed her sales pitch into foul-mouthed taunts aimed at their departing backs as she abrasively heckled their inability to satisfy a *real* woman. I shook my head in disbelief, but continued on, not wanting to risk one of the men in the street spotting our silhouettes in the pale mist.

I kept my eyes on her as I slipped by, taking special note of her tail even though the rest of her looked mainly human. I bit back a laugh upon realizing she was offering up some tail for anyone willing to suffer her unbelievably scandalous suggestions.

I reached the edge of the cemetery and was confronted by a veritable wall of reeds taller than me—like a cornfield in the peak season—and squishy, swampy earth. I glanced back at Xylo and he nodded, motioning me forward. I winced uneasily, recalling several movies that involved a character trying to flee into a cornfield to escape a murderer.

It usually didn't end well for them.

Xylo suddenly hissed out a muffled warning and I ducked into a crouch, turning to look back at him. I heard a familiar *thud* and glanced over his shoulder to see that a gargoyle had dropped out of the sky to land outside the pub a few paces away from the hell harlot.

He said something to her that I couldn't hear, and she paused to assess him up and down in a withering fashion. My pulse slowed when I realized that we weren't about to be assaulted like Xylo had presumed upon seeing the gargoyle descending so rapidly.

The woman finally held out her hand, seeming to want a deposit or proof that he was good for the money.

He handed her a small pouch and she hefted it critically. Then she shook her head after a few moments—probably choosing to charge more for the stone gargoyle than her usual price for those with flesh and blood.

He looked crestfallen for a moment and then hurriedly reached into another pouch at his belt and he pulled out—

I blinked incredulously. No fucking way.

He had resorted to bartering, and I was pretty sure that the long stone shaft he was waving animatedly at her was the dismembered gargoyle wang I had broken off that poor bastard on the bridge.

This sick puppy had stolen his pal's wang, and rather than alerting the others about his fallen comrades, he'd absconded with the phallic souvenir so he could trade it away for an hour of pleasure!

Talk about a wingman.

She cocked her head thoughtfully, grasping the shaft in a practiced manner. Finally, she nodded, slipping the pocket rocket into the bosom of her dress as she grabbed the gargoyle by the hand and tugged him inside the pub, looking more excited about her new girl toy than her patron.

I couldn't help it. I laughed.

Xylo swiveled his head my way, looking alarmed, and I immediately cut it short with a cough, sweeping the street with my eyes for any sign that someone had heard me.

No one had, thankfully. I let out a breath of relief, but Xylo was already anxiously shuffling my way, lightly shoving me into the reeds and out of sight of the pub. In my haste to comply, I tripped over a rotten log and landed on my knees with a disgusting squelching sound. I had reached out with one of my hands to catch my fall and it had landed on something squishy and warm.

I pulled my hand back, intending to give Xylo a piece of my mind.

But a bubbling croak stopped me cold. I slowly looked up to see that my hand hadn't landed in more mud. It had found a *body*.

Xylo let out a rattling growl, but I didn't dare turn away to look.

Because I was face-to-face with a slimy, dark green frogman who had been leaning back against a dead stump as tall as me, apparently taking a nap. I watched his bulging, golden eyes flutter open from beneath his conical, lily-pad hat. Without knowing to look for him, he very easily blended into his surroundings. If I hadn't touched him, I might not have ever seen him.

He looked just as stunned as me, as if he wasn't entirely sure whether he had woken up or was still dreaming.

Then his throat began to bubble outward as if he was taking a deep breath to croak out an alarm.

Without consciously realizing it, I'd already set my hand on the hilt of my katana and the blade left my belt with a faint whisper before slicing upward with as much force and speed as I could muster.

My blade sliced clean through the frogman's leg, severing the delectable hunk of meat as efficiently as a filet knife in a pricey French restaurant. It crashed to the ground, forcing the frog to remain leaning against the log for support as he squealed breathlessly, grabbing onto his stump in a panicked gesture.

I spotted his trident propped up beside him, swept it up in my free hand, and then stabbed it straight into his bulbous throat, still fearing he was about to emit his ear-shattering croak. His wet, webbed hands darted weakly to his trident in an attempt to tug it free, and I used the distraction to slice off the belt holding his sticky, acidic, coiled whip on his hip, since I didn't dare take it away from him with my bare hands.

Xylo suddenly grabbed me by one shoulder, yanking me back.

"We must run!" he hissed, glancing back and forth at the field of reeds surrounding us—where any number of other frogs could be camouflaged and lying in wait.

"Oui," I murmured absently, holding my sword out before me as my eyes darted back and forth searching for any other frogmen.

"Yes, *we*," Xylo urged. "We *both* need to run. Now."

I frowned in confusion before realizing that I'd spoken the French word for *yes*—still thinking about frog legs—without realizing it.

"How about you lead, Xylo," I suggested. "And hop to it," I added, wanting to place as much distance as possible between me and the whimpering, dying frogman behind me.

We'd taken two steps before the frogman found the strength to remove the trident and use his last breath to belch out a bone-chilling, croaking ribbit of alarm—even I could tell it was a cry for backup, and I didn't speak frog.

What really concerned me was how many similar croaks replied.

And how close they all were. Some of them had to be in the reeds with us. And they had those handy tongue whips.

"Merde," I cursed in French, urging Xylo to run faster.

17

Luckily, we'd made it out of the reeds with minimal fuss—although the sounds of pursuit had come alarmingly close. We'd only escaped by covering ourselves in the swampy mud—hair, clothes, and every inch of our bodies.

It smelled positively delightful, if you were wondering.

Then, rather than running, we'd sat down in the deepest, thickest part of the reeds and were perfectly still for almost an hour.

The frogmen had walked past us about a dozen times, and somehow, they did so in complete silence, unlike when I had seen them outside the cemetery. Soft croaks had bubbled up from their throats—some signal to tell their buddies that this area was clear—before they slipped away to expand their search, assuming we had run for our lives and wouldn't have been stupid enough to stay in the reeds.

After they'd left, we'd still waited about twenty minutes before risking our escape—in a slightly different direction than we'd originally intended.

We slipped from the edge of the reeds and into a silent, aromatic garden blooming with dozens of flowers I had never seen nor heard of before.

Which only made me hyper-aware of the filth covering our bodies, tainting the pleasant scent of flowery heaven.

We knelt down in a thick patch of tall, white flowers—which let us keep an eye on the reeds while remaining concealed—just in case any of the frogmen had the bright idea to check the adjacent Eternal Gardens.

I let out a breath of relief. "That went well," I said dryly.

Xylo nodded. "You are still alive, so I agree. But we should be more careful in the future. Until you get some of your powers back."

I nodded, knowing we wouldn't have stood a chance if more than a handful of those frogs had caught us. I was a good fighter, but there was something to be said for having greater numbers—since I had no magic to balance the scales.

The distant sound of screams, cheers, and roars carried to us on the breeze from the direction of the Coliseum, which I could see much more clearly from here. I shivered, not wanting to know what had caused it.

"The Coliseum must be open tonight," Xylo said absently, staring off into the distance at the domed structure. "Two potential targets reside in that area, but there will be hordes of guests watching the event, depending on who is participating tonight. There will be no opportunity for stealth."

"Some kind of show?" I asked, grimacing.

"The Menagerie volunteers prisoners for fights. Although it was scheduled for tomorrow." He looked suddenly uncertain. "Perhaps I made a mistake. What if I have my days mixed—"

I placed a finger over his lips. Well, where his lips would have been. The bone was surprisingly warm to the touch—almost hot. "I'm sure you're right. Dracula is probably just trying to make things interesting for us, or putting on a special show for Samael," I mused, taking away my finger. "What is the menagerie?"

Xylo gritted his teeth. "A prison for shifters—those who refuse to work here. Dracula sends out hunting parties to capture them from the outside world. Although, it has been some time since anyone has been able to leave."

I grimaced distastefully, only marginally satisfied to hear that Roland's barrier had come with an unintended benefit—preventing Dracula from leaving to acquire new victims. "And he puts them into fights in the Coliseum?" I asked, furiously.

Xylo nodded. "Entertainment."

I clenched my fists, closing my eyes for a three-count. Just another reason to end this farce. Dracula had to die. "Do you think he sensed me breaking your bond to him?" I asked, opening my eyes suddenly as I realized that I hadn't even considered it before now.

Xylo shrugged slightly. "I do not think he uses it. I'm always right there to do his bidding."

"Right." I wasn't necessarily reassured by that answer, but I knew Dracula wanted me to succeed to some extent—enough to meet him for dinner—so I was pretty sure he would give me enough rope to hang myself. This was all a game to him. And the odds were already stacked against me.

He would leave us alone for a while longer. Things would change as I drew closer to our date.

But I had my own suspicions about how that would play out. Bits and pieces of the past few days had begun to shift and spin in my brain, rearranging and realigning comments, advice, and other things people had told me. Because I'd learned very well how words could be twisted. That was what had brought me here. Misleading statements. Double entendres. Wordplay.

Put another way, Papa Homonym and Mama Synonym had bought a bottle of Boone's Farm, some whip cream, and silk blindfolds to bump uglies like uglies had never been bumped before—to pervert Schoolhouse Rock into a late-night Cinemax special—in hopes of conceiving a phonetic paradox.

And it had worked, wasting a lot of my time as I tried to figure out what everyone really meant when their lips began moving.

But I no longer had time for games. This was a house of monsters, and I needed to make a statement—to remind them what fear tasted like, and that she had a name.

Callie Penrose. The White Rose. And that she was as sweetly spicy as candy-coated ghost peppers.

There really was no better place to cut loose. Any collateral damage from an all-out brawl would only harm other monsters. Like the infamous Marine, Chesty Puller, said when he was told his division of Marines was surrounded by enemy soldiers.

Great. Now we can shoot at those bastards from every direction.

If I couldn't cut loose here, where could I? Everyone here had earned a shallow grave to feed the scavengers.

I was the Circle of Life.

Well, I would introduce everyone to their new position on the food chain, at least.

I turned to Xylo to find him openly staring at my chest, looking thoughtful. I frowned, snapping my fingers to get his attention.

"Hey! You have to be more discreet if you're going to stare at boobs all day," I said, frowning in surprise.

He quickly jerked his head away, the smoke in his eye-sockets swirling rapidly. "Not your breasts. I was looking at the blood painted there," he said defensively. "I find myself drawn to it, but also disgusted by it," he admitted, indicating the Cross Pattée that I had painted on my chest before my fight with Roland in Kansas City.

"Why are you interested in it all of a sudden?" I asked. He'd seen it often enough already. Then again, I'd had my coat buckled closed in order to give me as much protection as possible—and to give us better chances at stealth, since it was practically a flashing neon sign. But I'd opened my coat after the frogs left, feeling like the swampy humidity was about to boil me alive from the inside out. At the same time, this was potentially huge if it had sparked some memory of his, so I tried not to act too defensively. "Do you recognize it?" I asked carefully.

He finally shook his head. "No. I do not know why it drew my attention," he admitted, sounding frustrated. "I'm sorry for staring at your boobs."

I nodded, not letting my own frustration show. It was a step in the right direction, at least. "Don't worry. It happens to me all the time, Xylo. Both fending off the boob-watchers and thinking I recognize something but not being able to explain it. Just relax and it might come back to you, okay?"

He nodded, looking relieved.

"Now, what do I need to know about these Eternal Gardens?" I asked, gesturing at the flowers all around us. "It doesn't look so bad. Does it have venom-spitting nymphs or carnivorous plants?"

Xylo was silent for a time. "Worse," he said, climbing to his feet. "We shouldn't linger once we get there..."

"Wait. This isn't the Eternal Gardens?" I asked, frowning.

Xylo shook his head. "Hardly. It's at least an hour away."

Well. This was shaping up to be all sorts of fun. I'd had to kill pansies before, but never literally.

"Lead on," I said with a sigh.

I followed behind him, keeping an eye out for more patrols as I let my mind wander, analyzing my current situation.

Like Xylo, something was bothering me too, and I couldn't quite pinpoint what it was. Just a faint but persistent nagging sensation. I replayed my conversation with Dracula and Samael, wondering if one of them had said something that I had missed, but nothing jumped out at me, and I found myself growing angrier with each step—angry that they thought to constrict me by giving me this stupid quest. To give me something to focus on other than them.

Was it some kind of purposeful distraction? What business had Dracula really been referring to that would occupy them for the next three days, and why was the Coliseum hosting an event a day earlier than Xylo had thought?

And what about this prison Xylo had mentioned—the Menagerie? Was there a way to release the captive shifters? I needed to take care of myself before turning this into a rescue mission.

Were the two men doing something nefarious that they didn't want me knowing about? Most definitely, but what was it?

I stewed over that and my godfather's role in all of this, playing out every theory I could think of. It all came back to what he had to gain and what he wanted.

Primarily, Dracula probably wanted the barrier taken down so he could finally enjoy the luxury of take-out meals again.

But what had he wanted with Roland? He'd said he needed a vampire. Was he looking for a protégé of some kind?

And Samael's comment about why he had really agreed to serve my mother and become my godfather—but then how much rage he had shown in front of Dracula when she was mentioned. Talk about bipolar.

No matter how hard I tried, I couldn't come up with a logical explanation that checked all the boxes, and nothing came close to enlightening me on the nagging sensation I felt. It was just the annoying buzzing of an insect in my ear.

I felt like a lion staring at a raw steak hanging just outside my cage. I wanted to burn this place to ash—all of it. Except I didn't have the power to risk taking out minions and attracting unwanted attention. I needed to be surgical, hitting only my six targets. So I told myself I would take out all my pent-up aggression on those with the ruby amulets.

But I vowed I would return when it was all over, and I had my powers back. Because Castle Dracula needed the White Rose—a silent, invisible killer who slipped from shadow to shadow, never leaving a trace behind. Just a disturbing crime scene.

If I couldn't create mayhem by leaving behind an overwhelming number of corpses everywhere I went or by setting off an Apocalyptic magnitude of architectural destruction, then I would have to kill them with fear—from the inside out.

I needed to get them talking to each other at the blood cooler about how old Jimmy had been eviscerated in the privacy of his own rooms while moisturizing his scales and filing his talons, and that any one of them could be next. Get them looking over their shoulders, staring at the shadows.

Show them Despair.

My Mask still wasn't functioning in any useful way, but I'd been a monster slayer long before I'd gotten the Mask. I'd worked for the Vatican Shepherds, the Holy Hitmen. Even though I wasn't the best little Catholic, I knew one thing for certain.

These motherfuckers needed Jesus.

So I decided I would be their personal concierge for their trip to the afterlife and the fields of judgment—of whichever pantheon they desired.

18

Like Xylo had said, it had taken close to an hour to get to our next destination. The red glow of the moon washed over the garden, making it look like a murder scene. But I had to admit, it was beautiful. Flowers thick with buds—some blooming, some not—and lush vines and foliage crossed the cobblestone paths. A blanketed silence settled over the Eternal Garden like we were cut off from the rest of Dracula's estate.

We had definitely climbed in elevation, so we might have the chance to see some spectacular views depending on where we went from here.

But sightseeing wasn't a priority. I had only two priorities—getting the demon to squeal out any helpful information she might have and stealing Dracula's Bane.

Which meant maintaining our course for the Observatory and the Infernal Armory, which were both on the far side of the huge Eternal Garden. To put it into perspective, the garden was probably the size of Central Park, or close enough as to make no difference.

For the most part, lush, dense trees formed a canopy overhead, but certain areas had been cultivated in order to allow unobstructed moonlight to hit the flowers. The winding, serpentine paths climbed up and down rolling hills, making the patches of wildflowers resemble splashes of dripping paint, and the place itself was a labyrinth of decisions.

From within our hiding place of a particularly tall section of wildflowers, Xylo gave me a look, silently asking if I was ready. I nodded and he slipped out of sight around the corner. He didn't weigh much, which was a benefit when stalking, but his ill-fitted boots were not conducive to sneakiness.

In fact, he sounded like a lame horse that dreamt of becoming a professional tap dancer, despite obvious limitations and constructive criticism from concerned loved ones. So I gritted my teeth as I watched him clomp across the path to the flower garden on the opposite side.

I waited until the count of three, just like we'd agreed, and then rose.

I took one step before hurriedly crouching back down again as a woman suddenly appeared from around a blind corner on the path about a dozen yards away, moving in utter silence.

Damn it. I would have to wait. I saw Xylo slowly peeping up from the foliage on the other side of the path, probably wondering what was taking me so long. He noticed the woman—who was now almost directly between us, but luckily she was fidgeting with a basket tucked under her arm so she hadn't noticed the two of us hiding in the bushes and flowers—and he very slowly, very intently, shook his head at me, emphatically telling me *no* in perfect silence. Since he didn't typically show facial gestures—he'd told me it was hard to make his face move—I couldn't surmise what he was trying to tell me *not to do*.

Not to wait? Not to be seen? Not to attack?

Because I had been considering a swift, brutal assassination the moment I saw the precious ruby amulet hanging around her delicate neck. It was a beautiful, priceless ruby set in white gold and dangling from a similar chain that was so fine it looked like spider silk coated in dew. The ruby was also surrounded by diamonds, making the amulet itself easily the diameter of a plum. I had no reference on what this meant, though, since I hadn't seen any other necklaces yet. Were they all this flashy?

It rested invitingly against her pale bosom. She wore a green, low-cut silk gown that showed off more than the recommended daily dose of cleavage, but it wasn't so much that it looked scandalous. She might have been my height, and she was barefoot, believe it or not—a stark contrast to her elegant dress that looked to be intended for a formal dinner or perhaps even a debutante ball rather than skipping about through gardens. I looked up at her face to see she was finished fiddling with her basket and that a faint, genuine smile split her cheeks as she took a deep inhale through her nose.

Then she began to hum in a melodic, lilting singsong, dancing back and forth across the path to pluck flowers from either side and gently tuck them into her woven basket. The glow of the crimson moon suddenly washed over her as she sashayed over to a section of the path that wasn't blocked from the sky by the overhead trees. Her ruby amulet practically caught fire whenever she danced out of the shadows and into the moonlight, making her look like some mythical, Fae-like creature of joy and happiness.

One of the amulets. She was one of my potential targets. This jubilant, beautiful young woman picking flowers needed to die by my hand. I felt a flutter of fear dance across my heart, though. This slip of a woman had earned Dracula's favor? Did that mean she had a particularly fine bouquet of blood that he favored, or was she much more dangerous than she appeared?

The beams of moonlight also made her fine skin appear to glow from within as if flushed with blood—which only served to highlight how pale she actually was. Shining a red light on a white canvas had a much more noticeable impact than shining a red light over a shade of pink.

She was stunning, her wavy dark hair bouncing off her shoulders as she sashayed and twirled, pivoted and skipped, her eyes actually closing for long stretches as she seemed to be imagining a dance partner twirling her up in a dizzying, cookie-cutter-romance, Hallmark Channel flick. I couldn't get a clear view of her face due to all her dancing and me hiding in the bushes, but I saw enough to notice it was long and thin, emphasizing her cheek bones.

She was definitely a ten on the beauty scale, that much was obvious. Closer examination would have only served to tack on extra decimal places to her score.

I peered through the flowers rather than lifting my head from my hiding spot, hoping Xylo had written words on a sign or something. But he was ducked out of sight, leaving me to fend for myself or to get better at Charades. Had he been trying to warn me that she wasn't alone and to stay still?

Or maybe he had been warning me *not* to stay still and to instead run away to one of our rendezvous points—like he'd apparently done thirty seconds ago, leaving me behind.

I turned back to check on the woman only to find her staring directly at the patch of flowers concealing me, no longer dancing or humming. She stood in a shaded section of the path, as if trying to hide her features from me. And although it should have been impossible with me hidden from sight, it felt like she was staring directly into my eyes.

My every muscle tensed, hoping she was simply staring at a flower near my head. Maybe she had heard something and was looking in my direction to find out if it was a cause for concern. If I remained perfectly still...

"Why are you hiding, girl?" the woman spoke. Her voice sounded like her humming—a songbird heralding the rising sun in a Disney musical—light and lilting without sounding forced. Just a naturally perfect singing voice. My heart raced wildly, knowing I really had no other choice but to reveal myself—before she decided that I was, in fact, a threat, and killed me with whatever powers she had.

Or beat me over the head with her basket like when an opportunistic thief picked the wrong grandma to try mugging and got the ass-whooping of his life with her purse—which she had conveniently packed with cans of corn for her evening casserole—instead. The type of grandma who had woken up that morning with one fuck left to give, and that had been before she realized she was out of milk for her morning tea, forcing her to brave the city streets with her walker to pick some up at the convenience store three blocks away.

I slowly rose from my crouch, ready to run if she attacked. She didn't. She just appraised me thoughtfully. I found that my gaze kept drifting to her amulet, probably making me look like a greedy street urchin since I was also still covered in filth from the reeds. I tried reaching out to the amulet with my mind, hoping I would be able to sense some form of power hidden within—maybe even my own.

And which one of my powers it might be.

I was either too far away, it held no power, or maybe I was not able to sense it on the magical spectrum—since I had no magical spectrum at the moment. It looked like the only way to find out if this was one of the right necklaces was to follow Dracula's instructions—kill her and let the amulet drink her blood—and then shatter it in hopes that this twisted version of the *Price is Right* would give me my wizard's magic first.

Xylo—who apparently hadn't abandoned me—finally lifted his skull out of the foliage enough to reveal only his eye sockets—which looked about as panicked as I'd ever seen—but he suddenly dropped back beneath the foliage and I heard other voices approaching—more women—a moment later. The humming, dancing woman was suddenly directly in front of me, grabbing me by the hand and anxiously tugging me after her down the path, away from the voices. I was so surprised that I didn't question it, and the next thing I knew, I was running along beside her through a trellised tunnel blanketed with the vines of aromatic purple flowers. If this local was scared of the women behind us, she probably had very good reason. Plus, I decided that I would rather fight one woman than multiple.

We burst out of the tunnel and ran down more cobbled paths, weaving back and forth like a snake as the ground suddenly descended so that we were running down a sizable hill, allowing us to gain some real momentum. We skirted a pond full of croaking frogs—which made my shoulders instinctively tense before realizing it was not a gathering of frogmen—jumped over a few benches here and there, and then circled a massive fountain featuring a nude mermaid bathing in the sun. Then the woman let go of my hand and veered off into the garden itself, leaving the path—and me—behind.

She tore through a wall of foliage ahead of her and I hesitated for a few seconds, listening for sounds of pursuit. But it sounded like we had lost them, so I took a deep breath, eyed the wall of foliage, and jumped through after her.

I skidded to a halt to find her standing before me, her hair a mess, her basket sitting on the ground by her feet, and her hands folded one over the other in front of her waist—hopefully a peaceful gesture. I finally got a clear look at her face and, although still beautiful, I realized she wasn't as perfectly pretty as I'd first assumed. Or maybe that was just the leaves and twigs sticking out of her hair.

We stood on a secluded edge of the garden, and when I say edge, I mean that we were twenty feet away from a sheer drop of what looked to be well over a hundred feet. I couldn't see the immediate base of the cliff from my viewpoint, but the distant landscape let me know we were higher than I would have preferred. High enough that it would be instant death if I fell from it. Dracula didn't believe in safety railings either. Other than that, the area was grassy and featured a lone wooden bench and one giant, knotted, old tree clinging to the last section of earth near the edge of the cliff. That was pretty much it.

The crimson sky and moon, as always, cast everything in a ruby glow.

I hoped she hadn't lured me here for a quick kill. Without Xylo—and not knowing what this woman was capable of—I might just be out of my league.

Her head was cocked slightly, and she was studying me thoughtfully. In fact, she looked uncomfortable and slightly puzzled. I couldn't blame her. She'd just found a mud-covered bitch with a sword hiding in her flower bed. "My name is Mina," she said after a time.

My jaw dropped and I blinked dumbly, feeling slightly star-struck all of a sudden. "Mina..." I breathed. "Wilhelmina Harker?" I asked incredulously, recognizing the name from Bram Stoker's novel.

19

Mina Harker was the human that Dracula had tried turning into a vampire, cursing her with his blood. In the story, it was the action that had set everyone against him—proving that he really was a monster and not just some eccentric loner, and that he needed to be stopped.

The reason I was star-struck was because, in the story, Mina hadn't been a bad guy. Dracula had tried to turn her but had ultimately failed. This woman hated Dracula. As did her husband, Jonathan Harker—for what Dracula had done to Mina.

They were the *heroes* of the story.

So...why was she *here*? Was I dealing with a potential ally? Maybe she would just *give* me her necklace.

She smiled, looking amused. "Yes. And you are?" she asked patiently.

I felt my cheeks flush. "Callie Penrose."

Her smile stretched wider. "What a lovely name."

"Who were they?" I asked, pointing back the way we had come. I hoped Xylo had tracked us, because this area was new to me and I wasn't sure where to go next. We'd taken a lot of turns, and with the thick canopy overhead during our mad dash, I very easily could have gotten turned around. A quick glance out over the edge of the cliff didn't show me any recognizable landmarks, which wasn't a good sign.

Mina grimaced at my question. "They go by many names. The Vixens. The Sisters. The Brides of Dracula. The Weird Sisters. Whatever you choose to call them, they are three sadistic psychopaths. It is best to avoid them. They can do worse to you than kill you." I nodded, not needing any elaboration. I'd heard all about those three, and silently wondered why they hadn't been on Xylo's list, or if they had just been some of the names he hadn't mentioned since there were over forty potentials. "You look like a woman who does not want to be noticed," Mina said, eyeing my filthy, swamp-stained clothes up and down, growing more comfortable with my presence.

I grunted. "I look like a woman who needs a week-long bath."

Mina smiled, dipping her chin politely, too ladylike to verbally concur.

She hadn't attacked me, so maybe my first necklace would be an easy acquisition. Except...Dracula had told me I needed to *murder* and exsanguinate the guests, not just take their jewelry. Did he really want me to murder Mina, though? Hadn't he been obsessed with her? "What are you doing here?" I asked, shaking my head. In the stories, Mina and her fiancé, Jonathan, had defeated and killed Dracula, watching the castle burn.

Yet here I was. The novel had obviously taken liberties. I had met Dracula in his castle—not burned down in the slightest—and was now having a girl's chat with Mina Freaking Harker. Then again, I knew the castle was a Beast, and even if Bram Stoker's story had been true, a Beast would have the ability to survive a fire—or to easily recover.

Mina sighed, her eyes growing distant for a few moments. Then she turned to look out over the castle grounds beyond the ledge. "I never intended to stay, yet I was never able to leave. We thought we had won, that we had sent him back to hell where he belonged. We were so wrong. His Beast is everlasting," she breathed in a barely audible whisper, shaking her head back and forth before staring down at her bare feet.

I shuddered to hear the fear in her voice. The fact that she became stuck here, stuck in her own personal nightmare from so long ago.

And now that nightmare defined her entire—immortal—existence. Dracula was a cruel son-of-a-bitch, no question.

"Luckily for you, the Beast is resting for the next few days. You should flee while you have the chance," she told me somberly, "before someone puts you into the Menagerie or the Beast awakes. I imagine she will be hungry when she rises."

I swallowed, clamping my lips shut. How did she know Samael had put the Beast to sleep but not know about me? I very carefully considered my response, playing out my clumsy footedness as shyness upon meeting a celebrity. "I heard there is no way to escape this place," I said.

She nodded. "Truer than you know."

"Where is Jonathan Harker?" I asked cautiously.

She looked up at me, her eyes hollow and empty. "I haven't heard his name in centuries..." she whispered. "I miss him so much." A tear rolled down her cheeks.

I winced guiltily, deciding to take a moment to gather my thoughts before blurting out a million questions.

"Why are you here? How are you here?" I finally asked, unable to formulate a theory of my own beyond *magic*.

Mina let out a harsh, bitter laugh. "The Beast lets no one leave. She carries a grudge well. Anyone who shows her disrespect suffers for eternity. Burning down this castle so long ago damned us all. It just comes back during the next full moon. She is hungry to keep everyone here—whether alive or dead, she does not care." I thought about Xylo and nodded. That was...terrible.

"And what is your punishment?" I asked. "To live here forever?"

"I am the newest Bride of Dracula," she whispered forlornly. "For better or worse."

And it suddenly made sense why the three Brides of Dracula might be lurking about in the garden—and why Mina had fled. They had probably come to terrorize her somehow. Dracula had upgraded to a newer model car —Mina—but had selfishly kept the old models—the Weird Sisters—in the garage.

Mina cleared her throat, unclasping her hands. She had a sorrowful frown on her face—the resolve of a woman accepting her fate. "This is my burden. My cross to bear." She appraised me thoughtfully. "What is your cross to bear, Callie Penrose? You look like a determined woman, and determined women usually have short fates. In fact, you even remind me of someone I once met," she added, appraising me thoughtfully.

I hesitated, wondering how honest I should be. "I've just got one of those faces, I guess. Your husband gave me a job to do," I finally admitted. "I'm just doing as he requested."

Mina was entirely still for about five seconds. "Oh? And what job is that?

My husband did not mention it when I saw him less than an hour ago. He did not mention you at all, in fact, Callie Penrose."

The hair on the back of my neck began to rise at the chill in her tone—at the news that another woman secretly stood between her and her husband, even if it was a husband she did not particularly care for. Territory was territory.

"Well, to be honest, I was tricked into coming here by the same demon you mentioned earlier. The one who put the Beast to sleep." In my mind, I was getting a very clear idea of what Xylo had meant by shaking his head at me. It had been *no—to anything and everything involving Mina Harker.*

Was this a kind of Stockholm Syndrome or had he brainwashed her in some way? Because I couldn't accurately read which side of the fan club she was on—for or against Dracula.

"That demon?" Mina finally asked, pointing out over the cliff.

I frowned, not understanding. She walked over to the edge of the cliff, motioning for me to join her. I did so, my every muscle ready to keep my feet firmly planted in the earth if she tried anything funny.

I glanced down.

And down, and down, and down.

The Coliseum stood below us, telling me just how high Xylo and I had really climbed on our way to the Eternal Garden. It hadn't seemed this high, but proof was proof. And like a Salvador Dali painting, I couldn't understand how we had ended up with the Coliseum so close. That didn't make any geographic sense.

But all those thoughts evaporated in a heartbeat.

Despite our elevation, I could see with perfect clarity that a man stood in the center of the Coliseum, and he was wounded and bloody. But the way he stood—so confident and determined...

It was Samael. My Godfather. No question.

And he was facing a behemoth of a creature that I wasn't even sure how to classify. The arena was littered with tall, heaping mounds of other bodies from dozens of different types of monsters, and I realized that Samael had killed them all. That number of bodies had to mean that Samael had been inside the ring for hours upon hours.

As if the moment he'd left my sight, Dracula had thrown him in there.

Holy hell.

Mina cleared her throat, snapping me back to my own perilous situation.

"Dracula does not like loose ends. The demon Samael completed some service for Dracula, but he also overreached by putting Sanguina to sleep. Behold the fate of a job well done in service to Dracula," she said, her tone emotionless. "The demon has already broken the old record for highest consecutive kill-count, but not even his kind last forever. The stench of offal and stale blood from all the fallen warriors left to rot convinced me to take a break and visit the Eternal Gardens to instead inhale the perfume of life. They paused the fighting to give his opponents some water and food, but it looks like they are getting ready to resume."

She turned to me, gauging my reaction.

And...I wasn't entirely sure what to think. Did Samael deserve this?

Sure. No question. And not even for betraying me. He was a Greater Demon and had likely done enough in his past to earn this several times over.

But...fucking Dracula again, being the asshole he was, turning on everyone after their purpose had been served. I let out a tired sigh. "This has to stop, Mina. All of it."

She nodded absently. "Good luck stopping all of *them*," she said, pointing back down at the Coliseum.

I glanced down to notice that the place was packed to overflowing, which I hadn't realized before since I had been so focused on Samael. But I did remember the cheers and shouts I'd heard coming from the Coliseum over the past few hours—and that Xylo had been surprised about the change in schedule.

Now I knew why. The newest gladiator was setting records.

But Samael was an agent of chaos and the double-cross. He had to have known Dracula would ultimately betray him—and would have had a plan to prevent it.

My heart skipped a beat at a sudden new thought.

Was I the *plan*?

Had Samael gone to every possible effort to make sure I didn't get tossed into the ring with him—into a prison cell for Dracula to deal with later? Was that why he hadn't mentioned my Horseman's Mask when he took my other powers away? Had it been a show for Dracula? He'd told me that we all had our parts to play, whether we liked them or not.

Was my godfather still on Team Callie, or were we all on our own teams pitted against each other?

But as I began replaying his comments in my mind, I grew fairly certain that maybe Samael *had* set all of this up—for *me* to save *him*. Too bad he'd put on such a good show for Dracula that I had no idea—or ability with my powers taken away—about how to do that.

"Maybe I shouldn't shatter all the necklaces," I murmured, realizing too late that I'd spoken out loud.

Mina glanced over at me sharply. "Necklaces?" she asked.

Inwardly, I winced. It was too late to take back my words, though, so I pressed on, speaking carefully. "Dracula tasked me with acquiring and destroying them," I admitted, indicating her amulet with my eyes and chin, but keeping my hands neutrally at my side so as not to appear threatening.

"The only way to acquire these is to—" She pursed her lips suddenly, narrowing her eyes in alarm. "He intends for you to kill us."

I held up my hands. "Well...a little. Just six of you, though. He didn't tell me to kill *you*, if that's what you're thinking. We get to pick which amulets we take and destroy. Total coincidence that I ran into you—"

"We?" she interrupted, her tone high-pitched and incredulous as she took a few steps back from me. "You're not alone? How many assassins did that snake send?" she demanded. "Is he making a move for the Master's Library or the Infernal Armory?"

I had no idea what she was talking about, so shrugged very slowly. "Easy, Mina. I'm not your enemy. I was just trying to walk through the Garden when you showed up."

"WHO ELSE?!" she demanded, her shoulders actually twitching spastically.

That's when I heard a sudden roaring sound from back in the Garden.

We both spun as three women burst through the foliage, fleeing a flaming skeleton with a crimson hood over his head who was roaring at them like a demon, catching the entire hedge on fire behind him, and effectively blocking us off from escape.

"That guy," I admitted, deciding honesty was the best medicine. "Look!" I said, pointing a thumb at him as he began to hurl fiery ribs at the three vampire wenches. "He doesn't like the ex-wives either!"

Mina glared at Xylo with unbridled hatred and what looked like stunned disbelief. "*You!* How *dare* he send *you!*" she screamed, apparently recognizing —and not approving of—my assistant. Then she turned to glare at me. "He will *never* succeed in this foolish game," she snarled, and I wasn't sure if she was talking about Xylo or Dracula. "I fear it's time for me to go eat Callie Penrose."

I stared back at her, not following her segue or sudden need for munchies.

That's when I noticed her purposefully shifting her stance for better balance—and I suddenly recalled an old lesson that I'd learned in grade school.

That commas—and phonetic pauses—mattered.

It's time for me to go eat, Callie Penrose was very different from *it's time for me to go eat Callie Penrose.*

One was a polite excusal.

The other was both homicide and cannibalism.

Good thing I had nonverbal cues to really punctuate—heh—the difference.

Like the long black claws suddenly sprouting from Mina's delicate finger-tips and the fangs protruding from behind her plump lips as she dove for my face with a serious case of the *nom-noms* and obvious ill-intent.

I've always heard you should never meet your idols, heroes, or favorite celebrities. I'd just never heard it was because they might try to kill you and eat you.

Strangely enough, her face momentarily spasmed in mid-air, and when she recovered, her eyes looked surprised.

I guarantee they weren't as surprised as mine. Had she had a mental break mid-attack?

The screams of rage and pain from Xylo battling the Brides of Dracula behind her were not my concern. I was too busy trying to draw my katana against the bipolar Mina-Pire to worry about Xylo. He was undying anyway.

I, on the other hand, was adorably squishy and needed to actively worry about keeping my blood on the inside.

In the chaos and rush of adrenaline, my English teacher's parting lesson crossed my mind.

You may occasionally get away with poor punctuation and win some battles, but Grammar will always win the war.

❦ 20 ❦

I managed to lift my blade and slap away Mina's claws as I dodged to the side to avoid her tackle. She landed in a roll, spinning to face me, switching our places so that Xylo and his new harem of jealous housewives were now behind me. I couldn't remain standing with my back to the potential new threats in case Xylo lost track of one of the Weird Sisters and she decided to jump in on our fight. So that left me one option.

The cliff.

I backed towards it, keeping the majority of my attention on Mina—obviously a god-damned vampire—as I tried to gauge the immediate danger from the new guests. I saw a woman hurled into the base of the large tree clinging to the edge of the cliff, embers and sparks flying everywhere, and all of them screaming, hissing, and roaring, before I refocused on my own little Bridezilla.

Mina raced at me in a blur, not as agile as I would have expected after a hundred years of practice. I was dangerously close to the ledge, though, so I couldn't risk a prolonged dance. She looked both determined and disgusted, as if she was at war with herself.

What the hell was going on with her? Was Dracula making her do this? Puppeteering his own wife? As if I had needed more reasons to kill him.

She finally closed the distance, and I knew I only had a couple feet of room behind me before I would experience freefall without wings. She swiped at my face with her claws in a jab, before whipping out with her fangs to get a bite out of my neck.

Of course, my katana through her chest prevented all of this.

She'd been so focused on the goal that she hadn't kept her guard up.

She coughed up blood, gasping as I yanked the blade free and kicked her in the stomach to get some distance. I felt disgusted with myself for kicking Mina—knowing that she hadn't wanted to be used as Dracula's puppet, and should have been on my side helping to take down her husband. But my life was more important than her feelings.

So I imagined it was my old English teacher, and this was my battle to win. I'd always wanted to do that to her for painting my papers in red ink.

I heard a terrible, horrifying scream near the tree, but I was too focused on Mina to look. Dracula's newest bride crashed to the ground, clutching at her ruined chest—right over her heart. I wasn't sure if that was enough to kill her or not—not with Dracula controlling her—but it was enough to give me a second to get clear of the ledge and finally glance over at the other fight near the tree.

I slowly lowered my katana, blinking a few times to make sure I wasn't hallucinating.

The screaming sound was coming from Xylo, but what really impressed me was that he was leaning backwards at a forty-five-degree angle, using some kind of sparking, fiery rope to string up two of the women and hang them over a large branch high up in the tree. Black smoke liberally poured out of his eyes, making me cringe.

He...was using my Horseman power somehow, and I hadn't felt a thing. As I peered closer, I saw that his bone arms ended at the wrist, and that the two women were actually being choked out by his detached hands. The joints and ligaments connecting his wrist to his hands had elongated into a fiery rope of embers and sparks, looping over the overhead branch.

He had hellfire noose-hands. Jesus Christ.

He was *hanging* them. With his freaking *hands*. Like a twisted version of Ghost Rider and his fiery chains.

I saw ruby necklaces hanging from their necks and turned away with a resigned grimace. I wasn't happy about how he was killing them, but if they wore those amulets, they were fair game. I'd just learned what trying to talk someone out of their necklace got me.

I was more concerned with how Xylo was using my Horseman powers when I couldn't. And how Mina had recognized the supposed simpleton skeleton.

Mina was staring up at me, blood dripping from her mouth. "Thank you," she whispered, sounding sincere. Her bloody hand shifted to the necklace and she yanked it off with a pained jerk. She opened her mouth to speak, but her eyes filmed over before she could say anything else.

I sighed. "We all die the same," I whispered. "Pray you don't come back as a skeleton."

I wasn't sure whether to feel relieved or disgusted about killing Mina Harker—one of the main victims of Bram Stoker's story.

I bent down to take the ruby necklace from her dead hands and dipped it into her blood, curling my lip distastefully. Nothing magical happened and I grunted, frowning down at it. I shoved it into my pocket without looking at it. It tingled faintly in my hand, and that was enough for me. We had made a lot of noise here and needed to flee before someone came to check it out.

Xylo released the two women right as I sheathed my sword and turned around, of course. They crashed to the ground bonelessly as Xylo's hands whipped back up over the branch to reconnect with his wrists. He hurried over to their bodies and yanked off their necklaces. The third Sister suddenly stumbled clumsily to her feet from the base of the tree, eyes wide with panic at the sight of her dead sisters. Xylo didn't hesitate, flinging his whip hand out to grab onto her necklace from a dozen paces away and yank it free. The vampire promptly leapt off the edge of the cliff, great, bat-like wings whipping out from her back as she swept them hard and fast in an effort to escape.

Xylo watched for a moment before calmly snapping off one of his ribs and flinging it at her with a casual flick of his wrist. The flaming rib tore a great hole through her wing, the fire incinerating the fleshy membrane like flash paper and she plummeted down to the ground.

She spiraled out of control with an ear-splitting shriek and fell to either her death or long-term intensive care, depending on a vampire's healing ability.

Xylo paid no mind as he crouched over the other women. His rib whipped towards him, slamming back into place with a flare of sparks, but it obviously didn't hurt him since he didn't react in the slightest.

I began breathing faster, trying to ignore the sounds of outrage from the

Coliseum below. What the hell were we going to do now, and why had Mina so suddenly gone crazy?

I made my way over to him in a swift jog, watching as he dipped the amulets into the blood. Well, two of them. The third had landed out of our reach, so we had an amulet, but no blood for it.

I gasped as the ruby pulsed with blinding light upon contact with the blood.

"Mine didn't do that," I said, feeling a sickening sensation in the pit of my stomach.

He turned to look at me, his face blank.

Then he turned to dip the other amulet into the blood before grimacing at the third, unbloodied amulet. Then he climbed to his feet and handed them over to me. "Show me," he said, sounding exhausted.

I shoved the amulets into my other pocket and walked over to Mina, pointing down at her. "I dipped it in the blood, and nothing happened."

Xylo was eerily silent, and the sounds of outrage from the Coliseum below rose in volume. They were not cheers. Judging by the trajectory, Sister Number Three had to have landed smack-dab in the center of the Coliseum.

Xylo cleared his throat uncomfortably. "That is not Mina Harker," he finally said.

I blinked at him. "You're shitting me."

He shook his head. "I shit you not."

I cursed loudly. "You're telling me that out of the four amulets we just had in our grasp, only two of them count for this stupid quest?" I demanded, angrier at myself than anything.

"I'm sorry about the third one. She was too far away for me to actually grab her without her taking me out over the ledge and leaving you unprotected," he rasped guiltily.

I shook my head, gesturing dismissively. "I'm not mad at you, Xylo. Just the situation. I don't understand. This woman was Mina—she knew things."

Xylo shifted from foot-to-foot. "Perhaps she took possession of one of the other, younger vampires. That *is* her amulet," he added, frowning as if at a puzzle. "And I did see Mina in the Gardens between us. She must have made a switch somewhere between here and there."

I gritted my teeth. The only time she'd been out of my sight was when she'd let go of my hand and jumped through the foliage—the still burning foliage, by the way, which was pretty much a beacon for what had gone down here.

"Yeah," I admitted. "That makes sense." I sighed wearily, glaring down at the poor vampire who Mina had used like a puppet. "For all intents and purposes, we just killed all of Dracula's brides..." I said bluntly, fully expecting the bastard to appear directly behind me and rip my heart out.

Xylo nodded calmly. "They saw me trying to follow you and Mina Harker through the Gardens," he said. "I had no choice."

"Me neither. She went from pleasant to killer at the flip of a switch. And we made a lot of noise," I said. Actually, Xylo had made all the noise. I had been the perfect lady, killing my target with finesse and silence. Except, I'd picked the wrong target. "Let's get out of here before reinforcements show up."

He didn't even respond. He just grabbed my hand and led me back into a section of the foliage that hadn't caught fire yet.

I tried to ignore the faint buzzing sensation of the necklaces in my pocket. I did not ignore the strange thoughts and plans that suddenly began to whisper in the depths of my mind. Several things Mina-not-Mina had said were bothering me.

I let my wild thoughts play out in my mind like simulations, seeing if they led to any new insights in this fucked-up game I was apparently playing.

21

Security had definitely caught onto our wholesale slaughter in the Eternal Gardens, forcing Xylo to take a different route that would conveniently bring us past the Master's Library that Mina had mentioned. She had demanded to know if Dracula was making a move for it, whatever that meant.

I was coming to understand that Dracula loved his extravagant names when it came to inanimate objects—as if making up for his lack of interest in the names of living creatures.

Or Dracula was naming it exactly what it was—a *Master's* library. Either way, I was somewhat relieved that our escape from the Eternal Gardens gave us the opportunity to check it out. Because it was highly likely that the real Mina Harker might swing by in order to make sure Dracula didn't do whatever it was that she feared him doing.

Which meant I might get the chance to personally explain that if she really hated Dracula so much, we were actually on the same side.

I was also betting that with Dracula being such a collector of treasures—which Xylo had confirmed to be the case—he might have some books on the Omegabet or something equally dangerous that I could steal from him or destroy. Barring that, I still wanted to see what kind of books he considered to be valuable, or powerful.

Anything that might give me hints on the Master's master plan.

You know how after you bought a new car you suddenly saw it everywhere? When you could have sworn you had never seen one on the streets before that day? Like you were some local trendsetter in automobile aesthetics, and that everyone had been silently waiting for you to choose your new car so they could go out and copy your design, even down to the color of the valve caps on your tires.

It was absolutely true.

Because everywhere I turned lately, I seemed to find double connotations and entendres that tied back to the word *Master*. Was that by design or just my overactive imagination?

Xylo had led us around the perimeter of the Eternal Gardens and through the Terrible Timbers—what felt like an enchanted forest—which luckily had no terrible wood or wolves to speak of—because they were likely all scouring the Gardens for us. Our walk through the dark forest finally opened up onto a small clearing with a huge, multi-story building with a single, fifty-plus-foot tower on the end closest to us. The building was still within the Terrible Timbers, but through the trees about a hundred yards further on, I saw several vast marble structures that looked like a ritzy city butting up against the forest.

Likely where all the rich monsters kicked their feet up.

The tower was encircled by one of those gargantuan, serpent-like, spiral staircases like I had seen on the towers from the bridge closer to the Keep. Up close, it was mesmerizingly intricate and detailed—enough that I almost feared it would come to life like a giant gargoyle.

Anything was possible here.

Xylo confirmed that it was not alive, and that it had never moved in his time living here. That was good enough to get me to agree to climb it, but I didn't fully trust his answer. Just because he had never seen it come to life didn't mean that it couldn't, and I'd seen enough crazy shit here to believe any insanity thrown my way.

The stairs were easily wide enough for a vehicle to use, and the attention to detail was unbelievable. It truly looked as if it was about to take a breath and detach from the tower. The sculptor had even carved individual scales into the railing, each as large as my fist.

To be safe, we crouched as we climbed, in case any gargoyles had been dispatched to search for the assassin who had killed the Brides of Dracula.

I found myself wondering exactly how the Beast accomplished such wonders—how its magic actually worked to make this terribly beautiful place. Did Sanguina simply will the place into existence, tap into the magic from our world, or did she somehow teleport it, or the materials to make it, from some other realm?

Because even with magic-wielding engineers, this place should have taken decades, if not hundreds of years, to build.

And Mina—speaking through her possessed vampire—had claimed that the place returned to its full glory at every full moon since they had burned it down.

That was another thing. What exactly had gone down when they killed Dracula so long ago? Had they actually killed him and Sanguina brought him back to life, or had they just thought they'd killed him? Maybe he'd suffered burns and the Beast had healed him.

I didn't hold out much hope for Dracula explaining it all to me—not after he learned we'd just cock-blocked him by killing all three of his old wives and turned his new wife against him. That was going to be an awkward conversation. But...he'd sent me out here, given me a guide, and told me to find the amulet necklaces. If he knew his wives wore some, had he *intended* me to kill them?

Had I actually been roped into killing his wives for him? That made me feel decidedly icky. I pointedly ignored the four amulets in my pocket, only two of them worth a damn in helping to get my powers back. Despite that, they all had a gentle hum to them—like if you placed your hand over a running microwave. I could tell the amulets were giving off power, but I hadn't sensed anything that told me whether it was my stolen power or something related to their own power. Xylo had told me that the amulets were essentially keys to travel the property, granting the wearer access to restricted areas.

Xylo had also urged me to shatter one or two of them in order to at least get some of my powers back, but after talking with Mina's puppet and seeing Samael in the Coliseum, I had misgivings about sticking to Dracula's plan. Without Dracula's Bane, Sanguina would just bring him back to life after I killed him, but I was no closer to finding that relic than I had been when I first entered this cursed place.

Not that I had a better idea on how to defeat Dracula or get my powers back, but at least I could wait it out until absolutely necessary. Following Dracula's request wouldn't end well for me, no matter what he had said.

Hell, he'd told me that I would serve him no matter what happened, and I was beginning to believe it.

I still had strange thoughts drifting through my mind, strange possibilities that I hadn't decided whether or not were applicable to my situation. I let them play out in my head, hoping they came up with something helpful. Because now we had the attention of the entire Castle Dracula after killing the Sisters. So far, we had been lucky in avoiding the numerous patrols, because we were going out of our way to stay off any known paths. Xylo's knowledge of the castle—and all the secret, unknown or unused paths he had travelled over the years to avoid bullies—had proven invaluable.

That strange nagging sensation still continued to pop up here and there, but it was sporadic at best, so I still hadn't pinpointed what the subconscious thought was or what it was trying to tell me.

I realized I had stopped walking and was just standing on the stairs, lost in my thoughts. I glanced up to find Xylo staring at the bloody Cross Pattée on my chest again, and this time he was speaking wordlessly under his breath as if trying to remember something.

He noticed my attention and jerked his head away with a mumbled apology before continuing up the stairs. I watched him thoughtfully for a few moments, wondering how I could help him get his memory back, or if it was even possible.

One thing I had tried to keep silent about was how Mina had recognized Xylo. At first, I'd thought it had been Dracula using Mina against her will, but when I'd mentioned the amulets, the vampire had lost her mind. Which meant I had been talking to Mina's proxy—a minion vampire that Mina had possessed. And Mina had not been happy to hear that her dear husband had intended to take her amulet and kill her.

And Mina had been just as furious to see Xylo—clearly recognizing him. I'd casually brought it up to Xylo and he'd just stared back at me blankly, telling me he'd never even spoken to her—just seen her from afar.

And I knew he was telling me the truth. He simply didn't know how to lie. I'd briefly considered the possibility that maybe Xylo was Jonathan Harker, having his memory wiped by Dracula for pure cruelty. To have Harker—now Xylo—as his and Mina's personal servant, and Xylo having no idea who he'd been before becoming a skeleton soldier.

Xylo had looked over at me, reading my thoughts. Finally, he shrugged. "I don't think that's true, but how would I know?" he asked in a saddened tone.

And he was right, but he might also be wrong. Even those afflicted with mental maladies caused by magic often displayed reactions of some kind— on the subconscious level—when confronted with a subject that came too close to their wiped memory. They may grow silent if they were usually talk- ative, or sad if they were usually happy. Any kind of change to their typical attitude was a potential red flag.

Except Xylo didn't change at all when he read my thoughts. He just shrugged, looking helpless. "I wish you could read my mind and see how desolate it is," he finally said, staring down at the ground.

I closed my eyes and made an effort to read his mind. I found myself staring into an empty warehouse, but I wasn't sure if it was my imagination or not.

"Think of something happy," I told him absently.

In my mind, a lone balloon suddenly appeared, floating in the emptiness, and I found myself smiling excitedly—

Then the balloon popped, and I heard a low, growling laugh echoing from the shadows.

Jesus. His one happy thought, and that fucking werewolf had taken it from him. Even in his *memories*.

I opened my eyes to find Xylo hanging his head. "I tried. That always happens when I think about my balloon."

I smiled sadly, reaching out to squeeze his hand. "Where I live, balloons are easy to get," I told him. "And I was able to see your thoughts," I said, feeling proud of myself. It had been hit-or-miss.

He nodded with an empty smile. "Great job. Really."

So I let it go—and I decided to be very careful about my stray thoughts from here on out. We reached the top of the stairs at the top of the tower and Xylo opened the wooden door leading inside. Although my shoulders tensed, I was somewhat relieved to be back indoors. Walking around outside in the open had been a nerve-wracking ordeal. I closed the door behind me, shrouding the room in darkness. I lifted my hand to cast a ball of fire for light only to remember that I didn't have my magic.

Xylo murmured something under his breath and his ligaments suddenly began to glow brighter, casting the room in a soothing light. I smiled, nodding at him. Inwardly, I wanted to know exactly what his powers stemmed from. I doubted that his power was restrained to this castle, because having an army of skeletons that only functioned within its walls would be no help in the real world when Dracula chose to go on the warpath. They would serve as an incredible defense of the Castle, though.

I followed him through what was apparently an unimpressive storeroom, stepping over old discarded furniture that was almost stacked to the ceiling. Xylo suddenly held out a hand, glancing back at me. "We are not alone. Move in silence, and follow my footsteps," he whispered, his teeth clicking on the *T* sounds. I nodded at him, idly wondering how he was able to make the *S* sounds.

He crouched in the doorway and I saw enough to realize we were on a high balcony overlooking a vast space. Xylo glanced left and right before settling down on his hands and knees and crawling up to the railing lining the balcony. I carefully followed him to the railing and glanced down. What made sense was that we were five stories above the ground floor. What didn't make sense was that the library was significantly larger than it had appeared from the outside, and that several more balconies like ours rose over our heads—which was impossible since we'd climbed to the top of the tower before entering.

On each of those balconies were rows and rows of books.

Luckily, our balcony was dark and held no surprise guards or anything. I looked back down at the ground level to see a large, U-shaped desk in the center of the open space, and it was piled high with stacks of papers and old, leather-bound books.

That had to be Dracula's desk. Because there was a blind-folded baboon seated cross-legged on the floor in front of it, and he had an ancient looking bamboo staff resting across his knees. I frowned at him thoughtfully. He was obviously a guard of some sort, and I was betting he was a lot more dangerous than he looked—which was plenty dangerous enough. Baboons were vicious, violent creatures when provoked.

The fact that he had only a staff, no armor, and was blindfolded almost made him scarier, in my opinion.

I nearly yelped when a shape moved on the railing of the balcony directly across from us, not thirty paces away. And then a *third* baboon lazily slipped from his perch on a higher balcony to fall two levels down, snatching onto a railing with almost sloth-like grace, bobbing rhythmically for a two-count, and then letting go to repeat the process a few times until he reached the ground floor. He had two kamas—basically handheld sickles—tucked into the back of a yellow sash tied around his waist. He was also blindfolded, but he'd navigated down the balcony as if his eyes were unnecessary.

I glanced down at the wooden floor of our balcony, truly noticing how warped the wood was and how much detritus littered the area—crumpled paper, dried leaves, dehydrated sticks and twigs, and even a glass object or two. Luckily, our path had been relatively clear or else—

My heart froze.

Sound traps.

The baboons had made sound traps. The floorboards would creak or you would accidentally disturb something on your path as you kept your eyes fixed on the baboons.

And that's when they would come for you.

I squeezed Xylo's arm and pointed at the traps, shaking my head.

I decided that I didn't really need to see the library that badly. Xylo nodded, reaching out to tap my shoulder and point out where I should crawl to get back into the room we had just left. I studied his directions and prepared to move back to safety.

I heard a heavy *thud* on the metallic rail behind me and flinched— silently. Nothing happened. I slowly craned my neck to glance back and my eyes widened. Xylo had his back pressed up against the railing and he stared at me, not moving a millimeter.

Because a motherfucking baboon was standing on the railing, his elongated feet gripping the bar, implying he must have dropped or swung down from a higher level, but he didn't seem to have any interest in going any further than our balcony. He held a sai—a dagger with two sharp prongs curving outward from the hilt—in either hand, and his matted, shaggy fur was much thicker and longer than I would have thought, making him look two or three times larger than he probably was. It would also conceal his movements in a fight, the fur making it hard to see what his hands and feet were actually doing. The hair around his neck was even longer and thicker, resembling a mane of sorts. His back was to us or I would have tried killing him on the spot before he had a chance to raise an alarm.

The baboon's bare ass shone in the light of Xylo's glowing ligaments, giving me a too-close look at his crime scene. Simply put, it was impossible not to notice the stark contrast of bare skin compared to the long fur covering every other part of his body. Then he slowly, silently, began to crouch down to perch on the railing in a squat that only brought further attention to his anus.

Xylo didn't make a sound. I didn't make a sound, but I was confident my eyes looked as wide as Xylo's smoking sockets. I was relieved to see that it didn't appear that the baboon had any ability to smell or magically sense that smoke or we would have been in trouble. We'd seen at least three baboons so far, but more importantly, we'd seen three baboons in only our brief inspection of the immediate area.

This library was massive.

There could be dozens upon dozens of them in the library. All ready to pelt us with poo and then ka-bob us with their ka-nives. The baboon's tail slowly lowered, brushing across Xylo's face. I slowly shook my head from side-to-side, urging him not to move at all.

All it would take was one faint sound—perhaps even my breath—to make the baboon turn and sense us. Xylo glacially lifted a hand, gesturing with a finger for me to leave. I heard a faint scraping sound as bone scratched bone and my heart suddenly thundered in my chest as the baboon's tail froze and the creature cocked his head slightly.

I reached into my pocket, setting my jaw, hoping I would find something I could throw down the balcony to draw his attention. I found only the collection of necklaces and my butterfly charm. The baboon slowly began to turn, not making a sound as it moved.

He couldn't see. As long as I remained silent, we might be okay. Still, my other hand slowly hovered over the katana, fearing to even grab it in case the baboon could hear me drawing the blade or gripping the hilt too tightly. The baboon finally faced us, and I parted my lips in order to balance out my breathing so that I wasn't sucking air through my nose and possibly making a noise.

22

This baboon's elongated, black nose resembled more of a snout, and the long, fluffy, white hair covering his head and cheeks made him resemble a dandelion. A black blindfold covered his eyes, but I could see his nostrils flaring as they tried to pick up on our scent. He deftly hopped down from the railing, landing on all fours directly in front of me, cutting me off from Xylo. Despite the fact that Xylo had been the one to make a sound, the baboon slowly leaned closer to me, sniffing loudly. But from his lack of immediate reaction, he apparently couldn't sense me, for whatever reason. Was it the mud from the swamp still covering me?

Maybe I smelled just as stanky as him.

He let out a grunt, jerking his head back and cocking it left, then right, looking confused and agitated, as if he knew something was here and didn't understand why he couldn't smell it. I didn't know whether to laugh or cry. The baboon bared his fangs at me, saliva stretching from canine to canine in long, goopy strands. He even stood vertical, shaking his head left and right, his hair whipping back and forth in some kind of threatening warning.

Then, before I could react, even had I tried, the baboon reached back with one hand, took a record-breaking speed-crap in his palm, and hurled it right at my face, following it up with a hissing, silent roar.

Except…nothing hit me. I heard it strike things in the room behind me, but not hard enough to knock anything over and draw any of his allies for assistance, thankfully.

As much as I wanted to, I forced myself not to question it. I just gave credit to God for one of His lesser-known—yet still enforced—proverbs, found only in *The Bible—The Uncut Edition*.

Those who fling poo at thy neighbor shall be blinded with poor aim.

The second-hand stench of his obviously healthy digestive system now permeated the air, and it was sharp enough to actually make my eyes sting. His fur also smelled like stale sweat, making me wonder how long we could withstand his presence without giving ourselves away by gagging to death.

Xylo chose that moment to purposely make a faint noise. The baboon spun, raising one sai in a blur, and held the blade up to Xylo's neck vertebrae. He roared directly into Xylo's face, splattering him with saliva before hopping back a step, brandishing both sais now. I wondered how he could sense him now when he hadn't before. I doubted Xylo gave off a scent, so how had he verified his target?

He fell back down to all fours—even though he was still gripping his weapons in his ridiculously-long, front feet-hands—bringing his anus about an inch from my nose, which was an excellent way to give me double-barrel pink eye if he suddenly had a rumbly tummy.

I held my breath, not wanting to risk exhaling across his bare skin in case he felt it.

But trying to hold my breath with my nose only an inch away from his smooth ass—the semi-automatic AnusK47 that had just unloaded a fresh clip of feces at me—I couldn't help but visualize myself as a cowgirl blowing smoke off the tips of my pistols after a duel. I tried biting back my laugh, but it only resulted in a choking snort that sounded as loud as a gunshot.

I swiftly closed my hand around the hilt of my katana, ready to draw it and shove it down his barrel in hopes I could at least slow him down or wound him. But I froze before I even drew my blade. And then I blinked.

The baboon hadn't heard me. I glanced down in confusion and immediately stifled a gasp.

I had no visible legs or hands. I was just a faint, almost unnoticeable mist.

Just like when I had used my Horseman Mask for the first time. If not for the still very serious danger of the situation, I might have started to cry in sheer joy. I had some power back! Finally! I didn't understand how, and I honestly didn't care. To be even more honest, it had kind of ticked me off that Xylo had been able to interact with my Horseman Mask when I couldn't. So this was doubly rewarding—a soothing balm to my petty jealousy, and a healing poultice to my confidence.

Because a small part of me had entertained the fact that maybe I had failed—that the Mask had deemed me lacking, finding more value in an undying skeleton than it did in me.

I shook off the thought and considered this new development, wondering how I could use it to help Xylo appease the baboon. Because the baboon was glaring at Xylo, eager to rip his head off.

"Ruby!" the baboon barked in a guttural cough.

My eyes widened. Ruby. The baboon couldn't sense me, but he could sense Xylo—a skeleton. And skeletons were sometimes used to deliver messages across the castle. At least that had been one of Xylo's jobs. The baboon wanted proof that Xylo had permission to be here.

The monkey was asking for ID, and apparently one of Dracula's rubies was a VIP ticket.

I quickly closed my hand over one of the amulets in my pocket and pulled it out, not bothering with caution since the baboon obviously couldn't hear me. I wasn't sure how long my mist was going to last, though, so I didn't want to risk more movement than necessary. I kept my eyes on the baboon's shoulders as I crawled over to Xylo and carefully hung the necklace over his hand. He didn't flinch or react at my touch, leading me to believe he could still see me somehow, despite the mist. Perhaps it was because he shared an affinity with the Mask of Despair. I let go of the necklace and hoped for the best.

Xylo didn't waste a moment. "Here is my Ruby," he said in a soft, low tone, raising the amulet up. But the baboon had sensed a change in the air the moment I let go of the chain, chuffing softly under his breath. For the first time, I realized I had grabbed Mina Harker's necklace—the most ornate of the four ruby amulets. I really hoped that wouldn't backfire—that the baboon wouldn't recognize it as belonging to Mina and instantly accuse Xylo of theft.

The baboon sniffed the air several times and then abruptly leapt over Xylo's head to land on the railing. He sheathed his weapons behind his back, tucking them into his sash again, and turned his head slightly, directing his ears at Xylo.

"Sorry I question," he said in choppy English. "Wear ruby, no hide ruby. Library closed. Even for you, Death Spinner." Then he simply dropped off the ledge, obviously satisfied by Xylo's stolen ID. Maybe the baboon had recognized just how powerful Mina's necklace was and had chosen to take a long lunch in case Dracula showed up demanding to know why one of his most valued residents had been interrogated like a criminal.

Dracula didn't seem like the guy to put a written warning into his employee files.

His employee files probably consisted of death certificates—and only so he could keep track of the employees he had promoted into unpaid, eternally-indentured, skeleton slaves.

I wondered if Dracula had any skeleton baboons in his service—making use of them even after they died, like he did with Xylo's brothers.

Blind warrior baboons were bad enough, but *undying* warrior apes?

No thanks.

And what was a Death Spinner? One look at Xylo let me know he was just as baffled by the title as I was.

I also wondered why the baboon hadn't sensed the other necklaces stuffed inside my pocket. He'd gotten right up in my face and hadn't felt them, but Xylo holding one up a few feet away was noticeable? Was it because of my mist?

I realized Xylo was staring at me. Not knowing how to turn the mist off but not wanting to stick around, I waved at him. He waved back slowly.

"Can you hear me?" I whispered, surprised.

He nodded.

That was a relief. "Let's get out of here. I think we've used up all of our luck."

I drifted—such a strange mode of perambulation since I was mist—back to the room of unused or broken furniture and was about to reach for the door when I smiled. I took a deep breath and tried to press through the door like I had done with the barrier around Roland's church when I first put on the Mask of Despair.

And I grunted as I felt a spongy resistance. I pressed harder and, ever so slowly, slipped through the door and back outside. I stumbled slightly on the other side and abruptly saw my hands out in front of me. The mist was gone. Forcing my way through the door must have tapped out what little reserves of energy I had stored inside. I should probably figure out how to replenish that, seeing as how it was my only source of power at the moment. I crouched down, suddenly feeling entirely too vulnerable and naked after my stint at being invisible.

The door kicked open behind me and Xylo jumped out onto the stairs with his fists and teeth clenched. His ligaments flared brighter as he looked left and right for any sign of a threat. Then he saw me and visibly relaxed, lowering his hands as the embers slowly dimmed back to normal. He quickly joined me in a crouch, ducking beside the railing so we wouldn't be seen if any sentries were circling the skies.

"How do you feel?" he asked.

I shrugged, taking stock of myself in a clinical fashion. "Fine. I'm not sure how I used the mist, though. The Mask didn't respond to me back on the bridge when you bonded with it. Well, I was able to sense the power within, but I couldn't access it."

He considered that in silence. "That is how I felt when I threw hands," he said softly, as if startled by the revelation. "With the Sisters. It just happened."

"Throwing hands means boxing. Fist-fighting," I explained, biting back a laugh. "You hung the Weird Sisters with my powers?" I asked, having assumed as much upon seeing the dark smoke pouring from his eye sockets, but not having asked the direct question before now.

He averted his gaze, staring down at the ground. "I apologize," he said. "I didn't mean to use it without asking. I—"

I reached out and squeezed his arm, sensing the direction he was about to take—some self-defeating comment again. "I'm not angry, Xylo; I'm trying to understand it. If I'm ever angry with you, I promise to personally and directly let you know. You'll never have to guess." He nodded in relief, something no man would ever do. "As soon as Samael hit me with the Mark of the Beast, I thought he had also blocked my Horseman's power rather than taking it away from me. So I was surprised to see you bond with it—and me—but I was even more surprised that you were able to use it in the Gardens, and that I was able to access it just now. I didn't try to do anything. It just happened."

He nodded thoughtfully, looking relieved. "I did not try either. I just wanted them dead to make up for our delays."

"On the bridge, you said something about an echo," I said, deciding that I'd bottled up that question long enough.

He nodded. "It felt...familiar to me. Like an old friend, even though I don't have any friends."

I smiled. "You have me, Xylo. I'm your friend. What else is there?"

He opened his mouth in mute surprise, and I took it as a murmured *aww,* like one would do if they saw a puppy trip over his own feet.

I glanced around, wondering how long it had actually been since we started. I wasn't wearing a watch or anything, which I really should have considered sooner than now. I saw the Clocktower through the Terrible Timbers, but it was facing the opposite direction so I couldn't read it.

"You are right," he said, reading my thoughts. "We should get moving. Sorry you couldn't see the library. If I would have been more careful—"

"Stop, Xylo. No more of that, remember?"

He closed his teeth with a click and gave me a resigned nod.

"What is a Death Spinner, Xylo?" I asked carefully.

He shook his head after a few moments. "I'm not sure. Maybe that's what they call us skeletons?" he asked, glancing back at the door as if considering going back in to ask them.

I watched him for a few moments, picking up on his genuine concern over the question. He didn't know. Was that a good or bad development?

"Let's go see the demon," I told him, attempting to wall off my thoughts from his observation. Because I didn't want Xylo reading my mind until I was certain my vague idea had any merit, and I wouldn't know that until I asked the demon some very specific questions. My talk with Mina's puppet had been more helpful than I at first thought.

I hoped.

Xylo peered over the stairs, recalculating his path since we couldn't sneak through the Master's Library anymore. A few moments later, he motioned for me to follow him back down the stairs. I did, pulling out my butterfly charm and squeezing it in my palm.

Come on little butterfly. Give me some kind of hint...

It might have pulsed warmly—very faintly—but that could have just been my imagination.

I kept it in my palm, remembering how I'd spent a decent amount of time holding it before using it for the first time. Maybe it needed some love and attention before it opened up.

That didn't explain how my mist had worked with the baboon, but it was the only data I had to go on.

And it was progress. A flickering candle flame of hope that true despair conquers all, or whatever that Corinthians quote had been trying to say.

Thinking of that reminded me of Samael's comment about why he'd chosen to become my godfather, and I gritted my teeth, deciding he could spend a little more time in the Coliseum for that delusion alone.

That my mother would ever love him back. How ridiculous!

❧ 23 ❦

I t didn't take us very long to reach the area with the Observatory where the demon resided. It was near the opposite end of the Keep from where we had started, but I definitely understood why we had taken the long way around. The area between the two points consisted of broad, open streets and elegant marble structures that rivaled Rome in its prime. Walking down those streets would have been a death sentence.

The only reason it was marginally safe now was because the streets were entirely empty—everyone was out searching for us near the Coliseum and Eternal Gardens. Still, I felt like a million eyes were watching us, even though I had no justification for it, having not seen a single living thing since the baboons.

We crept down the fanciful hedgerows lining the street, peering over them to make sure we weren't caught by surprise.

Which let us get close enough to at least see the Infernal Armory that might or might not house Dracula's Bane, along with the rest of his collection of magical artifacts and weapons that he'd acquired over the many centuries that he'd stalked the earth. It was at least the size of the Nelson-Atkins Museum of Art in Kansas City

And by close enough, I meant we stopped about fifty yards away, at best, because it was teeming with guards. I counted over two dozen of them in a matter of seconds. Most were skeletons like Xylo, but I had seen at least half-a-dozen who looked like men but moved like predators—making them either vampires or shifters. Maybe something even worse than that. Judging by the thoughtful look on Xylo's face, this wasn't the usual level of security, which meant Dracula had beefed it up. For my sake? Or because of the murders in the Eternal Gardens?

What had Mina feared him doing? Wasn't this whole place his to do with as he pleased?

"That's where they keep the Eternal Metal," Xylo murmured, almost longingly.

I patted him on the shoulder. "Your ribs are way cooler, Xylo. And besides, with blades for hands, how would you hold your beer by the pool on a hot, sunny day?" I asked, teasingly.

He glanced down at his hands thoughtfully. "I can't drink beer, and I don't think I've ever seen the sun."

I sighed, trying to think of something else hands were good for that would apply to a skeleton. "High-fives," I finally blurted in an excited whisper. "You wouldn't be able to high-five without hands."

I lifted my palm at head level for him to give me some skin—bone.

He stared at my hand, looking confused. "What is this?" he asked.

"Slap my hand with yours," I urged. "It will make you feel empowered. Happy. Just try it."

He looked doubtful, but finally slapped my palm lightly.

And upon contact, an explosion of black lightning struck the distant Infernal Armory, obliterating one of the domes and about ten of the guards in a shower of crumbling stone and screaming guards.

A smoking, charred femur slammed into the stone beside us, sinking into the mortar as it melted the stone surrounding it. I hopped back a step, wondering what was hot enough to melt stone.

Apparently, Xylo's high-fives.

I stared incredulously at both the smoking femur and the damage to the distant structure.

"I like high-fives," Xylo said softly, staring down at his hand as if he'd never seen it before. "My brothers cannot do that."

He looked up at me, and I smiled crookedly, not sure what the hell had just happened, but not wanting to kill his buzz. I'd told him it was empowering, but I hadn't meant anything like that. I noticed that the smoke in his eyes was lighter than before—not as black.

Had that been my Horseman's power?

Alarm gongs suddenly rang out and I grabbed him by the shoulders as a dozen more guards spilled out from the building, turning to stare up at where the freak bolt of lightning had struck.

I also saw a band of necromantic blood slaves dry-washing their hands guiltily, as if fearing one of their associates had fucked up somehow.

"We need to leave. Now. We're the only other people on the street, so it's pretty hard to deny our involvement."

Xylo nodded. "Follow me."

And we fled, turning down a side street, ducking low behind the hedgerows so that no one noticed the escaping vampiric terrorists.

What in the living hell had *that* been? The bolt of black lightning had torn through the dome of the building like it was tissue paper.

Thankfully, the Observatory wasn't more than a few blocks away, and since it was around a corner, there would be no immediate line of sight from our most recent crime scene.

The Observatory was a tall, cylindrical building about fifty feet in diameter and twice as tall, with two squat, rectangular wings stretching out from either side. The top of the Observatory proper was a massive glass dome, but the opening for the telescope was pointed the opposite direction from us, aimed up at the Blood Moon. I shook my head in wonder, but Xylo was already making his way up the broad steps leading to the entrance. I followed, keeping an eye out for sentries or, really, anything with at least two appendages, a modicum of self-awareness, and a figurative axe to grind.

Thankfully, I saw no one—but that brought on its own brand of anxiety, like we were walking into a trap of some kind.

Xylo skipped the main entrance and made his way to a side door, glancing back over his shoulder to make sure we were still alone. Then his ligaments abruptly flared brighter, emitting fiery embers into the night air as he simply tore the handle off the apparently locked door. He tossed the handle into a nearby bush and motioned for me to follow. I slipped inside a gloomy interior that reminded me of an empty train station in a bustling city like New York.

Xylo stood perfectly still, cautiously scanning the area from one end to the other. The building was pretty unremarkable. A lot of desks and bookshelves, piles of loose paper, and furniture to lounge in. Xylo finally turned to me with a nod. Then he was walking.

As he strode deeper into the building, I pulled out my butterfly charm, considering our current situation.

So far, we'd only managed to take out four targets—which had netted us two functional amulets to use to get my power back. At the expense of killing the three ex-Brides of Dracula but leaving a hot and bothered Mina Harker still in the land of the living, and hungry to hunt us down like dogs even though we were technically on the same side.

We both wanted Dracula dead.

As I considered the list of demands Samael and Dracula had made for me, I found that I was grinding my teeth in frustration—not at our failure to do better but at the utter ridiculousness of it all.

It just didn't make much sense.

I wasn't going to even begin to attempt to understand Samael's personal motivations in all of this—him announcing he was my Godfather, proving we shared a solid Blood Bond, admitting he had the hots for my mother, and then immediately betraying—or possibly pretending to betray—me in order to aid the man we had supposedly come here to kill.

For his loyalty, Dracula had then tossed the Greater Demon into the Coliseum for a long, drawn-out execution and some wholesome family entertainment.

All of this was what had been bothering me ever since speaking with puppet-Mina, and what had put my subconscious mind into overdrive.

With a huge, apparently empty, building concealing us from curious, murderous eyes, I decided it was time for me to face the music and see if my subconscious analysis had shaken any answers loose.

Ultimately, it boiled down to motivations. If Samael or Dracula wanted me dead or imprisoned, I would have been dead or imprisoned already. Pretty much every explanation or scenario I'd come up with could have been solved more efficiently by them simply locking me up or killing me back when they'd taken all my powers.

In fact, I hadn't been able to come up with a single reason for them *not* to have entertained one of those two options.

Which meant that one—or both—of them *wanted* me out here, hitting the streets, killing the locals.

Even though Dracula could have likely done that for himself with a figurative snap of his fingers. What did I bring to the equation? Especially when Dracula had been expecting Roland—a vampire—not me. What had turned him from being disappointed to see me to suddenly excited to agree to Samael's overly complicated scheme to cut me loose?

Was it really as basic as them just wanting to watch me struggle and squirm to stay alive for three days?

But then Dracula had given me a guide—Xylo—to help me navigate his home. One that his wife did not apparently approve of. Then again, he hadn't told her anything important about this scheme, so maybe that was just his standard M.O. when dealing with Mina Harker.

And to give me a guide who almost immediately shared a strong bond with my Horseman's Mask—the Mask that Samael had conveniently failed to mention to Dracula. Taking away all my other powers but leaving me the Mask was akin to taking a butter knife away from a toddler but handing her a cocked and loaded pistol.

I knew Dracula's Beast wanted me dead as recompense for my mother apparently stealing her eyes but, again, that could have been resolved when Sanguina had me pinned down for Samael, but they had instead put my foe to sleep. No matter how I wished I could see things in a different light, Samael had saved my life with the Mark of the Beast. Otherwise I would already be dead.

The more I thought about it, the more convinced I became that Samael —in his own twisted fashion—had used the Mark of the Beast on me to give me the only chance he knew he could give me.

To let me be myself for three days while making me appear weak and helpless to Dracula—to make him underestimate me.

And Dracula had bought it.

To be honest, I hadn't even taken the time to really process what they'd said about my mother—that she had come here and freaking blinded Dracula's Beast. That was some straight-up, gangster-level heat.

I wasn't saying that the quest they had given me was easy. But it was strange. Like inviting the guy who beat up your friend over to your house for a long weekend and telling him—at gunpoint—to take out your trash as punishment.

Regardless, if I wanted to survive, I needed to assess my own situation.

I had none of my powers other than my years trained in the art of hand-to-hand combat, my tentative Horseman Mask, and Xylo—the depressed, under-appreciated Death Spinner who didn't know his own past. Oh, and my skin was tougher, now, and Xylo had a strange lightning bolt high-five.

The enemies were easier to line up.

Dracula had a job of some kind for me that he said I would take whether I wanted to or not. And I knew he wanted the barrier taken down.

The Beast wanted vengeance for my mother stealing her eyes.

Mina Harker was now gunning for me, thinking I was Dracula's pawn.

And Samael had brought me here, obviously knowing all of this ahead of time, meaning he'd been very busy while I was off exploring the Doors in my quest to enter Solomon's Temple.

And he hadn't been alone in that setup. Other godly beings in Kansas City had helped the Fallen Angel. And that had been before anyone knew about me becoming a Horseman, so it wasn't my powers they were interested in.

It...was *me*, Callie Penrose.

But I couldn't do anything until I found a way to neutralize Sanguina, otherwise she would just keep reviving my foes until I gave up or collapsed from exhaustion.

So, how could I defeat a Beast like her? My mother had tried a direct assault and had succeeded only in harming Sanguina. Even when I'd had all my powers at my disposal, I hadn't fared very well at all in a direct fight. Worse than my mother, in fact.

I followed Xylo up a flight of stairs, finding nothing worthy of even a second glance as we made our way closer to our target. Thankfully, everyone who lived or spent time in the Observatory seemed to either be out searching for us elsewhere or they had clocked out for the day, so we reached the top of the steps and continued walking through another large, open space without any sign of danger hitting our radars. We still *acted* as if dangers lurked around every corner, but we saw no one. The Observatory even *felt* empty—devoid of life. Abandoned. Vacant. Lifeless.

I had come here with one clear purpose: kill Dracula before he decided to come to Kansas City in retaliation for Roland's barrier. Roland had just been a pawn in that—and I didn't have the mental energy to consider where our relationship now stood—but Samael had orchestrated the barrier scheme with finesse. Totally unlike this scheme right now.

I decided that there really wasn't any easy way to predict what Samael and Dracula were up to. One was a Greater Demon and one was a Master —both known for manipulating events in truly bizarre and complicated ways.

Rather than wasting more time trying to understand what they wanted *from* me, I decided to flip the script—focusing on what *I* wanted.

No more playing by their rules—like Mina had implied. So, what did I want?

I knew I would like to hang Samael by his giggle-berries over a frozen pond in the middle of nowhere, with Lambchop's *The Song That Never Ends* playing on repeat on a boombox with blown-out speakers that was hooked up to a solar chargeable power source.

For example.

A close second was to figure out my Horseman Mask, because right now it was the only gun in my magical holster, and I knew I would need every advantage when confronting Dracula or his Beast.

Unless I wanted to risk shattering the amulets in my pocket, but I had a very strange feeling about that—especially because anytime I considered doing so, that nagging sensation came back with a vengeance.

❧ 24 ❧

The first time I'd used the Mask, I'd spent a considerable amount of time focusing on my failures and flaws, owning up to them. I'd also focused on my indomitable spirit—that I would always get back up one more time than I had been knocked down.

But that hadn't worked for me back on the bridge.

Xylo was very much in tune with his failings and flaws, owning up to them without question—even wallowing in them. I'd spent a little time trying to help him turn his self-esteem switch back on, but his default negative mental attitude was a hard habit to break.

On the bridge, he'd said he felt an echo from the Mask, and then he'd somehow tapped into it, absorbing black shadows into his eye-sockets and establishing some kind of bond with me and the Mask. But unlike my first time tapping into the Mask, he hadn't added a caveat to his flaws like I had —that he would overcome them in some way. He just relished in them.

If that was the key to using the Mask...

I started to grow angry. What kind of stupid power was that? Was I supposed to sit around for a few hours prior to every fight, wallowing in misery over my past failures so I could depress my enemies to death? That wasn't practical. Fights happened spontaneously most of the time, and my enemies weren't the kind to give me a few hours warning or to postpone their attack if I needed a Debbie Downer breather.

No. My enemies were assholes. Cruel, sadistic bastards who wanted only power. And the Masters were at the top of that chain. They wielded fear like a weapon, using it to break down both their enemies and those who worked for them. Those like Xylo—a guy who couldn't even remember his own life. Dracula chose to constantly remind him of his failures, kicking his feet out from under him at every—

I blinked. Dracula did to his enemies what I had done to myself the first time I used my Mask. He had used *despair* like a bludgeon to keep them in line, but I had chosen to use it like a self-flagellation whip, beating my own body with it. I had been my own Dracula. It had worked because it had still been me focusing on Despair—just in an unproductive way.

What if I flipped the direction?

Why had I chosen to become a Horseman in the first place?

Sure, I had needed power to fight Roland and to earn Xuanwu and Ryuu's help, but that hadn't been my true, underlying reason.

It hadn't even been to help Nate Temple.

I'd chosen this path because I wanted to sow seeds of despair in the hearts of my enemies. I wanted to show them fear in a handful of dust. To make them shake with it, constantly looking over their shoulders. To break them from the inside out.

Hope and Despair were two sides of the same coin.

Nate, the Horseman of Hope, had vowed to *take* all hope from his enemies.

I, the Horseman of Despair, had vowed to *give* unrelenting despair to my enemies.

This understanding wasn't news to me, although I hadn't really applied it as the dominating factor to *powering* my Mask—the ignition key. Instead, I'd used it to control the Mask's abilities once I already had it running—like gasoline or fuel. I had wanted to bond and open up to the Mask, baring my soul in order to show my true colors, and that I was worthy of its power—and it had worked.

So I had falsely assumed that it was the only way to get the engine running—introspection and humility.

To pour a ton of gasoline into it and wonder why it didn't start, even though I didn't have an ignition key.

But if I'd already bared my soul to the Mask, admitting my own Despair and that my will to overcome it would always be stronger...

What use was it to bare my failings to the Mask *all over again?* You couldn't really bare your soul twice—that nullified the very meaning of the phrase. Sure, things could change as time passed and you had more failings you needed to acknowledge and add to your diary, but that only reshaped your core, it didn't necessarily change it.

It was no wonder that opening up to the Mask on the bridge had produced no results for me but had worked for Xylo. I'd tried *reliving* my first date with the Mask, where Xylo had *gone* on a first date with the Mask.

On the way here, Xylo had asked me why I hadn't broken the necklaces to get my powers back yet. I'd shrugged it off, telling him it could wait, not wanting to voice my concerns out loud.

Because his simple question had shone a light on something I'd been hiding from without even knowing it. I'd failed. I'd tried to call up the power of the Mask only to be ignored. And then Xylo had succeeded without any apparent effort.

And I was way too competitive for that not to bother me. When I committed to something, I gave it my all. Excellence was the only acceptable result.

I had just become the Sixth Horseman—at least I had used the Mask one time. I hadn't received any kind of confirmation letter or anything, but I knew beyond a shadow of a doubt that it was mine. The Mask even looked like that dream vision I'd had of myself with the blindfold and crying silver tears.

Despair was written on my forehead in Enochian script.

I. Was. Despair.

No question. But that certainty had only made it worse, because on the bridge, I had failed where Xylo had succeeded.

Despair was a fickle, fleeting thing, apparently. Like a dog, if you gave it a little affection it would forget all about previous owners.

So I'd had my face rubbed in my failure by Xylo's success.

And that had apparently bothered me on a deeply subconscious level—brought to my attention only thanks to Xylo's innocent question about breaking the amulets. My failure with the Mask had led to me feeling undeserving of it. And that dark cloud had hovered over my head, growing darker and darker with each step—even as I cheerfully tried to help Xylo banish his own perpetual dark cloud.

But I had been too stubborn to give up, not wanting to run away from the problem and revert back to the easy path, the comfortable path—my wizard's magic, my Silvers, and my Heavenly abilities. Smashing those amulets—although smart—was also running from my Despair problem.

Even though I hadn't consciously been aware of any of this. I'd basically gone crazy all internally—splitting into different warring factions within my own heart and soul. Now that I was aware of it, I could get on with fixing it —like I would fix any other bout of internal insanity.

Women did that all the time. We were professionals at going crazy and then, just as swiftly, going uncrazy. Nine out of ten men disagreed with this fact, but upon further analysis by an independent group of women, it turned out that they had just been wrong.

It was rather concerning how that single failure on the bridge had festered, creeping through my self-confidence like...

I narrowed my eyes, realizing my problem with Despair mirrored something Xuanwu had once told me.

"Yeah. Okay. Fuck turtles," I growled.

Xylo jumped at the unexpected sound, my words crashing into the silent space like a broken glass. Then he crouched, snapping off one of his ribs to wield as a weapon. "I'll fuck the turtle," he rasped, glancing left and right, brandishing the rib bone over his head like a meat cleaver. "Wait. What is a turtle?" he asked, not seeing any nearby threats.

I laughed, shaking my head. "No. I was thinking out loud about something a friend once told me," I explained.

"Oh." He lowered his hands, opening and closing his mouth several times. "What is *fuck*?"

I laughed again. "Something you do with bad guys." My face instantly flushed beet red as I realized how that would have sounded to any of my other friends. "I mean that the word can be used in many ways. Most often it's used when you are angry about something or angry with someone. I was angry with the turtle," I said hurriedly, not wanting to have to explain the whole sex thing to my new skeleton friend. Anatomically, it didn't really apply to him anymore anyway, which would only make it harder to explain.

He nodded thoughtfully, repeating the word a few times under his breath. Thankfully, he was too preoccupied with the new vocabulary to read my thoughts. "Okay. Fuck Dracula," he said, glancing over at me as if to check whether or not he'd used it correctly.

I laughed, patting him on the shoulder. "Yes. Fuck Dracula."

He nodded satisfactorily, looking empowered by the spoken curse—especially that he'd directed it at his former boss, Dracula.

Which was a huge step, folks. Finally mouthing off to the bully who had terrorized—even if it was just to himself.

That was called backbone.

My skeleton was finding his backbone. And if his slowly-waking new powers were any indication of his future potential...

I almost felt bad for the bullies of the world.

Almost.

25

Xylo tucked his rib back into place with a brief flare of sparks before resuming our walk. Not seeing anything worthy of note in our surroundings, I returned to my thoughts, replaying the events on the bridge in my mind.

Rather than focusing on what I already knew about Despair—I had been more concerned about getting my hands on some power so that I could kill the things that scared me—that I hadn't approached my Mask with the respect it was due.

I had shoved a quarter in her slot and then waited for her to vibrate for me.

When she had nonverbally told me that a quarter wasn't enough, I had stubbornly dug my heels in and argued that a quarter was plenty, thank you very much.

It sucks to be wrong, but it's better than choking on ignorance.

Now that I understood where I had dropped the ball, I pulled out my butterfly charm, smiling down at it. I opened myself up, not entirely sure it was necessary, but wanting to show the Mask what I had learned. Nate had fed Souls from Hell into the Masks, and he'd talked about them like they were living beings. Mine had definitely acted like a jilted lover when I hadn't given her what she needed from me most—a purpose for our relationship.

Or at least *two* quarters.

First dates were cool. They were amazing. Not that awkward, first encounter dinner, but that first time you genuinely opened up to the other person and shared some *Stuff*—capital *S*. The kind of phone calls that ended up lasting three hours before either one of you looked at a clock. The picnics that ended up lasting most of the day, where you forgot all about the other things you had planned on doing later that afternoon.

Those were great.

But it was next to impossible to *relive* them.

Trying to live in the past meant that you were never looking to the future —which only resulted in stagnation. And the harder you tried to relive that moment in the past, the deeper your roots of stagnation grew—until neither one of you knew why you were always bickering.

No.

What you two were *supposed* to do was build on *top* of that first real date. Like building a house, that first real date was the concrete foundation. Next, you had to start going vertical, slap a roof on, throw in some drywall and paint, start picking furniture, and on and on...

You couldn't keep trying to rebuild the foundation and then wonder why your partner was always bitching about the rain getting their hair wet.

Neither one of you ever thought to build a fucking *roof!*

So.

I thought about a fucking roof.

I visualized what I wanted from the Mask, and what I would give in return. I wanted destruction, mayhem, terror, petrifying fear, pain, agony, loneliness, and so much more.

And I wanted to wrap those gifts up in a bow to give to my enemies—the motherfucking bullies of the monster world—those who thought to take what was not theirs.

My Mask must have thought those gifts were cruelly considerate, magically malicious, and perfectly perfect, because the butterfly charm suddenly grew warm in my palm.

Then it suddenly flickered into the white stone Mask of Despair, and I grinned with delight. We still had a lot to learn together, but I had a good idea what she wanted from me now.

First of all, she was tired of the rain getting her hair wet.

She wanted to get the roof up so we could get on with the fun stuff— picking paint colors and furniture.

Xylo made a strange sound and I looked over at him. He was staring at the Mask with a look of awe. "I *feel* it..." he breathed.

I frowned. "You feel it?" That wasn't good. If he could sense it, maybe others could as well.

He nodded. "I feel it through my bond with *you*. Like on the bridge. I felt it grow warm all of a sudden. Stronger. I can tell you feel excited right now," he said, staring at me.

I nodded, relieved to hear that I wasn't suddenly emitting a beacon for monsters to find us. I glanced down at the Mask. "Soon," I murmured, willing it back into the butterfly charm. I didn't know how much power it had stored up, but I didn't want to waste it. I would need it for Dracula and his Beast.

Feeling much better, I thought back on what I knew of Dracula, what everyone had said about him—both before I arrived and since. That he had taken Mina Harker for himself and killed her fiancé Jonathan. What Samael had said to me—both before and since we'd come here.

How everything I'd learned about him had categorically defined him as a tyrannical, schoolyard bully.

And I really hated bullies. Almost to an irrational degree.

So...how did you get a bully to stop? How did you beat a bully?

Playing their games and following their demands never worked—it just encouraged them.

I let all these thoughts play through my mind at the same time, like I was standing in a crowded cafeteria. Through the din, several voices and snippets of conversation rose up louder than others before fading away, only to be replaced by a different snippet or piece of information.

And strangely enough, that random assortment of highlighted comments actually painted a much clearer picture than when I had tried analyzing them sequentially, as they had happened, or grouped together in any categorical way, because this process allowed my subconscious to do the heavy lifting. Like a boat, your mind was an extremely capable vehicle—able to float downstream on its own, for the most part, subtly shifting and correcting course naturally. When you tried forcing it to go against the current, problems often arose.

Sometimes you just had to let the boat be a boat, not an extension of you. Part of being a good seaman was knowing when to get your oar wet and when to leave it tucked away.

So I sat in my mental cafeteria and let the hum of the crowd take over as I followed Xylo towards an arched entryway, wondering how close we were to the demon. My shoulders began to grow lighter as I casually observed the numerous voices—rearranging the pieces of the puzzle from what I had initially thought to be their proper place.

The picture it quickly began to reveal wasn't anything at all like I had expected—or hoped—to find. In fact, it was downright terrifying.

But a small part of me whispered that it was the right—the only—path.

And that the next steps would, ironically, require some deft steering if I wanted my boat to survive the storm. I went back through it all just to be sure I hadn't missed anything and let out an anxious sigh.

I had a few missing pieces I needed to find, but I was confident of the necessary outcome, because when I tried applying several different answers to those missing pieces, the puzzle still ended up as the same final picture. After I dealt with the demon, I needed to sit Xylo down for a chat.

Because if he saw what I intended without me explaining my reasoning...

Well, he might just run back to Dracula and tattle on me, choosing the lesser of two evils.

And I wouldn't necessarily blame him.

In fact, it might be better to tell him *before* we met with the demon.

I looked up, opening my mouth to catch his attention, only to find that he had already stopped and was staring at me. "I heard your thoughts. No need to explain. Which is good, because the demon should be just ahead."

I clicked my mouth shut, my eyes widening. "You *heard* me?" I asked, feeling the hair on the back of my neck stand straight up. "The whole thing?"

He nodded. "It's grown clearer since the bridge."

"Why isn't it that easy for me to read your thoughts?" I complained for what felt like the tenth time.

He shrugged. "I don't have much else to think about so it's easy to focus on your never-ending thought stream," he admitted. I shook my head, biting my tongue since I knew he hadn't meant it how it had come across—any other man would have gotten my wet hellcat impersonation for that comment.

Xylo's comment was more like your friendly neighbor of over a year finally telling you that you never closed the blinds in the bathroom when you were showering every morning at seven o'clock. Too little, too late.

"Your plan is dangerous, but it makes sense," Xylo assured me. "Well reasoned out. It's what I've been trying to suggest to you for some time, now. In your mind. I thought since you didn't respond that maybe you thought it a poor idea."

I stared at him in silence. "You were trying to tell me this?" I asked flatly. "In my mind."

He nodded. "Not as detailed as your plan, but the principle was the same —to change the game while making it look like you were still playing by their rules. It's usually how I had to approach things in my past duties working for Dracula. I had to think of alternate paths to take to follow his rules but in a way that limited the suffering or embarrassment he had wanted me to feel."

I nodded woodenly, suddenly recalling the persistent, strange, nagging sensation I had felt. That...had been Xylo? Damn. I wished I had known a way to unscramble it sooner. "Well. I guess I need to listen better," I muttered, shaking my head. "Thanks, I guess. But if any new weird things start happening and you don't think I'm paying attention, give a sister some warning."

He cocked his head. "A sister?" he choked, sounding alarmed. Then he stared at me very intently for a moment. "Oh. You mean tell you sooner. Okay." He nodded.

I shivered at how quickly he was picking up on this ability to read my mind. A girl just couldn't think in peace with men around. Even dead ones. Xylo studied me with his unreadable face and I just sighed. "Let's go see what she has to say. Be ready for anything."

He shrugged. "It's probably best if I prepare for her to kill me a few times before she learns it is a waste of energy. That is usually how these things work out."

I grunted. "Yeah. Well, not all of us can afford that luxury."

I rolled my shoulders and checked on my katana as I stared at the double doors just ahead. They were larger than others we had seen, but they weren't flashy or anything.

A big bad demon was on the other side, and I was about to go say *hello*.

✦ 26 ✦

The toes of my boots abruptly began to tingle as Xylo shoved the doors open, standing in my way like a bone shield since he couldn't die.

We entered a large, open room with a massive telescope on the far end, but that's not what caught my attention. In the center of the room, I saw a ten-foot-tall monster of a demon. Her gray scales were rough and rigid, she was extremely muscular, and she wore only a fur skirt that stopped at about mid-thigh. Like a lot of extreme athletes, she had more pectoral muscles than breasts, so it wasn't that scandalous. She had a long, wide lizard's tail, and her snout extended at least a few feet.

She looked like a mutant crocodile. She turned to glare at us with beady black eyes, but she didn't speak, and she didn't attack. Because one of her legs was chained to the floor by a manacle that was wide enough to wrap around my entire torso from neck to navel, and a ring of glowing runes marked the floor, trapping her within a powerful magical circle.

She had enough chain to walk around—I saw a huge cot, a table and chairs—but she wasn't close enough to reach the circle.

I met her eyes, not entirely sure what to make of this. Xylo said nothing, but he also didn't look surprised. This must have been what he meant when he'd told me I needed to see her *current situation* for myself. She definitely wasn't being treated like a queen as I had thought. Maybe I could use that to my advantage.

"Demoness?" I asked politely, figuring she saw very little of that.

Maybe she would be more open to answering my questions. If Dracula kept her locked up like this, then they obviously weren't friends.

She nodded slightly. "Who are you?" she asked suspiciously.

"Callie Penrose."

She took one critical look at Xylo, hesitating for a moment upon noticing his smoky black eyes, and then turned back to me, likely wondering how or why I had one of Dracula's henchmen at my side. "I do not know that name," she said, studying me thoughtfully. Maybe she could sense the Mark of the Beast on my forehead, or she just assumed I didn't have any magic. She probably thought I was an insane imbecile to confront a demon without any powers.

I let her think what she would and cleared my throat. "I'm going to hazard a guess and assume you're not pals with Dracula. We have that in common."

She scoffed. "Good for you. Take a look at your future, child," she muttered, indicating her manacles. But I could tell that I had definitely caught her attention, admitting I wasn't a fan of ol' Drac.

"How about your freedom for some answers?" I suggested casually, letting my eyes scan the room as I spoke, like I was asking something as unimportant as whether she liked milk with her coffee or not.

She was dead silent for a moment, and then she chuckled in a hollow, defeated manner. "More like I'll give you answers and then you'll renege on your word. How about you make both of us happy and just kill me already."

I stared at her thoughtfully, surprised that I felt slightly sympathetic towards this monster—a demon. Was I losing my touch, or was Dracula just that much of a suck-wad?

Instead of replying to her statement, I pointed at her restraints. "Why are you chained up like this?"

"Because I know the truth," she muttered. "And Dracula can't have anyone learning *that!*"

I frowned. "What truth?" I asked.

She spat at one of the runes and it flared up with crackling, purple light. "These cursed runes prevent me from speaking it. Unseen chains over my mouth and unbreakable chains over my feet," she cursed. "All forged from chains over my heart," she cursed, kicking out with her foot hard enough to obliterate a concrete wall. Her foot hit the limits of her reach and the heavy chain made a dull, metallic *thump*, not remotely weakened by her attempt. Wow. "See?" she muttered.

I nodded, glancing over at Xylo. He shrugged, not even turning to look at me. Right, he could read my thoughts. I really wished that I had caught onto how sharp he actually was earlier in our travels, because we could have been working together more closely this whole time. His unique ability to read a situation and come up with a clever plan had preceded my own bumbling attempt. I hadn't thought of him as much more than a navigator and a trusted friend—because he was always discrediting himself.

But he was a font of knowledge on multiple fronts, and apparently a clever tactician. Who the *hell* had he been before all of this?

Maybe it really was because he didn't have much to think about in his own headspace, like he'd told me, so he could more easily focus on my thoughts instead.

I studied the demon, weighing my options.

I'd expected a fight that would result in me threatening her freedom with the Seal of Solomon in order to get her to help me.

But here she was, already imprisoned.

And neatly tied up like a gift, making me wonder if this was a trap—if Samael or Dracula had expected me to come here, sent everyone away, and tied up the demon for me.

Maybe they wanted me to step inside that circle of runes to trap myself for some dark ritual. Maybe that was why they hadn't imprisoned me back when this all started. They had needed me to voluntarily walk into *this* specific circle.

Xylo cleared his throat, not looking over at me. "She's been imprisoned for one hundred years," he said, almost casually.

The demon looked up sharply, hissing at him. "And what does that have to do with anything? You don't even know who you are, *shepherd!*" She roared with laughter as if at a joke. "But this demon knows all, and knowledge is the chains of bondage in this paradise." She kicked out with her foot again, railing against her restraints to no noticeable effect.

I blinked incredulously at her flippant comment. Xylo was a Shepherd?

As in...a *Vatican Shepherd?* Holy shit.

Literally.

With Xylo being an ancient skeleton, did that make him one of the first Shepherds? Was that why he'd seemed troubled by the Cross Pattée I'd drawn on my chest—the mark of the Knights Templar?

A million questions suddenly raced through my mind, and I felt a straining tension in my bond with Xylo. He was gritting his teeth, seeming frustrated—as if he still had no recollection of what this new information might mean.

I began to seriously believe that someone had done this to him—like Dracula—in order to hide his true identity from himself—because if he ever remembered he was a Vatican Shepherd, he would be an immediate, powerful threat to absolutely everyone here.

But if that was the case, why would Dracula then hand him over to me as a guide, knowing I had worked for the Shepherds?

Maybe this demon was simply fishing for a reaction. Just because she was the enemy of my enemy didn't make her trustworthy. She would do or say anything to get out of her chains—or to goad me into killing her, apparently.

Did she really know who Xylo was? I sensed him shaking his head profusely, but it felt more like a frustrated gesture than a direct answer to my thought. He wasn't saying she was wrong; he was saying he didn't know if she was telling the truth. Because I could tell that her comment hadn't cleared up the cobwebs of his own memories, unfortunately.

I shook my head, tabling the topic.

Xylo had mentioned the length of her imprisonment in response to my thoughts that her circle prison might actually be a trap Dracula had set up specifically for me. The length of her imprisonment might not matter. Dracula could still be using her to trap me, even if she didn't know it.

I studied the circle of runes, gritting my teeth. At first, I had thought they were angelic, but the closer I looked, I realized they weren't just angelic. They were a smattering of all sorts of runes.

My shoulders tensed in alarm.

The Omegabet. Dracula had trapped her with the Omegabet.

As I stared at them, they seemed to come to life in a way, shimmering and flaring as strange words filled my mind. I quickly clamped my eyes shut, shaking my head. Without knowing exactly what they were or what they did, I didn't dare risk trying to study them.

I had some kind of natural understanding of the Omegabet, but that was more dangerous by far. The Omegabet was deadly.

Although...

I could always ruin just *one* of the runes—like I would any angelic rune—pretending I'd never even heard of the Omegabet. Because it really was just an angelic rune mixed in with others to make something greater. But if I destroyed only just one angelic symbol, would the spell drop? That still left me with the chain, and even if I had my magic, I wasn't sure I could break something strong enough to restrain a demon.

At least I couldn't be trapped inside with that ring of runes broken.

I decided to give the demon a choice. "Show me what I want to know, and I'll break the circle. I don't know what to do about the chain, though," I admitted.

She scoffed incredulously. "Lies. You can do no such thing, little girl. You have no power. Even if you could do such a thing, Dracula and his Beast would hunt me down before I managed to leave this room. No one escapes Sanguina."

I smiled. "Sanguina is currently taking a nap, and I'm planning on killing Dracula. So if you know all these secrets, why don't you tell me where Dracula's Bane really is. I don't think it's in the Infernal Armory. That's too obvious—"

She froze, looking like a bowling ball had just struck her between the eyes. "What did you just say?" she whispered in a strange, almost fragile, tone.

"Sanguina is taking a three-day nap—"

"No. Dracula's Bane," she said, leaning closer, her eyes seeming to burn with need. "Who told you about that?" she hissed, her eyes darting back and forth in an almost frantic or terrified manner.

I considered telling her, but remembering Samael's potential feud with her, I shook my head. "Agree to help me—"

"TELL ME!" she roared, her jaws spreading wide as she railed against her manacles. "I will agree to *anything* for this answer!"

"Fine," I said, holding up my hands. Demons were usually much better negotiators, so this was definitely a first. "You agree to answer all my questions truthfully and not try to kill me or my associates?" I asked, trying to cover every loophole. She nodded eagerly, licking her lips with a tongue as long as a cobra—unlike any crocodile tongue I'd ever seen.

I glanced at Xylo and he shrugged slightly, but he did look surprised by her sudden swell of emotions.

I turned back to her and let out a breath. "Samael told me I would need Dracula's Bane in order to truly kill Dracula, and that I could find it in the center of the castle, in the heart of the Beast—"

The badass crocodile demon abruptly collapsed to her knees like a puppet with cut strings and began to cry and laugh at the same time.

Xylo and I shared a long, confused look. I shrugged, not having any idea what the hell was going on here.

Through her tears, I heard what sounded like a demon praying for the first time in eons.

"Love is patient...love is kind...You came back for me, Samael..."

And the hair on every inch of my body suddenly tried to stand straight up on end. She was reciting First Corinthians chapter thirteen—the passage about unconditional, non-judgmental love.

That was the same passage Samael had mentioned when I had asked why he originally agreed to become my godfather and work for my mother.

I had thought he was trying to tell me that he had loved my mother.

But I had apparently been very wrong. He'd been talking about lady crocodile, here.

"Wait a minute. This is a goddamned *love story*?!" I demanded incredulously.

Which was also technically accurate since they were both fallen angels.

She looked up at me, tears streaming down her face. "Yes, child. Yes. Those words—*Dracula's Bane*, and that it was locked up in the *Heart of the Beast*—was a code phrase Samael promised I would one day hear, and that it would mean my freedom was at hand. I am the *Heart* to Samael's *Beast*, you see." My mind reeled in disbelief, but she continued on excitedly. "When you first walked in here, I thought you looked familiar, but I assumed my eyes were playing tricks on me after spending so long alone. Tell me your *real* name, dear. *Show* me your real name," she said, her voice almost feverish.

I hesitated, slowly reaching into my pocket for the Seal of Solomon.

As I pulled out the demon prison, it caught the light of the flickering torches, and the demon began to laugh gleefully—something no demon should have done upon seeing a device designed specifically to trap them. "It seems I get to fulfill my promise to your mother after all, goddaughter."

If Xylo wouldn't have grabbed me at the last moment, I would have fallen straight down on my ass.

27

I stared at the demonic crocodile, trying to organize my scrambling thoughts. Goddaughter? What kind of acid had my parents self-medicated with back in the day? Choosing not one, but two demons for godparents.

My soul was doomed.

"How am I supposed to believe any of this?" I asked, shaking my head. Just because it sort of made sense in a demented way didn't mean that she wasn't manipulating me, using my emotions against me.

The demon sighed empathetically. Then she cleared her throat, staring at me. "You were to be orphaned on the steps of a place called Abundant Angel Catholic Church. You were to be given the Mark of the Beast to make Dracula underestimate you. You were Named after Excalibur—literally." She cocked her head quizzically. "Although I do not sense it within you. Has the King risen already?" she asked. Then, under her breath, "I've missed so much!"

I stared back at her woodenly. Hardly anyone knew those things, and most who had known were dead.

She took my blank look as a suggestion to try harder. "Qinglong promised to guard your mother's laboratory in the event of her death." I flung up a hand to stop her, feeling tears come to my eyes for some reason.

It wasn't necessarily even heartache. I was just fucking overwhelmed. My life had been like a recipe for a cake, and I was only just learning how many chefs had been in the kitchen.

"Enough," I whispered. "Please. Just stop."

"Of course, Callie. I didn't mean to be inconsiderate. I've been waiting for this day longer than you've been alive, and I'll admit that my hope had turned to despair," she said in a soft tone, not emphasizing the words— which meant there was something she didn't know about me. Then again, becoming a Horseman had been my idea, not part of my mother's scheme.

I nodded, wiping at my eyes. Xylo was glaring at the demon like my own personal guard dog. I let him continue.

I finally looked back up at her. "How could you know any of those things? You've been locked up here for a hundred years, right?"

She nodded. "More or less." She waited a moment. "I can tell you as much or as little as you wish to know."

I waved a hand, remembering we were on the clock. I didn't have time for this crap, and I'd missed enough opportunities for answers that it was refreshing to have someone trying to convince me of how much they knew about me, for once. "Hit me."

"Samael and I have secretly been in love for centuries, but I fool-ishly became trapped here about a hundred years ago, my own arrogance getting the best of me. Your mother learned of these things—she never told me how—and approached Samael, who had been unsuccessful in his own attempts to save me since he couldn't risk letting anyone know how he truly felt for me or else Dracula would have executed me on the spot or used me as leverage against him, giving Dracula a Greater Demon in his pocket of tools. Your mother was determined to kill Dracula and his Beast, so she made a deal with Samael. Constance would do everything in her power to help save my life if Samael first promised to become your godfather and look after you in the years to come."

I felt like a piece of glass, riveted to the floor as I listened, unable to move for fear of shattering.

"Samael agreed, willing to do anything to get me back, even though it was foolish to meet his end of the bargain before she met hers. Men," she muttered.

"Love," I retorted, smiling faintly.

The demon smiled back, nodding. "But Constance was unable to defeat

Sanguina. She only succeeded in stealing her eyes. She was forced to flee before she—and you—became trapped here for good. Like me."

I frowned. "Wait. That means she was already pregnant with me when she came here," I said, all sorts of horrified to hear she had come here—of all places—with me in her belly.

"Irresponsible," Xylo murmured, looking thoughtful.

I glared up at him. "Don't tell me you were a part of this, too," I warned.

He shook his head fiercely. "I was in the bottom of the well at the time."

The demon blinked at him. Then she burst out laughing. "That was *you?*" she roared, crying crocodile tears. "Everyone knows that story! Even me! Did you ever get your balloon back?" she hooted.

The black smoke in Xylo's eyes shifted warningly, and his embers and sparks abruptly brightened. "No."

The demon turned back to me, wiping at her eyes. "Before Constance escaped Castle Dracula for good, she came to visit me. She believed she had a solution, but that it would take time to come to fruition, and that she couldn't do it alone. She promised to one day save me in exchange for my help with her plan and that I would become her unborn daughter's godmother once I was free." The silence stretched out. "And with you here, now, it seems her plan has gone off without a hitch."

I grimaced at that last part. I could think of one or two *hitches* I'd had to navigate, but I knew what she had meant.

It was hard to deny my mother's capabilities at planning long cons.

I was Exhibit A.

"I really hope she told you the part of the plan that involves me defeating a Beast that no one can apparently defeat," I muttered. "And all without my magic, since Samael so cleverly branded me with the Mark of the Beast.

She waved a claw. "You are blood bound to Samael, yes?" she asked. I frowned but nodded. "Then you can remove it yourself. I will show you how. You'll have your toys back in a snap."

I blinked at her. "Just like that."

She nodded. "That's the beauty of it. You two are blood bound—like family. Only Greater Demons can utilize the power in the Mark of the Beast." She smiled devilishly. "And look who is blood bound—family—to a Greater Demon. You, sulfur-sugar. You."

I grimaced distastefully at that pet name, preferring that it was never again used to indicate me. Xylo somehow let out a long whistle through his teeth. I frowned, glancing over at him, having never heard him do it before. He looked just as startled by his reaction as I was.

"But your powers won't help you anyway, just like they didn't help your mother. You see, you cannot defeat the Beast. That is the entire point—and where your mother failed. No one can *defeat* Sanguina—or any other Beast," the demon continued, grinning feverishly. "Only a Beast can defeat a Beast."

"This is such a great plan," I said with false cheer, turning to Xylo. "Right?"

He looked back at me dubiously. "No. This is a terrible plan."

I shrugged, turning back to her. "I would have preferred a much more optimistic godmother, you know."

She grinned wickedly. "How many godmothers do you know who would eat their goddaughter's foes?" she asked, licking her lips.

I grimaced. "Okay. Fair point."

She nodded primly. "Sanguina is the entire source of Dracula's power. With Sanguina in play, Dracula will live on for eternity. But your mother surmised a way for you—and only you—to win." She leaned closer, as if to verify I was paying attention. "You can only *dominate* a Beast, not *defeat* it. They are parasites and need a strong parental hand to keep them in line. You are quite literally the only person in the world strong enough to dominate Sanguina—who is probably the strongest Beast I have ever seen."

I stared back at her numbly, not feeling encouraged. "I'm not great at guessing games, and time is running out."

"You have Sanguina's Silver eyes within you, do you not?"

Xylo gasped. "The Eternal Metal?" he rasped.

My heart skipped a few beats. I had considered that my mother had hidden Sanguina's eyes somewhere, but to hear that they were the source of the Silvers inside my own body...

Maybe I had experienced too much shocking news lately, because I just felt numb at the revelation. If the Silvers were Xylo's Eternal Metal, why hadn't everyone freaked the hell out when I'd used them to fight all those skeletons in the Feast Hall?

Xylo leaned close, and he was staring at me like I was a Goddess. Apparently, he'd read my thoughts. "Dracula *was* startled to see your claws of Eternal Metal. Samael reassured him that they were gifts your mother had given to you. Then when they broke, Dracula dismissed them as unimportant." He glanced down at my katana thoughtfully. "Is that..." he trailed off wonderingly.

"Yes. Is this the Eternal Metal you've been going on about?" I asked.

He touched it with a finger bone and immediately shuddered. "Yes, although I never would have known had I not touched it. Something is different about it."

The demon interrupted us. "Biology is funny like that." We both glanced up, frowning. "Your mother believed that it would either grow stronger within you or weaker, but there was no way to tell which. So it is not as distinguishable as the purest form of Eternal Metal from Sanguina."

I nodded. That...actually made a lot of sense.

But it also perfectly reiterated a point. My mother had crafted me like a bacterial culture in a Petri dish. Mixing up all sorts of spiffy ingredients to make me.

I considered all of this in silence, trying to process everything. Then I looked up at her. "The Beast and I are bonded," I breathed. "We share life essence."

The demon grinned, snapping her claws. "Bingo. It's still going to be a fight, but you'll be more or less on equal footing. Your will against hers."

I nodded stiffly, climbing back to my feet. That hadn't gone so well for me during our first tussle, but I'd learned a lot since then. Gotten a lot angrier. Had obtained many more personal reasons to hate Dracula and everything he stood for.

And I had a Xylo.

And my Horseman Mask.

And apparently—although she'd told me it wouldn't be of any use—I was about to get all my powers back. Still, if I dominated Sanguina, I might still need my powers to fight Dracula.

"Dracula is going to be very upset," Xylo said, sounding amused.

I smiled back. "Fuck Dracula." I started to lift my hand for a high-five, but Xylo stepped back suddenly, looking alarmed that I wanted to hurl a bolt of lightning somewhere. I winced, lowering my hand. "Yeah. Good call."

"Where is Samael?" the demon asked impatiently. "I need to see him."

I slowly turned to look at her, my stomach churning nauseatingly.

"We need to get you out of your prison. He might need your help."

Her face darkened. "Oh?"

Even though she was brand new at this godmother thing...

she had the fucking glare down pat. I even wanted to say a couple *Hail Marys* just to be on the safe side. Or would that be *Hail Unnamed Demon Ladies?*

I had an inkling that this little sulfur-sugar was about to get blessed out by her demonic godmother when she mentioned the Coliseum.

28

I studied the demon warily, wondering if I should instead keep her locked up while I told her about Samael and his stint as Spartacus.

Then again, maybe I wanted her to go rage out all over Castle Dracula. Give her a head start before I woke up Sanguina in case the Beast was able to multitask and deal with both of us simultaneously.

"Yeah. Let's release you first. Trust me."

She clenched her jaws angrily but didn't argue.

I walked up to the Omegabet prison, singling out the lone angelic rune and studying it meticulously.

I paused, frowning up at her. "Why does no one here know your name?" I asked curiously.

She studied me over her snout, unblinking. "Bad connotations. You can call me Lily."

My forearms instantly turned to gooseflesh and I instinctively wanted to run away screaming. But I managed to keep my face blank, exuding a cool, calm and collected demeanor as I nodded casually.

The smile on Lily's face told me I had not succeeded in convincing her how brave I was, and that she was amused by it.

"Lily," I mused. "Short for—"

"Just Lily," she interrupted authoritatively. "No other name should be used. Especially not here."

"Right. Pretty name," I said, still trying to play it cool. Xylo was turning from Lily to me with a frown, trying to figure out what was going on and why it was important.

"The rune, Callie," Lily reminded me. "My lover is waiting on me."

"Of course," I said, focusing back on the rune and trying not to hyperventilate. Was my godmother Lilith? Pretty much the worst of the worst—that was like saying Lucifer was your Uncle.

Xylo cleared his throat and we both looked over at him. "The chain is marked just like the circle," he suggested, pointing to a spot I couldn't see from my position. "Perhaps the circle powers the chain?"

I nodded my agreement, impressed that he had grasped such an abstract concept. Lily studied Xylo very intently after that, but I got back to work. Even if I wasn't necessarily ready to forgive Samael for his deceit, I had to admit that I was very excited about the thought of Lily and Samael cutting loose through Castle Dracula, going on the murder spree of all murder sprees.

That bloody distraction would give me plenty of time to deal with Sanguina and Dracula without having to worry about an army of reinforcements flanking me.

I focused back on the specific rune I had targeted. In my peripheral vision, the other runes flickered and moved as if alive, begging for my attention. I pointedly ignored them, focusing on only this one angelic rune—refusing to acknowledge that it was part of anything greater. Then I carefully reached down to my katana. I needed blood, but with my newly strengthened skin, I wasn't sure if I would be able to obtain any.

The edge of my katana easily sliced my palm open, surprising me. Was that because it had been formed from my Silver magic—the Eternal Metal—back in Kansas City, making it strong enough to overpower the protection I'd gained from my bond with Xylo?

Handy and scary. And further proof to Lily's claims.

I stared down at the blood pooling in my palm, taking one last moment to consider my plan. I smiled at the serendipity of using my blood to defeat a creature so closely associated with blood as his source of power and sustenance, wondering if this small red puddle would be enough to take down Castle Dracula for good like my mother had wanted.

And I hadn't even tapped into my Silver blood yet—which I would get once I removed the mark of the Beast.

"I will show you fear in a handful of blood," I mused under my breath, grinning wickedly as I modified the famous quote. I heard Lily purr her agreement.

With a figurative roll of the dice, I used my blood to draw a mirrored version of the angelic rune, canceling it out.

With a faint puff, the rune evaporated—as did all the others around the ring. I let out a breath of relief. Typically, breaking the circle was enough, but since this had involved the Omegabet, I hadn't been certain of the outcome. Singling out a rune and negating it had allowed me to pretend the Omegabet wasn't even a factor, but with that rune gone, the Omegabet hadn't been able to continue functioning.

Thankfully.

Lily was studying me pensively, looking impressed. "Do you know how many witches it took to make that? They were here for days..."

I climbed to my feet, dusting off my hands and glancing down at my palm to see the wound had already closed back up—not perfectly, but it was no longer an open gash bleeding all over the place. "That's because Dracula didn't want to share the full knowledge of this magic with anyone, so he broke it down, probably giving each witch a rune or two."

Lily considered that for a few moments. "Perhaps. But that doesn't explain how haggard they looked after it was completed. Well, for those who survived, anyway."

I just stared back, not sure how to respond to that. "I'm more than just a pretty face and a sinister mind. I'm made from sulfur and spite, and all things that haunt the night."

Lily blinked a few times, and then burst out laughing. "That you are, girl. That you are," she agreed, before glancing down at her manacled foot. Then she grunted, leaning closer. With minimal effort, she bent down and snapped it off her ankle, hurling it behind her to crash into the stone wall. She looked back up at me. "The chain was indeed strengthened by the circle you just destroyed, simply mirroring the power."

I nodded absently, knowing that was exactly how I would have done it.

"Now. Where is my Samael," she asked in a foreboding tone, staring towards the door, looking anxious to get started.

"First, tell me how to remove the Mark of the Beast." Her features darkened, but I held up a finger. "If I fail, we all fail. Then both of you will be locked up forever, and your secret love won't be a secret anymore," I warned her—not as a threat, but as a simple statement of fact. "And I'm sure Dracula and Sanguina will have strong opinions about how many of his soldiers you're about to go murder."

She growled under her breath, but I could see that she agreed with my assessment. "Attend me, goddaughter," she said, crouching down.

She pointed at the ground, urging me to pay attention as she began drawing a symbol in the stone with her claw—as easily as if it were sand. "Only Greater Demons—or their family, in your case—can use such power. Still, we do not share this. Ever. The less who know, the better."

I nodded. That made sense. Secrets—like technological advancements— were power. If everyone had the same technology, the technology wasn't as effective as a weapon. Think of times of war—the first to wield superior weapons like arrows, guns, grenades, or nuclear bombs usually had the upper hand. The same principle applied to magic.

I studied her symbol and the sequence in which she had drawn it until I was confident I could replicate it. I finally looked up at her. "I just draw it in reverse."

She studied me thoughtfully for a moment, looking proud. "Aye. Now, where is my hot hunk of hell meat, sulfur-sugar?"

"Wow. Some things should not be said out loud, Godmother," I said, grimacing. "Otherwise I might have to wash your mouth out with holy water."

She leaned back and cackled. Xylo watched the two of us, not really following along but as if trying to learn normal human behavior.

He was studying the wrong two people if he wanted to learn that.

I climbed to my feet, dusting off my hands. "Dracula took Samael to the Coliseum. He's been there for a long time, now, but he was okay as of a few hours ago."

She stared at me for a good five seconds, grinding her teeth together loud enough for me to actually hear.

"He has broken the record for highest kill-streak," Xylo offered helpfully.

I snapped my fingers, pointing at him. "That. He definitely did that."

Instead of speaking, Lily turned on her heel and stormed over towards her cot. Then she calmly lifted it up—with one hand—and flung it across the room. It shattered against the far wall in a shower of splinters. Then she stomped down on the floor with one foot, obliterating the stone.

I frowned. Stone shouldn't have broken like that, no matter how strong she was. It was almost as if the stone was—

She bent down and pulled something out of the hole she had made, and I suddenly realized that it had been a concealed hiding place—hollow, just like I'd thought.

She came back over to me, holding out a bundle of fabric and two wicked sawed-off shotguns made of a rough, uncut dark stone with purple crystals.

"These belonged to your mother," Lily said reverently. "She asked me to give them to you. Perhaps it will frighten Sanguina to see them again. Like your mother had returned to finish what she started when she ripped Sanguina's eyes out."

My fingers shook as I reached out for the items. "Th-thank you," I stammered, caught completely off guard. My mother had left me a gift—back before I was even *born*.

"Don't thank me. My goddaughter looks like a filthy refugee. It's embarrassing, is all."

I smiled crookedly, staring down at the bundle of black fabric. "Right." It was a pair of smooth black pants, a thin hoodie, and a girdle-like vest with straps and pockets for weapons.

"That was your mother's slaughtering outfit."

I nodded, my hands tingling slightly—imagining that my fingers were touching hers in some alternate reality where I might have had the chance to know her.

Lily pointed at the sawed-off shotguns, which looked more like two stone clubs than any type of modern weapons. "These..." she murmured officiously, "are truly something to behold. No one else can get them to work. Your mother tied them to her bloodline, so they only function for a Solomon. There's a cloth satchel of spare bullets wrapped up in the clothes, because these only fire starstone ammunition. She said she had more in her laboratory, but this is all she gave me."

I smiled. "Perfect."

"I'm about to leave, and we will only see each other again if we are both successful. I have full confidence in you, Callie. Do you have confidence in yourself?"

I turned to look at her challenging glare. I nodded, feeling a fire ignite in my veins at her tone. "Yes, godmother."

"And you are sure you know just how capable your competition is?" she demanded like a drill instructor.

I narrowed my eyes. "Don't worry. My competition cannot see me."

Lily snorted. "Of course they can see you. Dracula and Sanguina see all."

I shook my head defiantly. "They aren't my competition," I said distractedly, feeling adrenaline suddenly pumping within my very soul. Xylo let out a dark, rasping chuckle, reading my thoughts.

Lily shifted her gaze from me to Xylo, and then back again. "Explain."

I smiled, drawing out my answer as I met her eyes. "My competition cannot see me...because I do not own a *mirror*," I said, winking.

Lily smiled a terrible, approving, crocodile smile. "Oh, I think we will get along splendidly, sulfur-sugar." And surprisingly, she bent low to wrap me up in a hug. Since my hands were full, I had no way to stop her.

Like a grandmother pinching your cheeks or using a spit-soaked napkin to clean your chin in front of your friends at school.

She finally leaned back, looking mildly embarrassed that she had shown such emotion. "Yes, well. I'm off to go round up your godfather. He's been helpless without me."

I nodded with a faint smile. "Utterly."

She turned to Xylo. "You harm her, and I will gobble you up. You will spend the rest of eternity reanimating in my gullet."

He snorted. "That would be unpleasant. For you more than me." His tone was a gust of frozen wind in a forgotten cemetery.

She arched a stunned eyebrow. I probably did the same. "Oh?"

"A Death Spinner doesn't digest easily. Would likely wreak havoc on your delicate digestive system. All those internal organs to sear and sizzle. I'm willing to give it a try."

We both kind of just stared at him for a few moments. "I see," she finally said. "Do you want to know any secrets? Who you really are?"

Xylo stared at her with absolutely no reaction. "No, thank you. I have Callie. What else would I need?"

Lily frowned, moving her mouth wordlessly. I just stared at Xylo in disbelief. He hadn't wanted to learn who he really was?

And that line! He'd just become my favorite skeleton.

Lily finally turned to me. "Give the bitches hell," she hissed. And then she was running from the room with an earth-shattering roar.

"You too!" I cheered, even though she couldn't hear me.

Then I frowned, replaying her words. "Why did she say bitches?" I asked, turning to Xylo. "Is there more than one Beast?"

Xylo frowned uncertainly. "Not that I know of."

I shook my head. Too late now.

"I'm going to get changed and then we're going to party. You might even get to high-five again."

Xylo grinned toothily. "Goodie."

"What was up with your sudden confidence? It was amazing."

He nodded satisfactorily. "Did I do it right? I guessed that she wouldn't know what Death Spinners can do either, so I decided to make something up."

I nodded with a smile. "You nailed it, Xylo."

"Good. I decided that I do not like bullies. I do not like them at all. Fuck bullies. Fuck turtles. And fuck Dracula."

I grinned, trying not to laugh. "Fuck all of them," I agreed.

❧ 29 ❧

All things considered, Lily's news that I had a secret weapon inside of me was a much-needed, favorable development for the plan I'd already concocted.

The only way to defeat a bully was to bully him back, to take away his power and authority, revealing the sniveling coward beneath.

To take down Sanguina. What I hadn't known was that defeating her wasn't an option, and that I had to try and dominate her. I'd already known that I would have Xylo and my Horseman's Mask as power sources, having decided not to use the amulets at all.

Because I was finished playing by Dracula's rules.

With Lily showing me how to remove the Mark of the Beast, I no longer needed the amulets anyway. The Beast would wake up the moment I nullified the Mark.

And then—at about two-million-miles-per-hour—the shitstorm would unload upon Castle Dracula.

Well, Lily was probably already making up for one hundred years of abstinence with an orgy of murder, mayhem, and excessive bloodshed as she searched out her...hot hunk of hell meat, Samael.

She might even be hungry, now that I thought about it. I should have told her about the frog legs at the waterfront pub...

Despite all the answers I'd received on how to defeat Dracula and how my mother had set all this up, I couldn't help but wonder what Dracula had originally wanted with Roland. And why he had so quickly decided that I would qualify as a replacement—perhaps even a better one.

And why had Mina Harker—speaking through her possessed puppet—been so concerned about Dracula making a move for the Master's Library or the Infernal Armory. They were all his to begin with. Well, Sanguina's, technically.

Since I hadn't spoken with Samael, I had no way of knowing what other games or schemes he might have spun up since he'd been unsupervised for so long.

So I was really hoping that I didn't have any more shockers on the horizon. Lily had told me quite a bit of history, but she'd been locked up in an Observatory for one hundred years. Not really up-to-date on current events. There was no way of changing that, so I just readied myself to hear more potentially bad news.

Thinking of Samael and how he had worked so hard to get Lily back—even lying to Dracula about hating her...

It was pretty goddamned cute, to be honest. That old childhood jingle came to mind—with a few appropriate modifications, of course...

Samael and Lily sitting in a tree. S.I.N.N.I.N.G. First comes Hell, then comes bondage, then comes lil' Callie from a messed-up marriage.

I sighed, wishing I could have gotten something about an apple in there.

I had changed into my mother's slaughtering outfit and was sitting down on a wooden chair I had found tucked under a desk. A tall mirror stood across from me, but I hadn't approached it yet.

I glanced down at the two shotguns beside me. I'd loaded them with the strange-looking shells I'd found in the satchel that Lily had told me about, but there was no way to test the guns without drawing unwanted attention.

Because sawed-off meant they would be real fucking firecrackers in the sound department. Hell, maybe these starstone shells shot out miniature supernovas or something.

Have you ever tried to suppress a miniature supernova?

Me neither.

Xylo cleared his throat—the fact that he didn't have a throat made the sound a poorly concealed hint that we had things to do.

I sighed, climbing to my feet. I left the guns where they were and walked up to the mirror, knowing I needed a way to observe my work while I drew the inverse of the Mark of the Beast on my forehead. I couldn't afford to make a mistake.

But instead of doing that, I stared at my reflection for the first time in what felt like years. I'd found a trough full of water—triple-checking to make sure it wasn't actually a crocodile toilet—and used it to dip my old clothes in so I could wipe off the majority of the blood, mud, and grime from my hair and skin. It was better than nothing.

And my mother had been similar enough in size to me that her clothes all fit like a glove. I had the hood up—to hide some of the blood and mud I hadn't been able to wash out—and to be honest, I looked pretty badass.

All that was left was to reverse the Mark of the Beast on my forehead and get ready to throw my willpower against the strongest Beast even Lily had ever seen.

One advantage to this crazy plan—rather than waiting the three days Dracula had given me—was that no one would expect it. I'd found a shortcut before the first day was even up.

Xylo walked up to me, carrying the shotguns like my own personal golf caddie. He'd also pulled his impenetrable crimson hood up over his head so that we were twinsies. "Where do we go after this?" he asked.

I shook my head. "I have no idea. Stay close just in case the Beast decides to come here."

He nodded.

I took a deep breath as I cut my palm with my katana. Then I looked into the mirror and drew the inverse of the Mark of the Beast on my forehead with a bloody finger. The moment my finger finished the symbol, I doubled over, clutching at my abdomen.

Pain crippled me, just like it had in the Feast Hall when Samael had done it the first time. My scalp and forehead blazed with what felt like napalm, and I gasped, trying to stay conscious. As intense as it was, the pain was over in mere moments and I found that Xylo was supporting me, preventing me from falling over.

"Are you okay, Callie?" he asked, sounding frightened, staring into my face. I nodded, letting out a shaky breath. Then I straightened my spine, opening myself up to my old powers—

And I almost let out a scream of joy to find them within my reach again. I knew I wouldn't need them for the Beast—that they wouldn't do me any good—but simply knowing that I had them back made me feel whole again. Complete.

Ready to throw some elbows.

I calmly prepared for something bad to happen next, knowing that the Beast was somewhere rubbing at her eyes, yawning as she woke up from her nap earlier than intended.

"Your eyes are shining...just like the Eternal Metal," Xylo murmured, sounding awed.

I glanced back at the mirror and saw that my eyes were indeed shining with bright silver light.

Seeing them like this, with Xylo claiming they were his Eternal Metal... really brought it home for me.

I shared life essence with Sanguina. My mother really had fused her eyes into me somehow. The Silvers, as I'd always called them.

The strange part was that I'd had several supernatural factions try to claim credit for the Silvers. And now I knew they had all been lying to me. Even angels had tried to take credit for them.

I'd even spoken with them before, which sent a deep shiver down my spine, now knowing that the Silvers were actually Sanguina's eyes. Had I been talking to her, or some other Beast? Had the Silvers acted like some kind of Police Scanner out in Celestialtopia?

Now that I thought about it, I'd used the Silvers in any number of ways before—from trapping an angel to navigating the Doors. Silver tears even marked my Horseman's Mask.

How much of me was Beast and how much of me was Callie?

As alarming as that question was...

It also gave me a boost of confidence.

Because I'd done all of those things with my Silvers. And I'd done it all by myself. Without even knowing what they truly were. Which meant my willpower must be pretty fucking strong. Stronger than I would have thought. I was a natural at being a Beast.

More of a natural than I had been as a Horseman, anyway.

Xylo gasped, pointing at the mirror suddenly. I glanced over to see a horizontal, Silver crescent moon—points up—in the center of my forehead. And Silver tears—three from each glowing eye—streaked down my cheeks like rays of moonlight. The dried blood from the inverted Mark of the Beast I had drawn seemed to have vaporized in that first wave of pain I had felt.

I stared at the symbol on my forehead and I suddenly knew what it said.

"Despair," I murmured, smiling devilishly, marveling at the Silver warpaint on my face.

Okay, maybe I was getting a good handle on the Horseman thing, too.

Before I could say anything else, the stone floor began to rumble and quake, and I heard a furious scream from far, far away—a vaguely human sound.

Dracula must have caught onto my ploy and thrown a vamper-tantrum. Because that had not been the cry of a man whose sinister scheme had gone according to plan.

That had been the cry of a man at the end of his rope, willing to abandon everyone he had once loved unconditionally and everything he had once held dear, because his heart and soul were now only desiccated husks of ash and regret. A man ready to burn his house down from the front lawn—wearing only his tighty-whities and knee-length dress socks—in full-view of his neighbors.

Because he'd just lost a four hour game of Monopoly to his wife and kids.

It was music to my ears.

I straightened my shoulders and gripped Xylo's hand, giving it a tight squeeze to let him know I wouldn't abandon him to his old master. We were bonded by blood, but also friendship.

I wondered which big bad would show up first—Dracula, since I'd ruined his plan and stopped playing his game, or the Beast—who I'd just woken up.

I opened my mouth and cried out at the top of my lungs. "An eye for an eye, Sanguina! Come get some!"

The Beast obliged.

30

I found myself standing in a frozen clearing surrounded by a forest of strange, illuminated trees. Except they definitely weren't trees. They looked more like they had been pulled from a coral reef near the equator, plopped onto dry, frozen land, and then had grown thirty feet tall. They emitted a soothing, pale-blue glow.

Snowflakes as large as bottle caps swirled all around me as if I was in the center of a shaken snow globe, but I felt no wind.

And it wasn't as cold as I would have thought.

Despite the obviously winter climate, hundreds of flowers grew from the mounds of snow, in vibrant, almost painful, colors that I hadn't ever seen in nature before. Neon purple and green ribbons of light danced across the twilight sky in a world that had...three moons.

I double-checked to make sure I wasn't imagining things.

Yep. I'd definitely made a wrong turn somewhere. I'd slipped into a new solar system or something.

At least I could still breathe.

I was unstoppable, now.

"How are you holding up, Xylo?" I asked, my voice echoing across the frozen world. He didn't answer. I turned and instantly gasped. He stood beside me, but he was entirely encased in a block of dark, purple ice, along with my shotguns. I could vaguely make out his embers and sparks trying to fight off the cold, but they weren't hot enough to free him from his prison.

I gritted my teeth. "Hold on, buddy. I'll get you out of there."

At least I knew he couldn't die, but it was apparently much colder than I'd first thought. Was I able to survive it only due to my shared life essence with Sanguina? Speaking of...

I scanned my surroundings and instantly noticed that we weren't alone. A single creature stared at me from across the clearing. The fact that it looked like someone had taken a soldering iron to her eyes let me know this was Sanguina.

And seeing her in person, I wondered exactly how the hell I was supposed to physically fight such a creature. We were entirely different in every way imaginable. It simply wasn't physically possible. Period. At the same time, I'd always known this would be more than a physical confrontation. Lily had told me it would be a battle of wills.

I squared my shoulders and glared at her. Then I drew my katana very slowly and pointed it at the Beast. "You. Are. Mine."

Sanguina—although blind—curled her lips at me but did not speak. That meant she recognized the Silver sword, which had been my intent.

I took a step to the side, and Sanguina tracked me. Not entirely blind, then. That was a disappointment.

"I CAN SEE POWER, HUMAN. EYES SEE ONLY SO MUCH, BUT POWER SEES POWER," her voice screamed directly into my mind.

"What do you want, Sanguina?" I demanded, trying to duplicate Lily's authoritative godmotherly tone. I'd also decided I was going to speak out loud rather than risk embarrassing myself by trying to converse telepathically. I knew my limits, and Xylo had taught me how bad I was at reading minds. "Why all of this? Why ally yourself with a cowardly snake like Dracula?" I demanded, truly wanting to understand.

Because the Beasts I'd heard about had always partnered with individuals who had already been strong in their own right. Dracula's only source of strength seemed to be his bond with Sanguina. It didn't seem like a give and take relationship.

"I WANT AN ALLY. A PARTNER. BUT YOU ARE ALL TOO WEAK."

I smiled invitingly. "Step right up, honey. You won't find any weakness from me. I came here to chew bubblegum and kick ass, and I'm all out of bubblegum." Sanguina stared back at me, killing the punchline, so I tried a different tactic. "That means I came here to finish what my mother started. Do you remember my mother? She looked just like me—oh. Wait."

"YOUR MOTHER COULD HAVE BEEN WORTHY. BETTER THAN HARKER OR THE OTHERS, BUT SHE TOOK MY EYES AND FLED. WEAK. DISAPPOINTING."

I blinked at that. Harker? Others? What was she talking about?

I felt a sudden blazing fury raging up within me. "Did you know I was inside my mother's womb when you fought her? That she battled you while pregnant with me? That was the *only* reason she fled. Not out of fear for herself or any measure of weakness, but to keep *me* safe," I snarled savagely. "That isn't weakness. That's the strength of a *mother*. Something you will *never* understand, you poor, deluded, parasitic worm!"

Silence rang out in the clearing, and I could see I had stunned Sanguina. I realized I was panting, and that I had slammed my katana into the frozen earth. It crackled and flickered with Silver light—something I had never seen it do. I took a calming breath, going back over my words. I hadn't ever actually thought about my mother's decision like that before. I'd just been thinking out loud, running on autopilot.

But it was true.

And it was pretty damned cool, actually. In a totally unhealthy, psychotic way—like all true love.

"I THOUGHT YOUR MOTHER HAD FAILED," Sanguina finally said. "THAT SHE HAD BEEN WEAK. BUT I SEE SHE HAS GIVEN YOU WHAT SHE STOLE FROM ME, BONDING US IN A WAY I HADN'T THOUGHT POSSIBLE. WE ARE THE SAME, YET DIFFER-ENT. AND I SENSE OTHER POWERS WITHIN YOU. GREAT POWERS..." She trailed off, cocking her head as she studied me from across the clearing. Her lips didn't move when she spoke, almost making her look like she was wearing a mask. "WE COULD DO GREAT THINGS TOGETHER. JOIN ME."

I set my boots into the snow, readying for a fight. "I'm a fan of pants, Sanguina, so you better own a nice dress."

"THEN WE SHALL DANCE, HUMAN."

I drew up my Silvers in a way I hadn't ever done before. A column of flowing silver that stabbed at the Heavens suddenly erupted before me, swirling and spinning like a vortex of molten chrome.

I fed thoughts of all my victories into it, all my wins, all my accomplishments—and how I had done all those things despite usually working all by myself and always having only half the answers or explanations I should have had—because I hadn't known the truth about my past, the truth about my ties to Heaven, the truth about my parents, the truth about my Silvers.

Yet I had still taken home the victory trophies.

I built upon my tower of power, my tower of victory, drawing up every proud aspect of myself that I could think of.

I had never let myself rely on others to carry my weight. I had welcomed help at times but had never expected it or depended on it.

Long story short, I had always been my own woman.

Never, *ever*, having to submit or subjugate myself to another person or group or master. Not a church. Not any of the supernatural factions in my city. Not Nate Temple and his gang of monsters and gods from St. Louis. Not even angels or demons.

It was simply part of my spirit. I was not the type of person to curtsy, bob my head, and shuffle about meekly.

I'd never *needed* someone else. Sure, I'd *wanted* or *desired* help from others at times, but true *need* had never been a motivating factor.

Simply put, I was the antithesis of Sanguina. She needed a host, an ally. Because she was a parasite.

I just needed a goddamned mirror, baby—and someone ballsy enough to tell me that I couldn't do something.

Because I craved the challenge. The thrill. I wanted a mountain to scale. Some teeth to sink my knuckles into. I wanted a D.i.D. to save—whether that was a Damsel or a Dude in Distress, didn't really matter to me.

I hungered for a fight. A cause. Someone to avenge.

Hell, it was why I'd briefly gone postal and earned the moniker the *White Rose* in Kansas City—going vigilante on criminals and putting them six-feet-under when they tried to abuse loopholes to escape justice.

Which makes it pretty clear that I wasn't infallible. I also wasn't arrogant and didn't think I was better than anyone else. To be blunt, it was just that I never really thought to compare myself to others or to care what they might think of my actions. Roland Haviar had taught me to be self-reliant and to have a strong moral code, and I had welded those tenets deep into the foundation of my soul. I'd adopted his code of ethics so strongly that I'd even taken him to task—almost killing him—when he'd broken that code.

Less than two days ago.

So if I found myself stuck between a rock and a hard place, it rarely occurred to me to stay there crying out for help—even if that was the smarter, more efficient, solution.

If I had to wiggle out one centimeter at a time, then that's what I would start doing. I probably wouldn't even think of calling out for help until hours later. So, you could definitely say I was stubborn.

Although orphaned on the steps of a church, I'd been lucky enough to have a handful of father figures in my life.

And each of them—in their own unique way—had taught a spindly, snot-nosed, white-haired, orphan girl that if she learned how to define her *I*, she would own her corner of the world one day.

So I had defined my *I*.

And it had made all the difference. Because if you had that, you rarely needed anyone else's opinion. You were only competing with the strongest person you knew.

Yourself.

Just like I'd told Lily.

And as my mind raced with these thoughts and layers of self-analysis, I very pointedly tried to use my limited experience with telepathy to show Sanguina that she had *none* of these virtues or strengths. That in a vacuum, she was nothing. Because she had never defined her *I*, choosing to instead measure the value of her existence based on the strength of her partnerships.

Her *we*.

Which was a recipe for disaster.

Every. Single. Time.

My tower of power screamed as it seemed to reach the stratosphere, climbing out of sight through the wisps of clouds miles above.

I was surprised to see Sanguina's own tower rising up on the opposite side of the clearing.

Surprised at how *itty-bitty* it was.

But it was strange, because I could sense the immense level of power she was hurling into it, which meant it should have been significantly taller or wider.

A closer look revealed the reason. Vines of Silver light were actually peeling off her tower and braiding into mine—abandoning Team Sanguina and forcing her to work twice as hard to maintain her tower.

I watched as she panted desperately, refusing to give up, refusing to accept the spears of truth I had mentally thrown at her about her flaws and weaknesses.

The despair I had peppered her with.

That *I* trumped *we* every time but one.

When the *we* was actually comprised of two people who had solidly defined their own *I* and had joined forces.

I smiled and lifted my palm into the air and gently blew across it.

And my titanic tower of power exploded into a billion Silver butterflays —razor-winged butterflies—that swept out like a tidal wave to utterly annihilate Sanguina's tower. It collapsed and then evaporated like mist before sunlight.

Sanguina turned to stare at me incredulously with her soldered, empty eye-sockets. I sat down on the snow and slowly, distinctly patted the ground beside me three times in a silent command. Sanguina slowly approached, shuffling her feet as if still reeling over her crushing defeat.

As I watched her approach, I forced myself not to laugh giddily with joy, and instead tried to further analyze her earlier statements.

She wanted a partner. She really was a parasite. She'd spent her life looking for a worthwhile host, only to be repeatedly disappointed.

Did that explain where vampires came from? Some effect of her bond?

She lifted her head, her eyeless face staring straight into mine, having apparently read my thoughts.

"MY HOST WAS NOT STRONG ENOUGH TO KEEP ME SATED. I HAD TO FIND AN ALTERNATIVE SOURCE OF NOURISHMENT. HAVING MY HOST FEED ON THE BLOOD OF HIS BROTHERS AND SISTERS SUSTAINED ME. I DID NOT KNOW IT WOULD BE CONTAGIOUS."

I nodded in understanding, masking my disgust. She'd *accidentally* created vampires. *Whoopsies. I was just so hangry*.

So Dracula hadn't been strong enough to keep her in line, and she'd been forced to fend for herself in the food department.

And like a child, she'd discovered the joys of snacks.

Taking a little bit here, a little bit there. Some sweet. Some spicy.

But she was malnourished, never having gotten her full-course meal from a partner strong enough to handle her—one who could give her a quality relationship of give and take.

This whole thing was a cry for help. A child demanding attention.

I'd once spoken with Nate Temple, who knew a thing or two about Beasts. The three he had met hadn't needed blood to survive. But...they'd had a strong partner. A Tiny God or a Maker, as they were also known.

Sanguina had no Tiny God.

She was...Godless.

And as far as I knew, I wasn't either of those.

But...I *was* a genetically hybrid Beast, thanks to my mother's experiments. And I had access to lots of power in my own right. Maybe that was even better than having a Tiny God for a host. A little bit of home and a little bit of the exotic.

Still, Sanguina had needed proof. In a strange way, it had almost been like those old martial arts movies where the student had to prove they were worthy of being taught by the master.

Except in our case, I had been the master and had needed to prove to the already naturally-talented student that I—unlike the other masters who had disappointed her lately—could help her become the best martial artist the world had ever seen.

Sanguina really was an unruly child, not knowing how else to get what she needed. And the fact that she was naturally powerful only made her more dangerous.

She sat down meekly before me, a faint smile tugging at her cheeks. She'd finally accepted her defeat, and now she was practically radiating eagerness for us to team up. I grunted. This was definitely the strangest altercation I'd ever had.

And this was only Round One. I had plenty more still to do.

"First, you're going to unfreeze my buddy, Xylo."

She glanced over at him and the ice abruptly melted. Xylo stumbled, looking around frantically before seeing me seated on the ground with Sanguina. His jaw dropped so fast it fell entirely off.

I reached over, scooped it up and handed it back to him. "Grab my sword and sit down, Xylo. I might need your knowledge of Castle Dracula to ask Sanguina, my new buddy, some questions."

He nodded stiffly, slamming his jaw back into place and pulling my sword from the ground before sitting down. He stared at Sanguina, fascinated by the majestic creature.

I gathered my thoughts and leaned forward. "Here's what I want to know..."

Sanguina had no problem answering my questions—no matter how grim some of the answers were. To put it into perspective, Xylo lost track of his jaw three more times during the course of our conversation. And I didn't laugh about it even once. I was too busy staring at Sanguina in stunned disbelief.

And I had been saving all of my big questions for *after* I succeeded in reducing Dracula to a sooty smear.

As Sanguina continued to roll back the curtain on Castle Dracula, my mind began to race with endless possibilities.

31

Between one step and the next, we were back in the Observatory. It was nothing like my Shadow Walking. It was like waking from a dream.

I had a lot to learn about our new relationship, as long as my brain didn't melt trying to process it all. I had managed to dominate Sanguina, proving that I would never be the weaker partner—and I was beyond relieved to know that it had nothing to do with our relative level of mastery over the Silvers.

It was about mentality.

Owning the fastest car in the world meant nothing if you didn't have the key to the ignition. As fast as Sanguina's car was, she wasn't old enough to drive. She never *wanted* to be old enough to drive. She wanted a big sister to drive her around all the time. She wanted to lend her power out. In exchange for getting her sustenance and never being left alone.

It was kind of sad, really. Like an orphan.

She was stuck here on this strange planet, surrounded by humans who were too fragile to survive playing games with her. Leaving her with no other friends or family to turn to.

I grimaced at my poor analogy. Sanguina definitely wasn't as naive as a child. Not after some of the things she'd just told me. It wasn't that she was evil, but that her sense of right and wrong was so vastly different from ours that it made her seem evil.

Murder was bad, right?

What about when you stomped on that cockroach for daring to take a walk across your kitchen floor? Or when you stomped on it again just to be sure. Or when you flushed the potentially still breathing cockroach down the toilet. That was murder and torture, too, depending on your perspective.

That was Sanguina's mentality. She was just stomping on cockroaches.

But there was a type of innocence about her.

So maybe it was best to say I was her guardian. I'd have to spend more time thinking on it, but I had more pressing matters to consider at the moment.

Xylo handed me my shotguns. He'd already given me back my Silver katana, and I had tucked it into a loop on my new pants.

"You remember the plan?" I asked him, scanning the room for any sign of Dracula. He should have been here by now. If he didn't show, we'd have to go hunt him down ourselves. Since I now had all my powers back, I no longer had any fear of walking down the center of the street in full view of Dracula's army.

Hell, I kind of felt like a walk. I would *skip* down the street, and even whistle showtunes as loud as humanly possible as I hurled fireballs and bolts of lightning at anything that moved—at all the little cockroaches.

But it would waste precious time.

"Yes. I'm ready," he murmured.

I let out an annoyed huff, not seeing Dracula. "Then I guess—"

And he suddenly entered the room in a shifting cloud of crimson mist. He froze, hovering in place for a moment before solidifying into the handsome man we'd last seen in the Feast Hall.

He stared at me, looking bewildered.

Probably because I still had the Silver tears and crescent moon on my forehead, and my eyes were still glowing, molten chrome.

So Dracula was having a situational crisis. Here I was, obviously having retrieved some of my powers—powers he hadn't even known about in the first place—yet he knew his Beast was awake.

That was why he'd come to this exact spot. Sanguina had traveled back from that other world to join them, letting them know they had a problem to deal with in the Observatory—essentially tossing up her Beast Signal over Castle Dracula.

Oh, and Dracula was astutely aware of the empty chains across the room, and the obvious fact that the resident crocodile demon who had lived here for the past one hundred years was nowhere in sight. That was probably very concerning to him since she apparently knew all the secrets of this fucked up place.

I was pretty sure they were the same secrets Sanguina had just told me.

Xylo took an aggressive step forward, standing between me and Dracula. "Get ready, Master. One or both of us is going to fuck you," he promised, the black shadows in his eye-sockets flickering wildly.

Okay. *That* hadn't been part of our plan. Xylo was going off script. *Play it cool, Xylo*, I thought to myself, hoping he would read my mind. His definition of the F-bomb was getting looser by the hour. I really should have done a better job of explaining it to him.

Dracula's eyes widened in disbelief. Then he burst out laughing, unable to help himself. "Well, *that* is an interesting tactic," he finally said.

Xylo nodded, his bones quivering and clacking like a pissed off rattlesnake. Seeing the cause of his lifelong torment—and finally having found a modicum of confidence—was proving almost too much for him to handle.

"I fucked all three of your wives, and now I will fuck *you*," he snarled.

Sweet Jesus.

Dracula's face went slack, and my heart dropped into my stomach.

Damn it, Xylo. No more teaching him curse words without making him promise to take a vocabulary test before using them out in the world. He was no longer using a loose definition of the word; he was just applying it to any negative emotion he felt towards a person.

"You ungrateful little shit," Dracula seethed. "I knew you weren't worth the trouble when I acquired you, no matter what she said—"

"And what did I say, dear?" Mina Harker asked in a cool tone, sauntering into the room with a small pet fox, of all things, tucked under her arm. It was sleeping peacefully.

Dracula spun, looking alarmed. "Oh, there you are, Mina. I hope all is well?"

She gave him a very dry look. "No more games, husband. You've been avoiding me all day. And I've heard the most disturbing news," she said with barely restrained fury, her voice dripping with venom.

I kept my face blank, staring at Mina Harker for the second time today. "I missed you in the Gardens."

She nodded, rewarding me with a brief, amused grin before turning back to her husband, even before she replied. "You missed me twice, technically." Then her eyes widened, and her gaze jerked back to mine, noticing my fancy warpaint. The fox let out a muffled, sleepy *yip* at the sudden motion but didn't bother waking.

I smiled back at her through my teeth, understanding her meaning. Firstly, when she'd pulled her switcheroo and quickly possessed a similar-looking vampire to use as a mouthpiece, and secondly when I'd stabbed that mouthpiece through the heart in self-defense when Mina had turned her into a kamikaze pilot before relinquishing her control.

"Third time's the charm, I guess," I admitted, shrugging. "And isn't the Eternal Metal awesome for facepaint? Sorry we blew a hole through the roof of your Armory...Mr. and Mrs. Harker," I said.

They both froze, turning to stare at me incredulously. Then their eyes shot to where Lily—the unnamed demon—should have been imprisoned. The demon that they had locked up for the secrets she knew. They wrongly assumed Lily had spilled the beans on their true identities—Jonathan and Mina Harker.

And I could tell their minds were racing with what other secrets might have been spilled. They had no idea.

I grinned. "You can't trust anyone these days, am I right? We had a little chat before I let her go. She has a lot of pent-up aggression to make up for after one hundred years of imprisonment. But I'm pretty sure she's anxious to talk to you two, personally."

They shared a long, silent look, and then Jonathan gritted his teeth. "San-guina will destroy you. She will rip your soul from your body and tear it to shreds. You have no idea what you've done—"

I backhanded him across the jaw so fast and hard that he stumbled. When he recovered—blindingly fast—and made a move to bite me, he took six inches of Solomon's shotgun down his throat instead. His eyes widened incredulously as he made muffled sounds around the barrel of starstone justice. I hefted the other shotgun up against my shoulder in a casual, devil-may-care gesture. "What's it taste like, Jonny?" He glared back at me and I laughed. "I found these relics just lying around in a closet. You guys ever seen the aftermath of starstone buckshot from point-blank range?"

They were both deathly silent.

I leaned closer to Jonathan and spoke in a conspiratorial whisper. "Do you want to?"

He shook his head anxiously and gave me another muffled response. I frowned in disappointment. "Maybe later, then." I pulled the shotgun out of his mouth, so that it was no longer tickling his tonsils, and lowered it to hang by my side.

Unsurprisingly, they were speechless, obviously recognizing my mother's old shotguns.

"I've gotta admit. I'm mighty curious how loud they will be..." I trailed off, still staring down at them.

Jonathan regained some of his backbone since he no longer had a mouthful of gun barrel. Or he was frantically trying to seize an opportunity. "Destroy them, Sanguina!" he snarled viciously.

I nudged Xylo excitedly. "Look out! Here comes trouble."

The skeleton snorted, folding his arms and yawning.

Seconds stretched by, and still nothing happened. I looked up to see the panicked looks on both of their faces.

Because I hadn't severed Dracula's tie to Sanguina yet, they thought they were still in control. Except...Sanguina wasn't answering her phone.

"While we're waiting for Sanguina to come exsanguinate me," I began, "why did you two agree to it? After killing the real Dracula, I mean. Did you think you two would fare any better than he did? That you would be better vampires? That your hearts might be pure enough to withstand the curse from the Beast where the real Dracula had been too weak?"

Because that was exactly how it had played out, according to Sanguina. Bonding Sanguina had turned the original Dracula into a vampire. Years later, when the Beast had seen her host fail, she had thought that rather than bringing Dracula back to life, maybe Mina—who had been bitten by Dracula —might be a stronger host for her. More compatible.

They flinched as if I'd slapped them. Mina looked sick to her stomach.

"And why do you let this dingleberry play at being Dracula when it's really *your* job, Mina?" I asked, jerking a chin at Jonathan. "Do you have no dignity? No pride?"

Jonathan stammered furiously, his face turning purple. "This is absurd. Of course I'm the real—"

He cut off as I leveled the shotgun one-handed on his face, not bothering to even make eye-contact with him. If he sneezed, he would headbutt the barrel. "Be silent. The women are talking."

Mina looked like a fish out of water, opening and closing her mouth wordlessly. She also shook her pet fox anxiously, as if none of us could see her doing it.

I smirked. "Oh, fine. Let's just get that part out of the way, shall we? False hope is only going to make this conversation drag on longer than it needs to." I turned to the fox, smiling animatedly. "Wakey, wakey, Sanguina," I cooed.

The fox lifted her head, yawning in that adorable way that only tiny little Beasts could pull off after a nap. When she opened her eye-sockets, they were just divots of melted chrome, just like I had seen when I'd confronted her in that strange world. Seeing her now all cuddled up and sleepy, I was doubly glad I hadn't had to physically fight her.

No matter how evil or powerful the fox might be, how could you live with yourself after physically fighting a spitting image of Copper's best friend, Tod from the *Fox and the Hound* movie? That story had wrecked me as a child. I knew I wouldn't have been able to put Tod in a chokehold or anything like that. Let the world burn instead.

Tod was the shit.

Sanguina hopped out of Mina's arms and obediently trotted over to me, her bushy tail sashaying back and forth before she settled down on her haunches at my feet.

"Good girl," I murmured. Then I turned back to Mina, who looked ready to make a run for it. "I really wouldn't, Mina. It would be a shame for Sanguina to get your guts all over her fur or for me to test out my mother's other boomstick on your deceitful little face." She flinched, her wide, terri-fied eyes latching onto mine. "Does Jonathan look like he's having very much fun right now?" I asked dryly.

"How?" she whispered incredulously. "I'm still bonded to the Beast," she argued, staring down at the fox. "I can feel it."

Sanguina panted openly, making it look like she was laughing.

Silly little fox.

"Good point," I said thoughtfully. I closed my eyes and called up my

Silvers vision. Almost immediately, I saw the blood bond connecting Mina to Sanguina—just like I had first seen while questioning Sanguina in that other world.

Without fanfare, I formed my Silvers like a guillotine and sliced through it, severing Mina's ties to Sanguina. I'd needed it intact up until now, so as not to make the two vampires suspicious and have them flee to god knows where.

Mina choked, gasping audibly. I opened my eyes to see her own eyes bulging as she clawed at her pretty little face—the vampiric powers given to her a hundred years ago suddenly ripped away.

I glanced at Jonathan and gave him a casual shrug. "Give her a minute. Probably hurts like hell. You should take this time to really smell the roses." He stared at me from over the barrel of my shotgun, his eyes wide and panicked, having no idea how to react to such a drastic change of events. He wasn't mentally equipped to handle it.

The bully had just gotten popped in the mouth in front of his gang and the rest of the school, and this was the moment of silence where all the other kids stared on as the bully reached a hand to wipe a smear of blood from his lips, and a strange watery substance from his eyes, as he debated whether or not he wanted to have a cry.

And decided that he did, in fact, want to go see his mommy.

Shotguns were great at enunciating things. So educational and informative.

32

I waited a few moments for Mina to regain her composure, not sure if she was only minutes away from disintegrating into a pile of ash as the stolen years of her extended life caught up with her. I felt no sympathy for Mina Harker.

She'd used a vampire puppet to try and kill me, first of all.

But Sanguina had also told me—in a calm, clinical recital—the long list of crimes Mina Harker had orchestrated over the years. She was no saint. She may have started out as a victim, but in some ways, she had become *more* terrible than the original Dracula, because she hadn't been equipped, hadn't had the defenses, to handle the corruption. She'd been too innocent by half.

Sanguina had been mistaken to think Mina might be a stronger host. She had been significantly *weaker*. The only reason she had defeated Dracula in the first place was because she'd had a gang of friends assisting her. Sanguina would have been better off reincarnating the original rather than trying to trade up.

Hindsight.

My real interest was with Jonathan anyway. Speaking with Mina was just to satisfy my own curiosity—and because I felt my mother would have wanted to know the full story.

"I asked you a question," I reminded her. "I know the outcome, but I want to understand your motivations. Sanguina wasn't able to share that part. Oh, and with your bond to Sanguina now severed, you're on borrowed time. Consider this your chance to repent. Soon you'll be living in a world of demons—lovely individuals like the one you held as a prisoner for a hundred years. I'm sure they will take much better care of you, though," I said sarcastically. I paused, letting her imagination run wild for a few moments. "But if you give me a clear, unfiltered explanation now, I might be convinced to put in a good word for you. It won't help much, but it's better than nothing."

Mina shuddered, lowering her chin in defeat. I noticed that the tips of her fingers had already turned gray, but I didn't say anything as she began to speak.

"When we burned the Castle down and killed Dracula, we thought it was all over. But I never actually recovered from his bites. During the next full moon, she came to me," Mina said, glancing briefly at Sanguina. "And she asked me to be her friend. She believed I might be a better...host...than Dracula had been. Realizing I couldn't escape what he'd done to me, I agreed, hoping that Sanguina could help me manage it without becoming a monster. But it didn't work. I couldn't control it. Sanguina taught me the Omegabet, and that only made me *worse*. Darker. If I had known how it would change me over the years..." she shuddered.

I froze, my blood curdling at the mention of the Omegabet. I shot an uncomfortable look at the cute little fox cleaning her paws at my feet—that this cute little fox knew the language of the end.

I'd already assumed the rest of Mina's explanation, but to hear Sanguina had taught her the Omegabet...

Another thought came to me. When they had killed the original Dracula, the rest of the vampires in the world—like the Weird Sisters—hadn't died, so the curse was everlasting, not tied to the top vampire.

That was unfortunate—being able to kill all vampires at once would be handy.

I turned to Jonathan, who was still staring down the barrel of my shotgun. "And when you found out Mina had become a vampire like Dracula, your love knew no bounds. You joined her," I said, grimacing.

He nodded slowly—but only after a quick glance at Mina to silently ask how much he was allowed to say. I permitted it, even though I was the only one making the decisions in this room. He cleared his throat. "Mina didn't want the attention of becoming the new Dracula, and she thought the fact that she was a woman would only draw the interest of more vampire hunters. Perhaps catch the attention of our old friend Van Helsing since he knew Mina had been bitten. So she decided to let me be the face of Dracula for all of our residents and, as far as the world was concerned, to let them continue thinking that the Harkers had succeeded in killing Dracula and destroying his castle. Good riddance."

"None of the people living here had any idea that you weren't the real Dracula?" I asked incredulously. I also wondered how Van Helsing had never learned about this. Nate Temple was apparently friends with the guy, and he was supposed to be a real badass—nothing like Bram Stoker's novel had depicted him.

Mina nodded sadly. "But someone discovered the truth. The Masters."

I looked up sharply, not having heard anything about this from Sanguina. Then again, I hadn't thought to ask her, more focused on the immediate dangers of Dracula—at least who I *thought* had been Dracula.

"They helped us organize the Sanguine Council, setting everything up so that we could run the world's vampires from the shadows. They told us that they would call on us for help one day and that we must be ready to answer with an army, or else they would tell the world the truth about me. About Dracula's curse passing to a new host. That the heroes of the story had become the villains."

Damn.

I turned to Jonathan. "And they later offered you something better, didn't they Jon? You grew to like your fake position as Dracula, and they offered to give you the throne in fact."

He clamped his lips shut.

Mina narrowed her eyes dangerously. "What?"

I nodded. "True love never dies."

Since he hadn't immediately denied it, Mina looked about ready to eat him alive. Her entire arm was now a sickly, mottled gray color. "Why?" she demanded.

"You never wanted the power anyway!" he snapped defensively. "I wasn't going to *kill* you, Mina. I *love* you. But someone did need to start actually *leading* the Sanguine Council—directly, rather than from the shadows. They need a firm hand. Like mine. One that doesn't feel guilt. Like you *used* to be. For better or worse, we are monsters, Mina. It's time to go back to what you used to be, to start owning the fact before we get rolled over. Case in point," he muttered, shooting a glare in my direction.

She thought about that in chilled silence for a time. "And what were you going to do about Sanguina? She knows that deep down you are weak. She only tolerates you because I told her to."

Jonathan's face darkened at that. "I found fresh blood to bring to the castle. I'd arranged for Roland Haviar—the infamous ex-Shepherd from Kansas City—to come here and complete a quest, absorbing power from some of our local residents. I was going to then sacrifice him and his accumulated power to her to win her favor. Except that bastard demon, Samael, brought me this one instead," he snapped, pointing at me. "The daughter of the woman who took Sanguina's eyes!"

He glared at pretty much everyone, looking like he was stomping his feet and shouting *it's not fair!*

I kind of understood his position. How had I, of all people, become buddy-buddy with Sanguina? She should have hated me most. I wasn't about to answer that.

I curled my lip angrily. I *knew* the amulet thing had been a ruse. He had been trying to fatten me up for Sanguina to eat. Bastard. Since the bully wasn't strong enough to get the power himself, he had resorted to using others—Roland or me—to bribe the Beast into working with him.

Good thing I'd found an alternative way to confront Sanguina. I wondered if completing his task with the amulets would have even given me my powers back at all.

"I was going to give Sanguina a choice—remain with you as a bored lapdog or to go out and explore the world. Release her from this prison. But it seems she found a new friend."

Sanguina looked up at that, and then over at me. "You'll see plenty of the world with me. Don't worry," I promised her, already having considered potential plans.

"You're not even a vampire!" Harker whined. "Everyone she bonds with becomes a vampire so she can feed."

Part of me smiled, because you could take that as him being upset the new owner of his puppy wasn't going to feed it as well as he had. *But she has to have one can of wet food every night after you brush her fur! She'll get depressed if you don't!*

But I also wondered about his statement. I was not a vampire, so what did that mean for our future relationship? For Castle Dracula? And should I have felt some sensation when I cut Mina's bond to Sanguina? Felt our new bond slide into place? Since we had shared life essence already, was it not necessary?

"None of that matters, Jonathan," Mina muttered. "It is what it is. It's not like we can deny the truth of it," Mina snapped, pointing down at Sanguina. "She obviously sees something in Callie, or their bond never would have worked. What I want to know is why you gave her my skeleton?" Mina asked, her eyes flicking towards Xylo.

He frowned at her, probably wondering why he was *her skeleton* to begin with. Xylo had said he hadn't ever spoken with her directly.

Jonathan let out a dismissive grunt. "He's of no use to anyone, no matter what you think. I needed someone to point her in the right direction of her targets or none of it would have mattered. He's a worthless bag of bones anyway. Utterly incompetent—"

Xylo snarled, his joints and ligaments suddenly crackling and hissing as the embers and sparks flared. "I. HAVE. A. *NAME!*" he roared, and gave Jonny Harkula the uppercut of all uppercuts, knocking him twelve feet into the air.

Harker shifted into crimson mist too late to avoid the blow, but early enough so that he didn't hit the ceiling. Mina gawked incredulously and tried to take a step, but her legs gave out and she stumbled to her knees. I glanced down to see that her face was now a pale, corpse-like shade, and her breath was a rattling wheeze.

Jonathan slammed into Xylo—and sailed right through him, forgetting about Xylo's ability to withstand that type of power.

But Xylo didn't let him go out the other side. Instead, he somehow trapped him inside his chest cavity.

Even though Harkula was a cloud of crimson mist, he began to scream as Xylo's bones—not just his joints—flared with embers and sparks that were hot and bright enough for me to take a step back, shielding my eyes.

And the mist began to pop and fizzle, evaporating with a noxious stench of burned meat, unable to escape the prison.

"How does it feel, *Master?*" Xylo cackled viciously. "To die slowly in a cage where everyone can watch you suffer. Where everyone can laugh at you!"

"Please! Stop! You don't understand—"

"No!" Xylo interrupted. "*You* don't understand. But you will."

Harkula continued to scream and wail, clawing at Xylo's ribs from the inside. Xylo set his teeth, grunting and hissing, and I noticed that his ribs were cracking and splitting.

Harker was hurting him. Damaging him. And Xylo didn't seem to care, as long as he took Dracula down with him.

Without thinking, I reached out and placed my hand on Xylo's chest. He shuddered, lifting his head to stare at my face from within the depths of his crimson hood. His smoky black eye sockets stared at me, and I watched as his teeth cracked and chipped at the force he was using to keep them clenched—at whatever Jonathan Harker was doing to him.

I closed my eyes and tapped into the Silvers.

I drew them into a single focal point, condensing them into a physical liquid over my hand. And then I pushed it into Xylo.

He gasped and I opened my eyes, still pouring the Silvers into him in hopes it would hold him together long enough for him to complete his vengeance.

I very easily could have demanded he stop hurting Harker so that I could kill the bastard myself and save Xylo's life.

But...

A man needed to learn that he had what it took to stand up to a bully, to face his demons. Taking this away from him would have taught him—subconsciously—that he wasn't strong enough to stand up for himself.

That only other people were strong enough to stand up to a bully.

Like asking your parents to yell at so-and-so's dad because their son had stolen your lunch money and poured milk on your head in the cafeteria.

Regardless that Xylo's bully was a ridiculously powerful vampire. Even though Harker wasn't the *real* Dracula, he had been bitten by the most recent Dracula, and that put him on a power level above and beyond about ninety-nine percent of bloodsuckers.

Xylo *needed* this.

And I needed my Xylo.

So, like all parents should do, I simply strengthened him, empowered him, figuratively told him he had what it took to make that bully squeal, and that all he needed was a hug from mom and a *go get 'em, tiger* attitude.

I did this subconsciously, recalling everything I had used to dominate Sanguina, and letting Xylo know that he had all these same strengths buried deep within him somewhere, even if he hadn't found them yet.

And then I fused my Silvers into his very bones much like my mother had fused them into my blood. To give him what he needed to fight his own battles. To make his own legend.

It didn't matter whether or not he remembered who he had been.

I would show him who the fuck he was *now*.

Because I was adopting this orphan.

Xylo Harker-fucking Penrose was about to make a name for himself.

Veins of Silver suddenly filled in the fissures and cracks that had been threatening to shatter his body and reduce it to bone fragments. He gasped. The veins of Silver raced through his body like the roots of a colossal tree growing in fast-forward. Soon, his teeth, ribs, and skull all showed jagged, erratic lines of Silver where they had begun to break—like he was tattooed with bolts of electricity from skull to toe.

And I watched as Xylo was reborn, a Silver and ivory hybrid, strengthened and reforged in his vaunted Eternal Metal—my life essence.

But I hadn't expected what happened to his hands. They seemed to absorb the Silvers the most, sucking them up like water poured on hot sand, until they were entirely coated in Silver magic rather than just reinforced by it like the rest of his body.

Like he'd dipped his hands into a basin of Eternal Metal.

And I watched as the black clouds of smoke in his eyes suddenly began to crackle with silver lightning from deep within the shifting black.

His spine straightened as he set his shoulders.

And then he reached inside his ribcage and grabbed the mist in one Silver claw. He ripped it out from his chest and lifted it to his eyes—the crimson mist resembling a wet towel, no longer able to vaporize and escape his grip.

Xylo began to laugh.

Harker's scream shifted to a chilling, desperate squeal.

And then Xylo fucking electrocuted him from the inside out. Black, acrid smoke billowed out from the wet, red towel that had been Jonathan Harker, until all that was left of the bully who had tormented Xylo was a scorched, smoking, handful of dried, threaded rags.

Xylo dropped them to the ground and they dispersed into a smear of dust. In the stunned silence, I heard a wretched sob. I spun—having forgotten all about Mina—to see a barely conscious, gaunt, balding corpse reaching a frail hand towards Harker's remains.

Her fingers never reached Harker before she, too, died, leaving Xylo and I alone in the empty Observatory.

Her body also broke down to dust, and the two piles did not touch.

"To dust, all things return," I murmured.

Sanguina began panting and wagging her bushy tail excitedly—the only other sound in the room.

Xylo was eerily silent, staring down at the two piles of dust with a look of satisfaction. "Fuck you, Harkers. Xylo just fucked you into oblivion."

Slow clapping drifted to us from the outer hall and we each spun to face the new threat.

33

S amael and Lily shuffled in, looking haggard and weary, covered in blood—both their own and that of their victims. Samael had no shirt and was covered in cuts and wounds. His eyes were white, but set against his bloody, muddy face, they seemed to glow.

Lily glistened with blood, leaving crimson claw prints behind her.

And they were laughing, the psychopaths.

"When you ripped that head off—with the spine still attached!" Samael crowed. "Oh, how I'd missed that. No one can debone a werewolf like you, Lily."

She smiled, supporting his weight. "Practice makes perfect," she said with a humble shrug.

Right. I cleared my throat, drawing their attention. "Godparents."

They paused, glancing about the room approvingly. Their eyes locked onto Sanguina at the same time, and their smiles were devilish. "Looks like we have cause to celebrate, *Dracula*," Samael said to me, grinning.

I frowned. "I'm not Dracula. I'm not even a vampire."

Samael shrugged. "Vampirism was a necessary effect so that Sanguina could feed and get the nourishment she required. The nourishment you can obviously provide is more...nutritional?" he said, searching for the right word. "Or else you would have already become a vampire. It's part of the bond. The trade between you two. You are Dracula, vampire or not."

I glanced down at Sanguina, considering.

"And Castle Dracula is now yours, of course. Your mother would be so proud, you little conqueror," Lily said, chuckling.

My heart skipped a beat. "What? All this is mine? A house of monsters?" I demanded, not even remotely excited. I already had Solomon's Temple, and I hadn't even begun to explore that one yet. Then again...I looked up sharply. "The Infernal Armory. The Master's Library. Those...are all mine, now?" I whispered.

Samael nodded, grinning wickedly.

"Why else would your mother have come here? Power, girl. To obtain power," Lily cooed.

I grimaced, knowing she was right.

"You did it, Callie. You bagged your first Master, and now Roland is safe. I'm glad to see you learned that Mina was the real threat. I always thought Jonathan was the one in power, but Lily caught me up to speed on the true power structures here." He smiled up at her—their differences in height were almost comical. I wondered if she had a human form, much like Samael could change from this into his demon form.

"I can't thank you enough, Callie. You brought us back together when everyone else had failed."

I sighed, waving a hand. "I was just glad to learn that you hadn't been talking about my mom."

He grunted. "I had to let you run with that assumption so that Dracula didn't find out the truth."

I nodded absently, thinking. Maybe Jonathan would have left battle plans lying about. Something to help me counter the Masters' plan to take over the world. Or maybe I would find books on the Omegabet. Sanguina could always help me learn it. She'd apparently taught Mina, after all.

I think I would prefer the book version over the lecture from Professor Fox. I glanced down at Sanguina thoughtfully, wondering if she—or even Xylo—was able to leave the property.

"YES."

Xylo jumped, almost scared back to life by the sudden telepathic shout.

Well. That meant we had time for a much-needed field trip.

Samael looked over at me. "The Masters have a meeting coming up in two months. Since you're technically Dracula, and Dracula is technically a Master...you are eligible—and likely expected—to attend."

I blinked at him. "The fuck what?"

"You're a Master, now. Whether they want you to be or not."

"The Sanguine Council also needs some guidance from Dracula. You just inherited two companies and an estate. How does royalty feel?" Lily asked.

Rather than worrying about that, I turned to Xylo, shaking my head regretfully. "I wish we could have learned who you really are, Xylo," I admitted.

Lily cleared her throat pointedly, but Xylo cut her off. "No. I don't need to know. If that changes, I will ask." He turned to me, confident Lily wasn't going to start blabbing. For her part, she studied Xylo acutely, looking very interested. "I already told you. I have a Callie. A friend. What more do I need?"

I smiled, dipping my head gratefully. The Silver coating his arms was chilling—a warning. And he hadn't had to give up his opposable thumbs to get his Eternal Metal!

I sat down, wondering exactly what I wanted to do next. I snapped my fingers and Sanguina hopped up onto my lap, walking in three full circles before settling down. "Do you have a way to make sure no one is able to enter or exit the property without my express permission?" I asked the little Beast.

Sanguina yipped softly and I felt a faint thrum to the air before she closed her eyes and went to sleep. I blinked. Okay. That had been less dramatic than I'd expected.

I looked up at Samael. "I think it's safe for us to remove your barrier now." He nodded, dry-washing his hands excitedly. He walked over and looked down at the two piles of dust that marked Mina and Jonathan Harker, then murmured something to Xylo. The Silver and ivory marbled skeleton studied him for a few moments before finally pointing at one of the two piles begrudgingly, as if not wanting to give up his prize.

Samael scooped up a pinch of the dust, chuckled, and closed his eyes, muttering under his breath. I felt a dull thump in the air that made my ears pop, and when he opened his fingers, the dust was gone. I glanced up past the telescope to see the sky above was no longer red—well, other than from the Blood Moon. The sky itself no longer had that crimson haze.

I glanced back at him. "Thank you. Now, we have a few things to catch up on, but that can wait until I return. Xylo and I are going on a field trip."

Samael and Lily shared a considering look, obviously wondering what I had to do that was more important than exploring my new real estate.

Xylo stood behind me. He might have ground the heel of his boot into the pile of dust that had once been Count Harkula, but he had such a good poker face, it was hard to tell.

I turned to Samael and Lily. "This place is still infested with monsters. I need you to whip the castle into shape and free the shifters from the Menagerie."

"Already did," they murmured in unison.

I nodded satisfactorily. "Great. Then you can make sure everyone else knows who the new boss is, and that I will address them in a few days."

They nodded, smiling excitedly at the hope that some of the residents might not take kindly to the news. "It's like a honeymoon," Lily clapped delightedly.

Right. Exactly like that.

I set Sanguina down on a nearby chair, petting her fur as she dozed on, not even waking when I moved her. I shook my head in wonder. So dangerous, and so small. "Be good while I'm gone, Sanguina. I won't be long." She made a whimpering sound, tucking her cute little nose into her belly as I scooped up a small package from the ground beside the chair.

Samael grunted, shaking his head.

"Come on, Xylo," I said, holding out my other hand. He grabbed it and I took a deep breath, opening myself up to my magic with a joyful smile. Then I Shadow Walked.

34

We Shadow Walked to a house with an immaculate front lawn, shaded and decorated with ornately cultivated trees. It was sunset, and we'd arrived beneath a tree with a thick canopy, partially leaving us in growing shadows. Steps led up to a house with a massive, wooden front door, and three bodyguards stood out front.

They looked like they'd just ruined their pants to see us appear so suddenly.

Xylo leaned closer to me. "Your eyes are still glowing."

"Oh. Right." I wasn't exactly sure how to turn that on and off, but I closed my eyes and took a stab at it, focusing on my Silvers. I felt a faint click in my mind, and opened my eyes, glancing at Xylo. He nodded approvingly, letting me know it had worked.

I turned back to the guards, and they looked even *more* troubled by this development. That this random chick just showed up on their lawn and she could just turn her glowing eyes on and off—like maybe one of them needed to go get a manager or someone higher up the food chain.

Remembering we were partially in the growing shadows, I stepped out to where they could see me more clearly and held out the bundle of clothes I had picked up from back at the Observatory—my white ninja outfit that I'd been given from the guards' boss, Xuanwu.

The guards gasped to see the familiar threads, and now that I was in the light, they put two and two together, and finally recognized who I was, and that I wasn't a threat.

"Mind if my good friend and I come inside?" I asked, smiling.

They practically fell over themselves, nodding and bowing as they hurried—backwards, since they didn't want to appear disrespectful by turning their backs on us—to open the doors and gesture us inside with open arms. I smiled at each one, meeting their eyes.

But most of them were too busy staring open-mouthed at Xylo, forgetting all about their manners. Then again, meeting a skeleton probably hadn't been covered in their lessons.

I led Xylo through the house and into the backyard area.

As I stepped out from the doorway, I smiled as the scent of apple blossoms filled the air. That mixed with the scent of sweat and dirt—since the men trained and honed their combat skills here—in a strange, complement.

And by men, I meant ninjas. Shinobi warriors. I wondered where Ryuu was. Something about him really drew me close. I wanted to know more about the mysterious leader of the ninjas. A lot more.

The sun had fully set on this side of the house—because I was pretty sure this was actually some kind of pocket dimension since the neighboring houses I had seen from the front were nowhere in sight, here. Also, in the distance, I could see a field full of apple blossom trees and mountain ranges —and there was nothing like that in downtown Kansas City.

A shirtless man was working a weapons form with a bo staff. He stopped mid movement, turning very slowly to face us. His chest was a raw red wound in the shape of a Crucifix, blackened around the edges.

From where I had burned him.

Roland Haviar, my old mentor. Ex-Shepherd turned Master Vampire.

He stared at me, dropping his staff, as his mouth worked wordlessly.

He didn't even look at or acknowledge Xylo.

"Can I borrow your keys, old man?" I asked.

He nodded very slowly, reaching into his pocket to grab the keys and extend them to me, never breaking eye contact.

I stepped forward and took them. "Thanks. Also, I need a favor, if you think you can help."

He nodded, still staring at me as if at a ghost. "Of—" he coughed, clearing his throat, wincing slightly as the flesh over his chest shifted at the sudden gesture. "Of course," he finished.

"I need you to contact the heads of the Sanguine Council. Tell them I demand a meeting—"

He cleared his throat politely but forcefully. "They are already here in Kansas City, waiting to meet with you. I told them you would be back in a few days," he said. "Alucard is with them right now. We've been taking turns keeping an eye on them," he admitted.

I blinked at him. I'd expected it to take a few days to gather them all up, giving me enough time to formulate exactly what I wanted to say to them. Because I had decided I didn't want to wait until their scheduled meeting that Samael had mentioned. I wanted to speak with them before anyone else had a chance to—any other Masters.

And I wanted them off their game, forcing them to come to me.

But it looked like my fight in the streets of Kansas City with Roland had already drawn them here like bees to honey.

Which meant I didn't have time to plan out my talk. It would be impromptu. Great. "Can you take me there?"

He nodded. "When?" he asked, finally seeming to notice Xylo. His eyes widened marginally and Xylo smiled at him.

"No time like the present."

Roland nodded. "Let me go change—"

"No. For what I have in mind, you're dressed perfectly." I glanced at Xylo and smiled. "Let's take a car. I need to make a quick stop on the way."

35

Roland had called Alucard to round up the members of the Sanguine Council—all of the oldest, most powerful vampires in the world—so that they were ready and waiting for us when we got to the hotel. We'd taken a service elevator up to the penthouse suite, which had a large meeting space. I'd told Roland that privacy would be a necessity, so none of the publicly visible meeting rooms on the main floor would work.

I glanced at the shirtless Roland. His fresh wound was impossible to miss. And Xylo...

I smiled for his sake, but silently wished the store would have had more options for me to choose from. Oh well, any port in a storm, as they say.

I opened the door and strode inside without pausing.

Roland and Xylo followed me on either side like bodyguards.

A long table stretched out before us, and dim lamps illuminated the room, revealing a dozen faces ranging from fat to thin, pale to dark, and young to old, even though they were all on the ancient side. Alucard was seated at the head of the table farthest from us, grinning excitedly at our entrance.

He took one look at Xylo and his smile froze.

Xylo stared down the dozen members of the Sanguine Council—Master Vampires who had all known that Dracula still lived and who had reported directly to him in secret, vowing not to ever let anyone else in the world know that they weren't actually the top of the food chain.

Most of the faces looked angry when they shot my way. Because they had come here to demand answers and explanations for whatever the hell had happened here, and to secretly find out why their boss, Dracula, had also been out of contact with them for so long.

Alucard stared at Xylo, shaking his head. "That is so fucked up," he murmured to himself, grimacing at what Xylo held in his hand. But in a room full of creatures with supernatural senses, everyone heard him. They all turned to stare at the skeleton. They didn't necessarily look surprised to see a living skeleton—because they had likely spent time at Castle Dracula and seen his guards.

But they definitely hadn't seen one with silver streaks and smoke for eyes. Or a skeleton clutching a red foil balloon on a string.

It said *Feel better soon!*

An obviously dead skeleton with a *Feel better soon!* balloon. Yeah. Alucard was right. That was pretty fucked up.

But the only other option had been one that said *Well done!*

And taking into consideration the fact that Xylo had spent a few years at the bottom of a well when he'd lost his first balloon, I'd decided the *Well done!* balloon would have been in even poorer taste.

But I'd promised myself that I would buy Xylo a goddamned balloon, so I wasn't about to be picky over the design. Xylo didn't seem to care at all about the words. I wasn't sure if he'd stopped smiling since I'd given it to him—other than the moment we'd walked through this door, anyway.

Because he'd put on his mean face for the vampires.

The Master Vampires also stared at Roland's chest with varying degrees of horror and disgust, letting me know he hadn't shared that with them yet. Perfect.

I clapped my hands, drawing their attention to me. "Alright, suck-heads. I wanted to remind you that you all work for Dracula."

They paled, looking uncertain how to respond to that since it was supposed to be a secret.

I rolled my eyes, pointing at Xylo. "Come on. I've been to Castle Dracula and brought back a souvenir. I'm not trying to trick you into giving up your secrets. I already *know* your secrets, because I just killed Dracula and took over his Castle. I'm your new boss, and I wanted to invite you to an Executive Retreat at Castle Dracula in three weeks. We need to do some serious team building to get through this change in management. Until that time, consider yourselves on probation and that you—and all your people—are on a blood bag-only diet. That's non-negotiable. No warnings. No forgiveness. If you do even the smallest thing that I might disapprove of, I won't even bother asking you about it. I'll just come to your city, kill you, and then bring your head to our Executive Retreat in three weeks. You kill someone, you die. You jaywalk, you die. You cut someone off in traffic, you die. You pay your employees a day late, you die. You ask a stupid question, I punch out your fangs for wasting my time. Then you die."

One of them jumped to his feet and began cursing violently, pointing a fat finger at me as his face grew purple with rage. I flung out my hand and decapitated him with a blade of air no thicker than a piece of paper and hot enough to instantly cauterize the wound.

His head thumped to the floor, still purple and still angry. The rest of the room was entirely speechless, stunned. Alucard was grinning widely, looking like he really wished he'd brought a bucket of popcorn.

Xylo calmly walked over, his helium-filled *Feel better soon!* balloon trailing after him on its string. He scooped up the head with one hand and set it down in the center of the table. He looked at it, cocking his head. Then he shifted it ever so slightly and brushed some of the man's hair out of his eyes. Then he nodded and walked back over to stand beside me.

One of the Italian vampires lifted a hand. He was old, but handsome.

I nodded at him. "Go ahead."

Xylo burst out laughing. "A head!" Even Roland grinned.

The Italian vampire did not. None of them did. He looked at me, and then the freshly decapitated vampire's head. "Ustafa...didn't speak any English," the Italian said in a careful tone. "He was demanding to know who you were and what you were saying..."

The room was deadly silent.

Well, that was unfortunate.

Then again, I didn't particularly hold any empathy for these men. They were Master Vampires of all the major cities in Europe and hadn't gotten there by being sweethearts.

I shrugged after a few minutes. "Anyone else need a translator, or is it safe to say that the example with Ustafa was understood across all languages?"

I went from person to person, staring into their eyes. Every single one of them nodded and bowed their heads—even if they didn't look very happy about it.

"Great. If you need anything prior to our retreat, Roland and Alucard are my generals." Roland and Alucard kept their surprise from their faces—especially Roland, who was on my shit list. "Now, you gentlemen have a pleasant evening, and in case anyone forgot to tell you..." I trailed off, smiling warmly at them, "welcome to Kansas City."

Then I turned to leave, motioning Xylo to follow me.

I made it a few steps before I stopped and held up a finger. I turned back around to face them. "I should probably mention that if Roland or Alucard so much as stub a toe in the next few days, I will *randomly* pick one of your heads to decorate my dining room table. Which means that even if you didn't do anything wrong, you might still be the one I pick to make an example of, so you should probably spend the rest of tonight making sure you're all on the same page."

Then I smiled at them and grabbed Xylo's hand. I Shadow Walked us directly from the room.

Balloon and all.

36

We arrived back at Xuanwu's home, and were instantly ushered in through the front doors like sorely missed family members. Xylo's balloon trailed after him, making that crinkling sound as it bumped into every doorway we stepped through.

He chuckled to himself each time, grinning like an idiot, and I couldn't help but smile. He'd finally gotten his damned balloon. We stepped out into the back garden and found quiet solitude. A few monks walked around here and there, but I saw no ninjas present. Just a quiet, peaceful evening.

Cain strolled down the path opposite us, carrying an armload of apples in his arms. He saw me and grinned widely, hurrying over. "Callie!" he crowed, dropping an apple here and there in his haste.

I smiled, wrapping him up in a tight hug. "I'm fine, you big oaf."

Cain took one look at Xylo, blinked, and then glanced up at his balloon, nodding approvingly. "Sweet balloon, man." Xylo nodded proudly but didn't really seem to care to join in our conversation. He was watching the wind shift and tug at his balloon.

Cain rounded on me. "I heard you came back, but you left before talking to me! Tell me everything."

I smiled, having missed his cheery, carefree attitude. "It was a love story, believe it or not. Like the Notebook," I said, thinking about Samael and Lily.

Then I remembered that Cain's parents were Adam and Eve, and that Adam had allegedly made some bad calls with Lilith. I clammed up.

When it was obvious that I wasn't going to elaborate, Cain turned to the skeleton with the balloon.

Xylo noticed our attention and nodded quickly, picking up on my anxiety. "Definitely a love story," he quickly said. Cain frowned dubiously, picking up on our obvious discomfort. Xylo pressed on hurriedly in an attempt to shift the subject away from the demons he apparently wasn't supposed to talk about. "We fucked Dracula and his Brides. No. *Her* brides," he said, correcting himself. "We fucked them all. Back-to-back. It was exhausting—"

"And that's quite enough out of you," I cut in, blushing furiously.

Cain burst out laughing, and Xylo lowered his eye sockets guiltily, not understanding exactly what he'd done but knowing that it had embarrassed me in front of my friend. He jolted suddenly, staring at Cain's apples.

"I like this guy. Where did you find him?" Cain asked me, still chuckling.

I was frowning at Xylo, though, watching as he narrowed his eye-sockets. If I hadn't known any better, I would have sworn Cain had just pissed Xylo right the hell off.

Xylo slowly lifted his head, glaring at Cain but speaking to me. "Who is this creature?" he asked in a dry, frigid tone.

Cain's smile withered away, and he dropped his apples, squaring his shoulders instinctively at Xylo's tone, let alone his words. "*Creature?* Who the fuck are *you* to call *me* a creature?"

"You dropped your apples," Xylo said, making it sound like a threat.

Cain shrugged. "I found them on the ground anyway. I'll pick them back up in a minute. Right after we work out your attitude problem."

I interrupted, not understanding the sudden tension. "Cain is my brother. He watches my back and keeps me safe. Take it easy, Xylo."

But Xylo didn't take it easy. "You mean like how I kept you safe in Castle Dracula? If he is your brother, shouldn't he have been there to keep you safe?" He leveled Cain with an open, judgmental glare. "As her brother, are you not your sister's keeper?"

Cain and I both froze. Ho boy. That was a very dangerous topic to bring up with Cain.

"Alright, boys. Let's table this for later. Cain, pick up your apples and take a walk. We've had a rough couple of days. I'll tell you all about it later."

Cain grunted, looking like he wanted more than anything to clock Xylo in the jaw. He bent over to pick up an apple. "Fine—"

Xylo chose that moment to lift his hand up to my face, as if telling me to shut my mouth.

"Hey!" Cain suddenly snarled, taking an aggressive step forward. "Don't you *dare* tell her to be quiet!"

Xylo didn't react. "High five," he told me through clenched teeth.

My eyes widened in alarm, and I shook my head anxiously. "I am *not* giving you a high five for this, Xylo. You'll kill him. Cain, you *really* need to go take a walk. Right the fuck now."

Xylo ground his teeth harder, his embers and sparks flaring uncontrollably. "I can control it," he lied. "Trust me."

And in my mind, there was a frantic desperation in his request. He was practically quivering with need. I thought about it, but still hesitated with his wildly flaring embers and sparks—that had really freaked Cain the hell out. Cain looked about as baffled as one could be with two people talking over his head about a nuclear high five and one of them spitting sparks from his joints.

"Please, Callie," Xylo rasped, letting go of his balloon and not even seeming to notice.

And that right there told me that this wasn't some simple pissing contest. Something was happening. Something I couldn't comprehend.

Still, I wasn't going to let Cain die for it. I took a quick step back, holding up my hands for both of them to calm down. Xylo gritted his teeth and lowered his hand, so I turned to Cain. "You *really* need to get out of here while I figure this—"

I was interrupted by a sudden flare of sparks and a faint slap of warm ivory on my sweating palm as Xylo flung his freaking hand at my outstretched hand for a long-distance high five.

Oh shit.

My heart stopped and I opened my mouth to shout a warning for Cain to fucking run for his life.

But I was too late.

A bolt of black lightning tore down from the night sky in a concussive explosion that sprayed me—and my open mouth—with sweet, pulpy gore.

I gagged, spitting it out as I tried to blink away the stars in my vision from the proximity of the blast.

Cain. I'd just tasted Cain's guts. I instantly gagged, wondering how the hell I was still alive.

Then I heard cursing. "You crazy son of a bitch! What the *fuck* was that?!" Cain roared.

"A high five, bitch," Xylo muttered.

"Little overkill, man. Now I'm covered in applesauce!" Cain muttered, disgustedly. "Who the hell high fives like that?"

Applesauce. Not Cain's guts.

I wiped heaps of apple pulp from my eyes to find Cain glaring at Xylo. I rounded on the skeleton, too. "You could have killed him!" I snapped.

He shook his head adamantly. "I know how to control it. The reason I destroyed the Infernal Armory was because I was angry at it—for denying me the Eternal Metal."

I harrumphed. "Hell of a way to test your theory, Xylo. You still could have killed him by accident."

"He deserves no less," Xylo said definitively.

I stopped short, as did Cain.

"What are you talking about, Xylo?" I asked, staring at him incredulously.

He was glaring at the apples on the ground, now. "You found these on the ground, you said," Xylo said, as if he'd discovered some great clue in the scattering of apples that Cain had dropped.

Cain grunted. "So? I was trying to be nice. Callie likes her juice boxes, but they don't have juice boxes here, so I was going to make her some fresh juice," he mumbled, avoiding eye contact with me as if embarrassed.

I smiled crookedly. That...was incredibly sweet.

"Perhaps she deserves better than fruit gathered from the ground," Xylo growled through clenched teeth.

Cain opened his mouth to argue and then cut short without actually saying anything. He remained like that for a few seconds, cocking his head as if at a bizarre thought.

"Xylo, you lost your balloon. Maybe you should go find it," I said, watching as the two of them stared at each other intensely.

"I'll get another one," he said distractedly. Before I could recover from my shock of him not caring about his balloon, he held out a hand towards Cain. "Give it to me. Now."

I had absolutely no idea what the hell was going on, but I realized we now had an audience. Xuanwu, the massive Black Tortoise stood a safe distance away, murmuring under his breath.

Roland stood beside him, eyes wide.

Alucard...

He'd found some peanuts and was tossing them back like it was the bottom of the ninth inning with bases loaded in the last game of the World Series—Royals versus Cardinals.

I didn't dare step away from Xylo and Cain, though.

Cain reached to his belt and slowly withdrew the long bone dagger he always had on his person. He never broke eye contact with Xylo, his face haggard and incredulous.

Xylo nodded back ever so slightly and took a step forward, holding out his Silver hand. "Yes, brothermine. Yes."

I gasped.

Cain held out his dagger, his hand shaking. And the dagger immediately began to glow with embers and sparks. Xylo touched it and the bone dagger flared brighter, almost too bright to stare at.

Cain crashed to his knees. "Abel," he whispered, tears streaming down his face.

"Yes, brother. Yes," Xylo said calmly.

Oh shit. The dagger...it was the blade Cain had used to kill his brother.

Abel, not Xylo. Motherfucking *Abel*. Cain's brother.

The brother he had murdered so long ago.

Family reunions were historically very dangerous events.

But this one was about to go down in the record books.

✣ 37 ✣

I jumped between them before I consciously considered the dangers. "What the hell, Xylo? I thought you couldn't remember anything?" I snapped, gripping him by the shoulders before he did something stupid with the bone dagger.

The bone dagger Cain had used to kill him so long ago.

Xylo looked back at me calmly, the shadows in his eyes shifting back and forth. "I didn't. Not until I saw the apples. Then the dagger tucked into his belt. It all came crashing back to me."

I stared back at him, shaking my head. "Apples?" I asked, not understanding how that had triggered his memory.

Cain spoke up from behind me. "When we were supposed to give a gift to God, Abel offered up the firstborn of his flock of sheep. He was a shepherd," he explained, his throat raw.

Shepherd...

That's what Lily had meant. Not *Vatican* Shepherd. But *literally*, a shepherd.

Cain continued. "I collected fruit already fallen from the trees, feeling lazy that day. God challenged me on the quality of my offering, rightly so. He accepted the sheep over my fruit, and I..."

"Killed me, Cain. You *killed* me. Your little brother!"

Cain nodded numbly. "Yes," he admitted without attempting to justify it. He stared up at Abel, the shame, disbelief, and guilt painted all over his cheeks in his tears.

I shook Xylo. "I'm not justifying what he did, Xylo, but he's *changed*. I helped him get past it. The guilt was crushing him from the inside. For thousands of years, he kept everyone at a distance, never trusting himself. I broke through that and convinced him to look at our relationship as a second chance at being a good brother."

"That doesn't change what I did, Callie," Cain whispered, his voice shaking. "My brother has every right. I submit. I think I might even welcome it, if it weren't for being concerned about *you*. I don't want to leave you alone."

Xylo glared down at him, gripping the dagger tightly. "She will never be alone, brother. She has *me*, now."

Cain nodded. "Then I am content. Show me peace. Please."

I cut in. "Well, I am *not* content. I beg you, Xylo, just hold off on your judgment. See for yourself if he has changed. Observe him. You are both my family, now, and I think we've all had enough of broken families. Two wrongs don't make a right."

Xylo slowly turned to look at me. "He is guilty. He killed me, his own brother. For no other reason than jealousy." I nodded. "He was supposed to watch out for me. He was his brother's keeper. He chose to become his brother's killer. And for that, I was somehow brought to serve at Castle Dracula like some prized pony, living a life of shame and guilt without even knowing why. I was bullied, laughed at, mocked, ridiculed. They all knew who I was. They had to," he whispered, his voice pained and furious.

Jesus. He...was right. Knowing Dracula, that was probably exactly how it had happened.

I grimaced, ignoring the tears misting across my vision. "Even still. He's been paying for that crime for thousands of years. He didn't know about Castle Dracula. You can't pin those crimes on him." Xylo lowered his gaze, nodding stiffly in acceptance. "I wouldn't have accepted him as my brother if I thought he was still the man you remember him as. He made a terrible, terrible mistake, but he has changed. Give him a chance."

Cain interrupted me. "No."

We both turned to look at him. His face was no longer torn, but relaxed and content.

"I will only agree to that if you agree to give Abel the chance to make the final decision on his own. No interfering. Give him a time limit, but after that you must let him choose as he wishes. I *demand* this, Callie. I want Abel to do as *he* needs. Not to simply agree to your plea. I accept death—now or later. But that is for him to decide."

I wanted to argue, but...

I couldn't. I had the unique perspective of having helped both men—no, brothers—through their personal torments. But each of them only knew their side of the story. And as much as I wanted to be their sister in this...

I wasn't. Maybe a step-sister.

But this was blood. Quite literally.

I finally nodded. "Okay. Can you give him two weeks to see what I see in him? That's all I ask." And I took a deep breath before stepping back, letting the two brothers face each other unobstructed, one of them armed, the other ready and willing to die.

I looked down at Cain and he smiled back at me, not a flicker of fear on his face. In fact, I'd never seen a bigger smile on his face. "Thank you, Callie," he whispered, his voice cracking. "No matter how this turns out, this is the greatest gift I've ever been given. To see Abel again. To have the chance to apologize to him, even if he doesn't want to hear it." He shook his head wondrously. "Only you, Callie. Only fucking *you* could pull something like this off." More tears poured down his cheeks and he laughed, a great, light-hearted sound. "Thank you," he finally whispered.

Xylo—Abel—studied the two of us thoughtfully, still gripping the dagger. But he no longer looked angry. He looked...pensive.

A small part of me realized that maybe Cain had something to teach Abel. That Cain's ridiculously cheerful demeanor was the exact thing Abel needed to learn himself. That the two actually needed each other. If only they could come to learn that.

Cain needed, wanted, forgiveness. He wanted to prove he could look after his brother. Hell, he had sacrificed his life for me in order to prove just that in the Doors. It had been part of the test to gain entrance to Solomon's Temple.

And Abel needed to learn happiness. How to escape his depression and the self-doubt heaped upon him by pseudo-Dracula—Jonathan Harker.

I nodded. "Remember that you aren't just each other's brothers. You are both *my* brothers now, too. And I am my brothers' keeper."

They both stiffened. I turned away, hiding my tears.

So sue me. If I had to use a little guilt to get the two idiot men to do what they needed to do, so be it. It was a woman's prerogative—to save idiot, stubborn, mule-headed men from killing each other.

I stumbled over to Xuanwu, not even bothering to say hello. "I need a drink," I muttered, ignoring Cain and Abel talking to each other behind me.

He smiled knowingly. "I have sake."

Alucard beamed and Roland nodded.

"Perfect. You better have a lot."

38

I stood in the pre-dawn chill, shivering, soaked, and trying to follow Xuanwu's strange, glacially slow, martial arts form. Tai Chi.

I felt like each individual brain cell needed its own dose of ibuprofen.

Xuanwu held more of a naturalistic philosophy and had woken me up with a pitcher of ice-water to the face.

I'd lurched out of bed with a shout—still feeling drunk—tripped over a table and then tore entirely through a rice-partition wall to fall head-first into the koi pond.

I'd never heard anyone laugh as hard as Xuanwu had. After I lunged out of the water, gasping for air, of course.

At least the pond had been warmer than the pitcher of ice-water.

After finishing the required martial arts training, I'd gone searching for Cain and Abel, only to find they had left Xuanwu's house, not telling anyone where they were going.

So I was in a foul mood when I decided to visit Solomon's Temple. Richard had taken one look at me, grunted, and had quickly brewed an entire pot of coffee as if by magic. Solomon soon joined us, healthy and hale, and I wrapped him up in a tight hug, laughing with joy to see his black veins entirely gone. Qinglong had been able to heal him without issue and was still shacking up in my mother's laboratory.

I spent the better part of an hour catching them up on my journey to Castle Dracula, pointedly avoiding the topic of Cain and Abel. I told them about Xylo instead. I showed them my mother's shotguns and they'd gasped in disbelief, having thought they'd been long lost or destroyed. I gave them a few moments to process my story and fondle the shotguns and then I asked them a question.

"Mind if I move some of my things here?" I asked. "Roland made some calls to my old landlord and cleared up the confusion by explaining that I hadn't actually died. When I didn't pay my HOA dues or respond to their demand letters, their standard procedure was to evict, even if I owned the place. But I'm thinking about selling it, if you have room here, of course."

Solomon and Richard both smiled eagerly. "Of course, Callie. This place could use a few more souls to keep it lively."

"You know, it's funny you should say that," I said casually. "How good is the security here?" I asked lamely.

His smile slowly slipped. "The best, of course. You know that."

They were both frowning at me.

"And no one from the Armory can just walk in here, right?" I asked.

Solomon nodded slowly. "We can ward off exterior doors to pocket dimensions. It's where your mother stored extra demons when her ring was getting full. What...exactly are you concerned about, Callie?" he asked, sounding nervous.

I let out a breath and asked them my real question.

Solomon choked on his coffee, jumping to his feet. "WHAT?!"

Richard had dropped one of the shotguns to stare at me, unable to even speak.

"Is it possible?" I repeated, ignoring their reactions.

Solomon cursed wildly for a few moments, arguing both sides of my question as if debating himself. I let him tire himself out before repeating my question for a third time.

He finally sat back down with a huff. "Yes," he finally admitted. "As much as I want to say no, this is your home, and we can keep it safe. It's just..." he trailed off, already having shouted out every reason he was both for and against it.

"It has a whole library," I said casually. "Things even you probably haven't seen before."

He glanced up sharply, and I gave him a slow nod. I'd held that part back as a bargaining chip, knowing this would be a hard sell.

"And we're just going to put it where? In the fucking back yard?" Richard blurted, shaking his head incredulously.

I shrugged. "It's like the Armory, right? We can move it here to restrict access for everyone else as a safety precaution. I just want to know it's safe. It's fucking huge, guys. Huge."

"And it has a library," Solomon repeated, scratching at his beard.

I nodded. "With ninja baboons," I added.

He arched a brow, mouthing *ninja baboons* a few times. "Well, we need to do it right. Let me do a little research, but I don't see any reason why you can't move Castle Dracula here," he finally said with a tired sigh.

Richard made his way over to a nearby liquor cabinet and began drinking straight from the bottle. I smiled at him. "Tons of monsters live there. We can go hunting," I said casually.

He lowered the bottle, looking up at me, his curiosity piqued. And as simple as that, I knew I had him.

Castle Dracula was going to be relocated.

"Is that a lily pad in your hair?" Richard asked curiously.

I scowled. "Yeah. I think I need a shower. It's been that kind of morning."

As Richard led me to the showers and Solomon took off to one of his libraries to research for the Castle Dracula move, I tried to think of anything else I could do to keep my mind off Cain and Abel. I knew I needed to visit Pandora to deliver the piece of Excalibur to the new King Arthur—whoever that was—but I didn't feel up to running into Nate and crew—the St. Lunatics, as I'd considered naming them. Not with lily pads in my hair—and hungover.

Claire would also be furious that I hadn't checked in on her, but I decided that I needed some real sleep after my shower. It had only been... how long had it been since I'd slept?

I counted back and grew very uncomfortable. Other than last night—when I'd passed out drunk—I hadn't slept in about a week or so. And I didn't feel even remotely sleepy or delirious.

I thought of Xylo and my new toughened skin. I also hadn't eaten in about the same length of time. I shuddered, wondering just how much I didn't know about my new bond with Xylo.

Abel.

And then my mind was back in that storm of emotions.

So I very pointedly focused on each step as Richard led me to the show-ers, studiously keeping my thoughts on the steps required for bathing.

Maybe I really did need some sleep.

Even if I didn't feel like it.

39

I sat in the Feast Hall of Castle Dracula with Claire. Even having visited the place twice in the past two weeks, she was still creeped out by everything. Especially the bevy of skeleton guards who constantly followed us around.

I'd called Nate Temple and set up a time to deliver Excalibur to him next week and had caught up on any other number of little things that had sat on my to-do list while I'd been traipsing about castles and other dimensions.

Sanguina sat curled up on a chair, dozing as she usually did. She hadn't minded the move to Solomon's Temple, but I hadn't introduced her to anyone but Claire yet. I knew Solomon would have a million questions for her, so hadn't let him meet her either. Even though he was technically her new landlord.

I sat at the piano, practicing. I had no experience with pianos, but everyone knew one song.

It took me a few tries—and plenty of heckles from Claire—to nail it, but I was soon playing it well enough to recognize. Kind of.

A voice cleared behind me and I turned to see Cain and Xylo standing at the other end of the room. Claire leaned forward nervously, knowing that this was about to be terrible or amazing.

Cain smirked at me. "Pretty sure you're supposed to play dark, haunting, creepy, foreboding music," he teased, eyeing the skeletons curiously.

Xylo stood motionless.

"I don't know any Nickelback," I said, shrugging.

Cain narrowed his eyes. "Ha." Cain was a huge Nickelback fan and didn't understand my fascination with lyrical rap artists. "Chopsticks is not very Dracula chic," he grumbled.

I shrugged anxiously, staring at the two of them. Waiting.

Xylo let out a breath and averted his gaze. "I've made my decision."

My heart thundered in my chest, but I kept my voice steady. "Oh?"

And without warning, Xylo turned and stabbed Cain in the chest.

I jumped to my feet, shouting as Cain fell to the floor, grunting and rolling back and forth, not dead, but wounded.

"What the living hell?" Claire demanded before exploding into her polar bear form. The skeleton army instantly crouched, ready to defend me from Xylo.

I held up my hands for everyone to calm down, my heart lurching in my chest. Maybe I could still save him. Maybe it wasn't fatal. Maybe Xylo had chosen some middle ground—to stab his brother but not kill him.

Cain continued to roll back and forth, moaning excessively, and I suddenly narrowed my eyes. No. They wouldn't dare...

"You..."

Xylo looked up at me sheepishly. "Prank?" he said weakly. "Cain told me you like pranks..." he explained, looking decidedly uncertain all of a sudden. Maybe it was the unbridled fury on my face. He must be learning cues that most men took decades to decipher.

Cain made a strange, choking noise, and I turned to fix Xylo to the wall with my glare. "Give me your dagger. I've changed my mind. I'm going to kill him for you."

Cain roared with laughter, jumping back to his feet hurriedly. "Not if you can't catch me!" he roared, jumping on top of the table.

Claire made a strange chuffing sound and I turned to find her seated on her haunches, looking like she was laughing.

I rounded back on Cain. "This is *not* funny, guys."

Cain hooted. "I'm trying to teach him how to laugh. To have fun. To be happy! You grumpy old woman!"

"That's it. You're both dead." And I began storming towards them.

Cain cackled like a madman.

"Run that way, Cain!" Xylo shouted, laughing himself. And then he ran the opposite direction forcing me to make a choice as my two brothers split up, racing for opposite escapes. I turned to Claire, realizing I was smiling. "Which one do you want?" I asked.

She glanced at both doors as they slammed shut, the sounds of hysterical laughter echoing from the walls on the other side. Then she began running after Xylo.

Sanguina lifted her head to look at me with her eyeless stare.

"DO YOU WANT ME TO KILL THEM FOR YOU?" she asked tiredly.

I shook my head, making sure the skeleton death squad also got the message. "No. We're just playing a game. It's probably safest if you don't join in on this one."

"OKAY. I'LL BE HERE WHEN YOUR'E FINISHED. WE CAN CONTINUE OUR STUDIES."

I nodded, suppressing a shudder. Studying the Omegabet had been... enlightening. And horrifying. "Sounds great."

Then I grinned, turning to run after Cain. "Ready or not, here I come!" I shouted at him, following the sounds of his laughter as he ran through the halls of the Castle Keep.

And a single tear rolled down my cheeks to hear laughter in this place.

To hear Xylo laughing in the place that had birthed his life of torment.

Although a terrible prank...

We were all kind of terrible people. Had all survived terrible things.

I still decided that I was going to dunk Cain in the Lake of Everlasting Woe.

Even if he had saved Xylo's life.

My brothers and sister laughed as we played for the first time in too long, and I knew that—for this singular moment, at least—all would be well.

Storms were coming soon. The seasons were changing. But not right now.

To every thing there is a season, and a time to every purpose under the heaven: a time to be born, a time to die; a time to plant, and a time to pluck up that which is planted; A time to kill, and a time to heal; a time to break down, and a time to build up; a time to weep, and a time to laugh; a time to mourn, and a time to dance; a time to cast away stones, and a time to gather stones together; a time to embrace, and a time to refrain from embracing; a time to get, and a time to lose; a time to keep, and a time to cast away; a time to rend, and a time to sew; a time to keep silence, and a time to speak; a time to love, and a time to hate; a time of war, and a time of peace.

Right now, it was a time for laughter.

A time for living.

A time for loving like only brothers and sisters could.

And that was good enough for me.

DON'T FORGET! VIP's get early access to all sorts of Temple-Verse goodies, including signed copies, private giveaways, and advance notice of future projects. AND A FREE NOVELLA! Click the image or join here:
www.shaynesilvers.com/l/219800

Callie returns in 2020... Subscribe to my NEWSLETTER to receive an email when it's live!

*Turn the page to read a sample of **OBSIDIAN SON** - The Nate Temple Series Book 1 - or **BUY ONLINE**. Nate Temple is a billionaire wizard from St. Louis. He rides a bloodthirsty unicorn and drinks with the Four Horsemen. He even cow-tipped the Minotaur. Once...*

(Note: Nate's books 1-6 happen prior to UNCHAINED, but they crossover from then on, the two series taking place in the same universe but also able to standalone if you prefer)

Full chronology of all books in the TempleVerse shown on the 'BOOKS BY SHAYNE SILVERS' page.

TRY: OBSIDIAN SON (NATE TEMPLE #1)

There was no room for emotion in a hate crime. I had to be cold. Heartless. This was just another victim. Nothing more. No face, no name.

Frosted blades of grass crunched under my feet, sounding to my ears like the symbolic glass that one would shatter under a napkin at a Jewish wedding. The noise would have threatened to give away my stealthy advance as I stalked through the moonlit field, but I was no novice and had planned accordingly. Being a wizard, I was able to muffle all sensory evidence with a fine cloud of magic—no sounds, and no smells. Nifty. But if I made the spell much stronger, the anomaly would be too obvious to my prey.

I knew the consequences for my dark deed tonight. If caught, jail time or possibly even a gruesome, painful death. But if I succeeded, the look of fear and surprise in my victim's eyes before his world collapsed around him, it was well worth the risk. I simply couldn't help myself; I had to take him down.

I knew the cops had been keeping tabs on my car, but I was confident that they hadn't followed me. I hadn't seen a tail on my way here but seeing as how they frowned on this kind of thing, I had taken a circuitous route just in case. I was safe. I hoped.

Then my phone chirped at me as I received a text.

I practically jumped out of my skin, hissing instinctively. "Motherf—" I cut off abruptly, remembering the whole stealth aspect of my mission. I was off to a stellar start. I had forgotten to silence the damned phone. *Stupid, stupid, stupid!*

My heart felt like it was on the verge of exploding inside my chest with such thunderous violence that I briefly envisioned a mystifying Rorschach blood-blot that would have made coroners and psychologists drool.

My body remained tense as I swept my gaze over the field, fearing that I had been made. Precious seconds ticked by without any change in my surroundings, and my breathing finally began to slow as my pulse returned to normal. Hopefully, my magic had muted the phone and my resulting outburst. I glanced down at the phone to scan the text and then typed back a quick and angry response before I switched the cursed device to vibrate.

Now, where were we?

I continued on, the lining of my coat constricting my breathing. Or maybe it was because I was leaning forward in anticipation. *Breathe*, I chided myself. *He doesn't know you're here*. All this risk for a book. It had better be worth it.

I'm taller than most, and not abnormally handsome, but I knew how to play the genetic cards I had been dealt. I had shaggy, dirty blonde hair—leaning more towards brown with each passing year—and my frame was thick with well-earned muscle, yet I was still lean. I had once been told that my eyes were like twin emeralds pitted against the golden-brown tufts of my hair—a face like a jewelry box. Of course, that was two bottles of wine into a date, so I could have been a little foggy on her quote. Still, I liked to imagine that was how everyone saw me.

But tonight, all that was masked by magic.

I grinned broadly as the outline of the hairy hulk finally came into view. He was blessedly alone—no nearby sentries to give me away. That was always a risk when performing this ancient rite-of-passage. I tried to keep the grin on my face from dissolving into a maniacal cackle.

My skin danced with energy, both natural and unnatural, as I manipulated the threads of magic floating all around me. My victim stood just ahead, oblivious to the world of hurt that I was about to unleash. Even with his millennia of experience, he didn't stand a chance. I had done this so many times that the routine of it was my only enemy. I lost count of how many times I had been told not to do it again; those who knew declared it *cruel, evil, and sadistic*. But what fun wasn't? Regardless, that wasn't enough to stop me from doing it again. And again. And again.

It was an addiction.

The pungent smell of manure filled the air, latching onto my nostril hairs. I took another step, trying to calm my racing pulse. A glint of gold reflected in the silver moonlight, but my victim remained motionless, hopefully unaware or all was lost. I wouldn't make it out alive if he knew I was here. Timing was everything.

I carefully took the last two steps, a lifetime between each, watching the legendary monster's ears, anxious and terrified that I would catch even so much as a twitch in my direction. Seeing nothing, a fierce grin split my unshaven cheeks. My spell had worked! I raised my palms an inch away from their target, firmly planted my feet, and squared my shoulders. I took one silent, calming breath, and then heaved forward with every ounce of physical strength I could muster. As well as a teensy-weensy boost of magic. Enough to goose him good.

"*MOOO!!!*" The sound tore through the cool October night like an unstoppable freight train. *Thud-splat*! The beast collapsed sideways onto the frosted grass; straight into a steaming patty of cow shit, cow dung, or, if you really wanted to church it up, a Meadow Muffin. But to me, shit is, and always will be, shit.

Cow tipping. It doesn't get any better than that in Missouri.

Especially when you're tipping the *Minotaur*. Capital M. I'd tipped plenty of ordinary cows before, but never the legendary variety.

Razor-blade hooves tore at the frozen earth as the beast struggled to stand, his grunts of rage vibrating the air. I raised my arms triumphantly. "Boo-yah! Temple 1, Minotaur 0!" I crowed. Then I very bravely prepared to protect myself. Some people just couldn't take a joke. *Cruel, evil,* and *sadistic* cow tipping may be, but by hell, it was a *rush*. The legendary beast turned his gaze on me after gaining his feet, eyes ablaze as his body...*shifted* from his bull disguise into his notorious, well-known bipedal form. He unfolded to his full height on two tree trunk-thick legs, his hooves having magically transformed into heavily booted feet. The thick, gold ring dangling from his snotty snout quivered as the Minotaur panted, and his dense, corded muscles contracted over his now human-like chest. As I stared up into those brown eyes, I actually felt sorry...for, well, myself.

"I have killed greater men than you for lesser offense," he growled.

His voice sounded like an angry James Earl Jones—like Mufasa talking to Scar.

"You have shit on your shoulder, Asterion." I ignited a roiling ball of fire in my palm in order to see his eyes more clearly. By no means was it a defensive gesture on my part. It was just dark. Under the weight of his glare, I somehow managed to keep my face composed, even though my fraudulent, self-denial had curled up into the fetal position and started whimpering. I hoped using a form of his ancient name would give me brownie points. Or maybe just not-worthy-of-killing points.

The beast grunted, eyes tightening, and I sensed the barest hesitation. "Nate Temple...your name would look splendid on my already long list of slain idiots." Asterion took a threatening step forward, and I thrust out my palm in warning, my roiling flame blue now.

"You lost fair and square, Asterion. Yield or perish." The beast's shoulders sagged slightly. Then he finally nodded to himself in resignation, appraising me with the scrutiny of a worthy adversary. "Your time comes, Temple, but I will grant you this. You've got a pair of stones on you to rival Hercules."

I reflexively glanced in the direction of the myth's own crown jewels before jerking my gaze away. Some things you simply couldn't un-see. "Well, I won't be needing a wheelbarrow any time soon, but overcompensating today keeps future lower-back pain away."

The Minotaur blinked once, and then he bellowed out a deep, contagious, snorting laughter. Realizing I wasn't about to become a murder statistic, I couldn't help but join in. It felt good. It had been a while since I had allowed myself to experience genuine laughter.

In the harsh moonlight, his bulk was even more intimidating as he towered head and shoulders above me. This was the beast that had fed upon human sacrifices for countless years while imprisoned in Daedalus' Labyrinth in Greece. And all that protein had not gone to waste, forming a heavily woven musculature over the beast's body that made even Mr. Olympia look puny.

From the neck up, he was now entirely bull, but the rest of his body more closely resembled a thickly furred man. But, as shown moments ago, he could adapt his form to his environment, never appearing fully human, but able to make his entire form appear as a bull when necessary. For instance, how he had looked just before I tipped him. Maybe he had been scouting the field for heifers before I had so efficiently killed the mood.

His bull face was also covered in thick, coarse hair—he even sported a long, wavy beard of sorts, and his eyes were the deepest brown I had ever seen. Cow-shit brown. His snout jutted out, emphasizing the golden ring dangling from his glistening nostrils, and both glinted in the luminous glow of the moon. The metal was at least an inch thick and etched with runes of a language long forgotten. Wide, aged ivory horns sprouted from each temple, long enough to skewer a wizard with little effort. He was nude except for a massive beaded necklace and a pair of worn leather boots that were big enough to stomp a size twenty-five imprint in my face if he felt so inclined.

I hoped our blossoming friendship wouldn't end that way. I really did.

Because friends didn't let friends wear boots naked...

Get your copy of **OBSIDIAN SON** *online today!*
http://www.shaynesilvers.com/l/38474

Turn the page to read a sample of **WHISKEY GINGER** *- Phantom Queen Diaries Book 1, or* **BUY ONLINE**. *Quinn MacKenna is a black magic arms dealer in Boston. She likes to fight monsters almost as much as she likes to drink.*

TRY: WHISKEY GINGER (PHANTOM QUEEN DIARIES BOOK 1)

The pasty guitarist hunched forward, thrust a rolled-up wad of paper deep into one nostril, and snorted a line of blood crystals—frozen hemoglobin that I'd smuggled over in a refrigerated canister—with the uncanny grace of a drug addict. He sat back, fangs gleaming, and pawed at his nose. "That's some bodacious shit. Hey, bros," he said, glancing at his fellow band members, "come hit this shit before it melts."

He fetched one of the backstage passes hanging nearby, pried the plastic badge from its lanyard, and used it to split up the crystals, murmuring something in an accent that reminded me of California. Not *the* California, but you know, Cali-foh-nia—the land of beaches, babes, and bros. I retrieved a toothpick from my pocket and punched it through its thin wrapper. "So," I asked no one in particular, "now that ye have the product, who's payin'?"

Another band member stepped out of the shadows to my left, and I don't mean that figuratively, either—the fucker literally stepped out of the shadows. I scowled at him, but hid my surprise, nonchalantly rolling the toothpick from one side of my mouth to the other.

The rest of the band gathered around the dressing room table, following the guitarist's lead by preparing their own snorting utensils—tattered magazine covers, mostly. Typically, you'd do this sort of thing with a dollar-bill, maybe even a Benjamin if you were flush. But fangers like this lot couldn't touch cash directly—in God We Trust and all that. Of course, I didn't really understand why sucking blood the old-fashioned way had suddenly gone out of style. More of a rush, maybe?

"It lasts longer," the vampire next to me explained, catching my mildly curious expression. "It's especially good for shows and stuff. Makes us look, like, less—"

"Creepy?" I offered, my Irish brogue lilting just enough to make it a question.

"Pale," he finished, frowning.

I shrugged. "Listen, I've got places to be," I said, holding out my hand.

"I'm sure you do," he replied, smiling. "Tell you what, why don't you, like, hang around for a bit? Once that wears off," he dipped his head toward the bloody powder smeared across the table's surface, "we may need a pick-me-up." He rested his hand on my arm and our gazes locked.

I blinked, realized what he was trying to pull, and rolled my eyes. His widened in surprise, then shock as I yanked out my toothpick and shoved it through his hand.

"Motherfuck—"

"I want what we agreed on," I declared. "Now. No tricks."

The rest of the band saw what happened and rose faster than I could blink. They circled me, their grins feral...they might have even seemed intimidating if it weren't for the fact that they each had a case of the sniffles —I had to work extra hard not to think about what it felt like to have someone else's blood dripping down my nasal cavity.

I held up a hand.

"Can I ask ye gentlemen a question before we get started?" I asked. "Do ye even *have* what I asked for?"

Two of the band members exchanged looks and shrugged. The guitarist, however, glanced back towards the dressing room, where a brown paper bag sat next to a case full of makeup. He caught me looking and bared his teeth, his fangs stretching until it looked like it would be uncomfortable for him to close his mouth without piercing his own lip.

"Follow-up question," I said, eyeing the vampire I'd stabbed as he gingerly withdrew the toothpick from his hand and flung it across the room with a snarl. "Do ye do each other's make-up? Since, ye know, ye can't use mirrors?"

I was genuinely curious.

The guitarist grunted. "Mike, we have to go on soon."

"Wait a minute. Mike?" I turned to the snarling vampire with a frown. "What happened to *The Vampire Prospero*?" I glanced at the numerous fliers in the dressing room, most of which depicted the band members wading through blood, with Mike in the lead, each one titled *The Vampire Prospero* in *Rocky Horror Picture Show* font. Come to think of it...Mike did look a little like Tim Curry in all that leather and lace.

I was about to comment on the resemblance when Mike spoke up, "Alright, change of plans, bros. We're gonna drain this bitch before the show. We'll look totally—"

"Creepy?" I offered, again.

"Kill her."

Get the full book ONLINE! http://www.shaynesilvers.com/l/206897

MAKE A DIFFERENCE

Reviews are the most powerful tools in my arsenal when it comes to getting attention for my books. Much as I'd like to, I don't have the financial muscle of a New York publisher.

But I do have something much more powerful and effective than that, and it's something that those publishers would kill to get their hands on.

A committed and loyal bunch of readers.

Honest reviews of my books help bring them to the attention of other readers.

If you've enjoyed this book, I would be very grateful if you could spend just five minutes leaving a review (it can be as short as you like) on my book's Amazon page.

Thank you very much in advance.

ACKNOWLEDGMENTS

First, I would like to thank my beta-readers, TEAM TEMPLE, those individuals who spent hours of their time to read, and re-re-read the Temple-Verse stories. Your dark, twisted, cunning sense of humor makes me feel right at home...

I would also like to thank you, the reader. I hope you enjoyed reading *GODLESS* as much as I enjoyed writing it. Be sure to check out the two crossover series in the TempleVerse: **The Nate Temple Series** and the **Phantom Queen Diaries**.

And last, but definitely not least, I thank my wife, Lexy. Without your support, none of this would have been possible.

ABOUT SHAYNE SILVERS

Shayne is a man of mystery and power, whose power is exceeded only by his mystery...

He currently writes the Amazon Bestselling **Nate Temple** Series, which features a foul-mouthed wizard from St. Louis. He rides a bloodthirsty unicorn, drinks with Achilles, and is pals with the Four Horsemen.

He also writes the Amazon Bestselling **Feathers and Fire** Series—a second series in the TempleVerse. The story follows a rookie spell-slinger named Callie Penrose who works for the Vatican in Kansas City. Her problem? Hell seems to know more about her past than she does.

He coauthors **The Phantom Queen Diaries**—a third series set in The TempleVerse—with Cameron O'Connell. The story follows Quinn MacKenna, a mouthy black magic arms dealer in Boston. All she wants? A round-trip ticket to the Fae realm...and maybe a drink on the house.

He also writes the **Shade of Devil Series**, which tells the story of Sorin Ambrogio—the world's FIRST vampire. He was put into a magical slumber by a Native American Medicine Man when the Americas were first discovered by Europeans. Sorin wakes up after five-hundred years to learn that his protege, Dracula, stole his reputation and that no one has ever even heard of Sorin Ambrogio. The streets of New York City will run with blood as Sorin reclaims his legend.

Shayne holds two high-ranking black belts, and can be found writing in a coffee shop, cackling madly into his computer screen while pounding shots of espresso. He's hard at work on the newest books in the TempleVerse— You can find updates on new releases or chronological reading order on the next page, his website, or any of his social media accounts. **Follow him online for all sorts of groovy goodies, giveaways, and new release updates:**

Get Down with Shayne Online
www.shaynesilvers.com
info@shaynesilvers.com

f facebook.com/shaynesilversfanpage
a amazon.com/author/shaynesilvers
BB bookbub.com/profile/shayne-silvers
O instagram.com/shaynesilversofficial
twitter.com/shaynesilvers
g goodreads.com/ShayneSilvers

BOOKS BY SHAYNE

CHRONOLOGY: All stories in the TempleVerse are shown in chronological order on the following page

FEATHERS AND FIRE SERIES

(Set in the TempleVerse)

by Shayne Silvers

UNCHAINED

RAGE

WHISPERS

ANGEL'S ROAR

MOTHERLUCKER (Novella #4.5 in the 'LAST CALL' anthology)

SINNER

BLACK SHEEP

GODLESS

NATE TEMPLE SERIES

(Main series in the TempleVerse)

by Shayne Silvers

FAIRY TALE - FREE prequel novella #0 for my subscribers

OBSIDIAN SON

BLOOD DEBTS

GRIMM

SILVER TONGUE

BEAST MASTER

BEERLYMPIAN (Novella #5.5 in the 'LAST CALL' anthology)

TINY GODS

DADDY DUTY (Novella #6.5)

WILD SIDE

WAR HAMMER

NINE SOULS

HORSEMAN

LEGEND

KNIGHTMARE

ASCENSION

PHANTOM QUEEN DIARIES

(Also set in the TempleVerse)

by Cameron O'Connell & Shayne Silvers

COLLINS (Prequel novella #0 in the 'LAST CALL' anthology)

WHISKEY GINGER

COSMOPOLITAN

OLD FASHIONED

MOTHERLUCKER (Novella #3.5 in the 'LAST CALL' anthology)

DARK AND STORMY

MOSCOW MULE

WITCHES BREW

SALTY DOG

SEA BREEZE

HURRICANE

CHRONOLOGICAL ORDER: TEMPLEVERSE

FAIRY TALE (TEMPLE PREQUEL)

OBSIDIAN SON (TEMPLE 1)

BLOOD DEBTS (TEMPLE 2)

GRIMM (TEMPLE 3)

SILVER TONGUE (TEMPLE 4)

BEAST MASTER (TEMPLE 5)

BEERLYMPIAN (TEMPLE 5.5)

TINY GODS (TEMPLE 6)

DADDY DUTY (TEMPLE NOVELLA 6.5)

UNCHAINED (FEATHERS... 1)

RAGE (FEATHERS... 2)

WILD SIDE (TEMPLE 7)

WAR HAMMER (TEMPLE 8)

WHISPERS (FEATHERS... 3)

COLLINS (PHANTOM 0)

WHISKEY GINGER (PHANTOM... 1)

NINE SOULS (TEMPLE 9)

COSMOPOLITAN (PHANTOM... 2)

ANGEL'S ROAR (FEATHERS... 4)

MOTHERLUCKER (FEATHERS 4.5, PHANTOM 3.5)

OLD FASHIONED (PHANTOM...3)

HORSEMAN (TEMPLE 10)

DARK AND STORMY (PHANTOM... 4)

MOSCOW MULE (PHANTOM...5)

SINNER (FEATHERS...5)

WITCHES BREW (PHANTOM...6)

LEGEND (TEMPLE...11)

SALTY DOG (PHANTOM...7)

BLACK SHEEP (FEATHERS...6)

GODLESS (FEATHERS...7)

KNIGHTMARE (TEMPLE 12)

ASCENSION (TEMPLE 13)

SEA BREEZE (PHANTOM...8)

HURRICANE (PHANTOM...9)

SHADE OF DEVIL SERIES

(Not part of the TempleVerse)

by Shayne Silvers

DEVIL'S DREAM
DEVIL'S CRY
DEVIL'S BLOOD

SHADE OF DEVIL SERIES

(Not part of the TempleVerse)

by Shayne Silvers

DEVIL'S DREAM
DEVIL'S CRY
DEVIL'S BLOOD

NOTHING TO SEE HERE.

Thanks for reaching the last page of the book, you over-achiever. Sniff the spine. You've earned it. Or sniff your Kindle.

Now this has gotten weird.

Alright. I'm leaving.